Special Thanks To:
The Ladies – you know who you are
Nario Saavedra – Never change
Mom – Your turn!
Grandpa C. – Keep on flying

Contents

Prologue 1
Chapter 1 3
Chapter 2 26
Chapter 3 44
Chapter 4 52
Chapter 5 68
Chapter 6 82
Chapter 7 95
Chapter 8 105
Chapter 9 119
Chapter 10 132
Chapter 11 149
Chapter 12 165
Chapter 13 176
Chapter 14 188
Chapter 15 200
Chapter 16 217
Chapter 17 235
A Most Unfortunate Man 1

Prologue

I often dream of flying. Not like flying myself, but in an airship. Though there's not a lot of difference. The open cockpit of the typical airship allows the wind, dirt, and bugs to pummel the pilot, and it's almost like soaring through the air without the help of a mechanical device. In my dreams, I don't think much about it. I just go and enjoy the feel of being up in the air by myself, the king of the sky.

My dreams always start out this way. I'm not going anywhere. I don't need to be somewhere. I fly for the sake of flying. It's a religious experience that can't be explained to anyone who hasn't felt it. I wish that my dreams would never end. At least not this part of them. I spent years trying to hold onto this joyous scene and not let my mind slip into what I know lurks underneath.

All too soon the pleasant flight ends. The rest of the world begins to fill in around me. War. Guns and screaming fill the air. I can hear explosions happening far too close for comfort. I can see faces filled with pain. I can see my own face, cold and hard against the horror. It's a damned good thing I don't have any loved ones. I don't think I could bare to face them like this.

That's what had to happen in those days. I had to pretend like I wasn't killing other men like me. No, not like me. I didn't have anyone who gave a damn if I came back. Most of the others had wives, children, families who waited day in and day out to hear if they were going to make it home, standing on their own two feet. I made sure a good number of them didn't.

Steamroller
Prologue

Their ghosts fill my dreams, asking me why. I don't have any answers for them. It wasn't my decision to murder them. It wasn't my fault the war happened. Yet they continue to blame me. I blame myself. I pulled the damned trigger. I shot their airships out of the sky. I ended their flights. I'm the one who has to live with the memory. I'm the one who wakes up screaming.

Chapter 1

I bolt upright, sharp pain filling my head. I cringe and grip my skull. The pounding in my temples reminds me of the long night of drinking. The drinking is the only thing that keeps the dreams down to a dull roar. My face is coated in sweat, and my heart feels like it's ready to jump out of my chest. Then I realize it's not the pounding in my head and heart I hear. A knock thumps on the door.

The hell? Avery never knocks. He's got a key so he can get in and head up to the roof any time he wants. Beyond Avery, there are a few other people living in the building, but they never bother coming up here. They got no reason. I stay out of their business and they stay out of mine.

Curious, I push myself up, my head swimming uncomfortably as I do. I had drunk myself to sleep on the couch. Again. It's how I spend my free time between jobs. Strip down, flop on the couch, and drink until I can't lift a bottle to my lips any more. Wake up, do it all over again while I wait for a job. It's a privileged life.

Jobs usually come in the form of paper slipped under my door by a kid, who also doesn't bother knocking. I have ears on the street who get the right information into the right hands. Word gets around someone is looking for certain service. Then a runner, a street kid, gets sent here with a piece of paper that has an address and the client jotted on it. I respond back that I'll show up at a specific time. It's a simple system that keeps the wrong people from knowing where I live. But it also leaves me wondering who in the hell could be knocking?

I glance at the old grandfather clock in the corner, which shows both hands pointing to the 12. With the window shades drawn there's only a small amount of light glowing around the edges that could be from murky smog-filled daylight or the constantly burning city lights. A short time of groggy thought leads me to believe it's noon. I'm fairly certain I had been elbow deep in a bottle of cheap whiskey somewhere around midnight, though that may have been a couple days ago.

Another loud knock thumps against the door. Maybe if I wait long enough, they'll go away. Chances are good, it's too important for that. Who would knock on my door if it's not important? Plus, I'm already up. With a resigned sigh and a scratch to my bare groin, I call out to the door, unsure if the person outside can even hear me. When I had taken over the old apartment building, I made a few security improvements on my personal space. Just in case. One of those had been putting in reinforced doors. "What is it? What do you want?"

A muffled voice comes from the other side of the wooden door. "Mr. Reed? Colton Reed? I'd like to speak with you a moment." A woman's voice. Guess this means I should put on some pants if I decide to open the door. Her presence brings questions. Who is she? Why is she here? How the hell did she find me? It's not like I advertise where I live.

"Yeah, just a..." Gebus H. Corbet. It sounds as if a badger crawled down my throat, had hot sex with my vocal cords, and died angry. Clearing my throat only does a little to move the crap. A good belt of whiskey would have been a lot better, but there's only so much time now. "Just a minute." Or three, depending on how long it takes to find a decent pair of trousers.

A.K. Child

Steamroller
Chapter 1

    The place is a mess. Piles of newspapers, empty bottles, and old crap litter the floor. I don't generally bother to impress anyone. Normally no one but Avery comes through here and he doesn't give a damn. From the greasy footprints across the scattered papers, I can see Avery's been through recently. When I get a job, everything happens out in New Foundis' crowded streets. People just don't come here. Not even my tenants, who keep to themselves. If they need something fixed, they turn to Avery, who's better at that kind of thing. So, when someone comes knocking, it has my hairs standing on end. And it has to be a woman. This is shaping up to be an interesting day.

    I own the whole building. Bought it after a particularly lucrative job, mostly so I could have the roof as a landing strip. Before that I rented the space and was always in danger of having it yanked out from under me when funds run low. After buying the building, I let the other tenants stay. They didn't have anywhere else to go and the extra scratch keeps me sitting pretty. When I'm not working, I stay in my own small space, more like a cave than a home, and keep to myself. It's not a bad existence, considering where I came from. Not everyone is born with a roof over their head.

    I finally locate a pair of dirty pants under a pile of old newspapers. They were the pair I had been wearing most recently, so I'm not sure how they managed to get there. I guess some mysteries aren't meant to be solved. I might have searched a little harder for a shirt as well, but I've already taken too long. I wouldn't be surprised if she is out there impatiently shifting from foot to foot and getting ready to knock again.

As if reading my thoughts, the woman outside does knock once more. The sound is hesitant as if she's not sure the door will ever open for her. "Mr. Reed? I'm sorry if I disturbed you, but I'm afraid this is an urgent matter."

It must be to bring her here. I still wonder how the hell she found me. Someone must have told her, and that someone is going to become real good friends with my fists when I find him. The rat is lucky I'm not a murderer. Then again, I know people if it comes to that.

"Hold on, I'm coming." But first a quick check in the mirror. While this may be my territory she's trespassing on, I shouldn't scare the crap out of her. Not that the mirror is much help. It's covered in a layer of filth, blurring the finer details of my aging face. The random streaks of grey in my shaggy hair and scruff of my face are easy to see, but the worn lines under them seem like nothing more than awkward shadows. Or dirt. Must be dirt. I can't remember when I got so old.

I rub at them, trying to make them go away, but they stick to my face as stubbornly as the deep, ugly scar stretching from about midway across my left cheek to my ear. It's a reminder of my personal war with Vann Horner. We'd fought a lot during the war. He was always trying to get revenge for the crooked nose I inflicted on him. And it hadn't ended once we finally managed to go our separate ways. Somehow that bastard had found his way into the same line of work, and the rivalry continued. Why he couldn't go back to whatever life of luxury he had before the war, I have no idea. Maybe he isn't pretty enough anymore.

The scar has been with me at least 20 years now. It seems like forever. It seems like yesterday. The impatient woman knocks again, breaking me from my thoughts. It's time to answer her urgent call. I stop at the door as she knocks a final time. "All right, all right." I put my hand on the rusty knob, but don't open the door yet. "How did you find this place? Why should I let you in?" I almost feel like telling her to leave her contact info and I would get in touch with her, but curiosity has other things in mind.

She pauses. I guess she didn't expect to meet with any resistance. But she finally answers, her voice shaking slightly. "My name is Samantha Loral. Dr. Harris Wisen sent me to contract you. He gave me this address. If you don't mind, I'd rather not discuss the details in the hall."

Wisen? Am I supposed to know who that is? She says it as if his name is the magic key to get me to let her in. It works, if only because I'm tired of talking through the door. I open it, expecting some mousey schoolmarm or a secretary. What I get is something completely different. Ms. Samantha Loral is knock-out gorgeous. She looks to be in her twenties, with long, dark ringlets of hair that frames her face and end midway down her chest, inevitably drawing my eyes there. In the brief moment I actually see her face, I notice that it's long and thin, with a perfect pale complexion, and her dark eyes hold a hint of sorrow and mystery. I'm suddenly very aware that I'm standing there in a dirty pair of trousers letting my base instincts take control. I'm also too aware of the grey, stringy hair across the aging muscle of my chest. I should have looked a little harder for a shirt. A clean shirt.

"Mr. Reed?" Thank all the very few good things in the world, her eyes are locked on my face. Her voice draws me back up to them, but her expression is somewhere between curiosity and concern. I realize I'm staring. "I'm sorry to disturb you. I hope I haven't come at a bad time." She frowns slightly, glancing down the hallway.

"I…" Damn it, say something useful, stupid ass. Nothing comes to mind. It's as if my brain has turned into a desert and all I can hear is the imagined rush of water somewhere in the distance. "I mean, no. It's fine. How can I help you? That's what I do. Help people." It is? The words are out there before I can stop them, followed by an awkward, schoolboy smile. Yeah. I'm smooth.

"May I come in?" Her look shifts from concern to anxious. She glances over her shoulder as if expecting someone to be watching her. Was this Dr. Wisen lurking down the hall? I can't see anything around her, but I wouldn't be surprised if she's a patsy sent to make sure it's safe. Or worse. My smile falters as I sense something suspicious going on.

If he is waiting out there, she's not going to say anything until I let her in. I finally get control of myself and step back from the door. "Yeah, sorry. I'm not used to people showing up at my door." The state of the room catches me once more. "Uh…as you can tell by the mess."

She steps in, quickly sweeping the door closed behind her. A grimace touches her face as she observes the state of my home, but she turns it into a nervous smile. "It's…all right. I realize this is an imposition. I wouldn't have come here if Dr. Wisen hadn't insisted."

Yeah. Though I'm glad this woman is here rather than Wisen.

Chances are she's better to look at than some crusty old doctor would be. Still, I wish I had more time to make some kind of order out of the place. Oh well, it's too late for good first impressions. I head over to the sofa. An empty bottle sticks out of the worn cushions, the remains of last night's binge. I yank it out and toss it off to the side to clear a patch of seat for her. "Please, sit. Er…make yourself comfortable. Would you like a drink?" I flinch as soon as the words leave my mouth. Empty bottles are scattered through the other junk, making it look worse than it is. I'm not a lush. Really. At least not when I'm working. I don't need to justify myself.

She looks at the sofa for a moment before shaking her head and turning her eyes back to me. Her brown, soulful eyes. A blink and she pulls them away again, focusing on something behind me. "I'm glad you've decided to help. They say you're the best. I…Dr. Wisen, needs the best."

I shift and watch her, feeling awkward in a way I hadn't felt since the first time I had a woman. She had been a streetwalker, and I found her more intimidating than alluring. I'm not quite sure what I'm supposed to be doing with my hands or eyes. I start to randomly pull some of the old newspapers into stacks in an attempt to straighten up the room. "I haven't decided yet. Just what do you and your…employer?" It would be my luck that Wisen would actually be her husband. "Need me to do?"

She seems to relax now that she's inside. Maybe Wisen is hiding in the hall, waiting for her to successfully convince me to take their job. I can't help but wonder if she's in some kind of trouble. Maybe she's indentured to him somehow. I would have to watch her and her reactions.

For now, she begins to pace through a small aisle between crap. "There is research he needs you to retrieve."

She doesn't take the seat on the couch and there's no hope for the piles on the floor, so I flop down in the cleared patch. And find another bottle under the cushion. I try not to show my discomfort. "Hold on. Ms. Loral…Samantha, right?" She nods and stops her pacing. "What's your place in this? Why'd he send you rather than contacting me himself?" And why the hell did he send you here instead of following the usual ways to contact me? I don't ask because I doubt she knows. My assumption is Wisen wants things to happen, and happen now. I'm picturing him as a demanding, controlling bastard. No wonder Samantha seems so afraid.

Samantha hesitates and looks toward the door. She bites her full lower lip slightly as she looks back. Yeah. He's got to be out there trying to listen. Good thing the structure is sound. He's not likely to get a damn thing out of this. "I'm his personal assistant. I'm afraid he's unable to be here at the moment. He hasn't exactly been well."

Having enough of the bottle, I stand again and move closer to her, scanning her face quickly for any signs of injury. She doesn't shy away from my observation, and instead seems to give me the once over as well. She's afraid of something, and it's not me. Samantha says Wisen isn't well, and that can mean a number of things. A guy who has someone this scared has got to be doing more than sending her on errands. But I don't see a mark on her. "Okay. And why does he need me to get this research for him? To keep his hands clean?" I'd seen that happen a lot over the years. It's like a mechanic taking care of a pilot's airship. The mechanic is the expert in all the inner workings of an airship, and I'm an expert in getting things others can't.

"I..." Her mouth hangs open a bit, showing perfect teeth behind those lips. This is not a woman who came from the streets. I can see from the way she dresses and carries herself, she's got wealth in her blood. But here she is, working for some shady doctor who put her up to hiring a guy like me for a job no legitimate entrepreneur could handle. Had she lost her standing somehow, or did he have something on her? She presses her mouth closed again and shakes her head. "You wouldn't be stealing it. It belongs to him."

That isn't the answer I expect. "Really? So is this just a transport job then?" I'm trying to understand the urgency. If this Wisen character owns the item outright, why bother with a smuggler when he can hire a legitimate transportation service? Unless it's contraband. It wouldn't be the first time I've had my hands on illegal items.

"It's a little more complicated than that." Samantha goes back to pacing that small aisle. Her skirts shift around her shapely hips and it distracts me from my questions. The tiny shudder in her voice is the only thing that keeps me listening to her. "He was working on a project. Something called 'Tick.' I'm afraid I don't know the details, though I understand it to be very advanced technology." She refuses to meet my eyes when she turns back toward me and I realize she hasn't been able to the whole time. Sure, she was looking at my face earlier, but not my eyes. Something's going on and she's holding back. "There was a dispute. Dr. Wisen ended up losing his position with the research facility and he no longer has access. He wants what he was working on."

Of course he does. It doesn't take a genius to know those are Wisen's words, straight from his mouth. "Okay. So what's the deal with this place? And the project? I'm going to need everything you have." I want to help her, but I don't want to walk into this blind and right now she hasn't told me much of anything.

She shakes her head as she stops pacing and turns to face me, her hands folded. "Have you heard of ReGen Corps?" I shake my head and motion for her to continue. Her voice evens out as she speaks the facts, taking her mind away from whatever has her worried. "Their primary research is designed to rebuild much of the land that has been striped by coal mining. This was Dr. Wisen's passion."

I raise a brow. Even though I've infiltrated several businesses around New Foundis, I'm not familiar with the work of most of them. That's not a requirement of my job. What she's telling me has me confused. "Sounds harmless. What was the dispute about?"

Samantha's face sours and she shakes her head. "Some of the researchers were more interested in making money than rebuilding the world. They began working on tools of war, intending to sell their research to the highest bidder. Dr. Wisen would have none of it. When they forced him out, he had to leave behind his research. There is something called Tick, which he considers most important of all."

I turn away from her, trying to work this out in my head. Everything she's said so far sounds legitimate, but it doesn't answer why she was so nervous when she showed up. I feel like I'm missing something and she isn't providing the answer. I fold my hands behind my back as I pace away from her. "So, what's the catch?" I turn back to look at her, watching her pale face grow even whiter.

"Catch?" she asks finally, stuttering a little. "I don't know what you mean. It's a very straight forward request, which you'll be well compensated for."

"No." I shake my head and move back toward her. I want to know is her part in this. What is she afraid of? What's it going to cost her personally? "You're not just relaying a message to me, are you? This job means something to you, just like it does to Wisen. What am I getting into? Why does it matter to you?"

"I..." Samantha pauses, her eyes going down to the trashed floor. I wonder if she'll admit what's really wrong. "I'm very concerned about him. He's a good man, Mr. Reed. He's dedicated to his research, and he's willing to spend his life savings to retain your services." Samantha purses her lips for a moment. She's hit me with the unexpected and I find myself having to rethink everything. "I think this may be his last wish. What happened to him...being cut away from his life's work. It's just wrong. You can help him get some justice. If you can't, maybe you could point me to someone who can? I heard another name, a Mr. Horner."

I cringe and shake my head, drawing back again. "No. You don't want to deal with him." Anyone but Horner. I scratch my chin, feeling the several days' growth. Maybe Wisen isn't so bad. And he definitely couldn't be lurking in the hallway if he's ill. Maybe all her hesitation is because she's on the wrong side of town. She has balls to come here and the job is straight forward. "I'll take the job. Dr. Wisen knows I don't come cheap though, right?" Even when justice is on the line, I still need to make a living.

"Of course" Samantha reaches into the clutch she carries and pulls out an envelope. She looks at it a moment and I get that sense of hesitation again, like she doesn't want to be here talking to me. She moves around a pile of newspapers and hands the envelope to me. "This is half. That's how it usually works right?" She pauses, frowning slightly. "It's very generous."

I take the envelope slide my thumb under the wax seal to flip it open. Tucked inside is a row of large bills, crisp and fresh from the bank. They look like they were minted yesterday. I glance at her with a raised brow. Half? Samantha had said Wisen was willing to give his life savings, and this isn't anything to sneeze at. Printed on the inner lip of the envelope in handwriting I assume belongs to Samantha, is an address. The location is just north of the city, where the wealthy tend to settle. Some property Wisen owns, no doubt. "And this is where I'm supposed to deliver the research?"

Samantha nods, a relieved look coming over her. She smiles, stepping back away from me again and bumping into the pile of papers behind her. "Yes. That's Dr. Wisen's estate. I would have arranged somewhere else, but…"

"But he's unwell and this is easier." I finish for her. I tuck the envelope and its contents into my trousers and nod. Job accepted. She's extending a lot of trust, letting me know where the old scientist lives. I can't help but believe her story with that behind it. "It shouldn't be a problem. Tell me everything you know about the place I'm supposed to find the research. I need location, security, bare minimum I need to bring back. Anything you can think of."

She reaches into her clutch again, pulling free a large piece of paper that's been heavily folded. She unfolds it and lays it on the coffee table. A map, with a large, black circle drawn on it. "It's a compound. It's lies to the west, out past the hills. Right here." She points to the circle, then draws her hand away so I can look over the location.

I can't remember the last time I needed a map. Most of the land near New Foundis is burned into my head from years of flying over it. But then, there are plenty of research compounds scattered out there, so having a vague location is better than nothing. I lean forward again and look it over. "I know that area all right. I should be able to find it."

Samantha nods, keeping her focus on the map as if it will tell her something she doesn't already know. She's calmed down a lot from when she first walked in. It had to have just been nerves. She had no idea if I would accept the job or turn her away, and this side of town isn't the kind of place you usually find a high-class lady. She speaks softly, her words falling out like she had memorized the lines of a play. "The compound is mostly underground, but has a few surface structures and a perimeter wall. Security guards are stationed on the walls, and patrol the grounds inside. The entry points are secured, but I don't know any details beyond that."

I'm already picturing the place in my head. These kinds of structures aren't unheard of. Invenio is land-rich. Outside of the coastal cities and towns are farmlands. Beyond these are vast expanses of land devastated by deforestation before iron and coal were discovered, and kept clear of civilization by the mining companies until there was nothing of any value left. The only thing worth putting in these areas are researcher facilities. I don't know how anyone could live out there. Give me the lights and sounds of the city any day. I'd go crazy with nothing but the sound of crickets chirping at night. Most of my jobs are right there in the city. Though I've heard of these compounds, even flew over a few from time to time, I've never been in one. "Anything else you know about this place?"

Samantha stops pacing again and shakes her head. "No. I've never been out there. I only assist with matters of his estate. Dr. Wisen only told me what he thought you needed to know to find his research. He sent me to you first. He seems to think you're the right man for the job."

Of course I'm the right man for the job. I'm the best there is. I smile, trying to reassure her Dr. Wisen is right about me. "That's all right. You've given me enough. And the research? What should I look for specifically?"

Samantha begins to shift toward the door. It's a none-too-subtle hint she's ready to get back to Wisen and out of this hellhole I call home. And she's trying her hardest not to knock over or trip on all the crap in her way. "Documents, of course. Any of the research you can find. Even on the war machines." Her voice hardens as she says this, and I picture a great big bonfire on the Wisen estate as war research goes up in flames. "But Tick is the most important thing to him. If nothing else, find Tick."

I nod, slowly following her toward the closed door. "And this tick thing, how big is it? How much effort is it going to take to get this thing out undetected?"

And then her hesitation returns, making her pause. "I…don't know," she says finally, shaking her head again. "He calls it the key. It can't be that big."

Something called Tick, a key? It doesn't make a lot of sense, but then I'm no scientist. Her word is about the best I have to go on for now. I nod and start to dig around in the mess for a shirt. "It's all right. I'll head out while it's still daylight. It is still daytime, right?" Samantha nods as I pull on one of the lesser stained shirts I own. "It'll take me a little while for surveillance and planning. Then execution. Give me a week. You all right with that?"

She draws in a sharp breath, looking at me with renewed concern. "A week?" she asks, biting her lip.

I raise a brow, stopping in my task of getting dressed. "That's the standard time I give people. May take more, may take less. If it takes more, I'll let you know. Is that a problem?" Clearly it is, and I'd like to know why. She said he was sick, maybe even dying, but if the old bastard is going to die in the next week, this job doesn't mean a hell of a lot anyway.

"No. No, it's all right," she says, taking a calming breath. "I didn't realize it would take so long. But there's no problem. Really." Samantha even flashes a smile, though it's not exactly the happiest I've ever seen. Maybe Wisen is about to die.

"Well. All right then. You'll hear from me in about a week." I return to getting my things together. My flight jacket, scarf, hat, boots, and goggles are easier to locate than my pants and shirt had been. I keep those by the back door that leads up to the rooftop landing pad. After all the horrible things I had seen and done during the war, flying is the only thing I care about. Even the jobs are just a way to pay for flying.

"Thank you, Mr. Reed," she says quietly as she turns toward the door. The motion is quick, and she almost trips over debris. Samantha seems to own all the grace in the world though as she finds her way over a pile and pulls the door open to the freedom of the hallway. "I'll let Dr. Wisen know right away. We'll be waiting for your contact."

I throw the jacket around my shoulders and look up as Samantha slides through the opening. "All right. And try not to worry too much, okay?" I give her my best, reassuring smile. "I'll be back before you know it."

Samantha smiles a little more brightly, but shakes her head as she starts to pull the door closed. "Just please, hurry."

I look down to adjust the boot that's hanging awkwardly from my foot. "I'll be back as soon as I can. Please, take care of yourself, Ms. Lor…" The door clicks, brining my eyes back up. She's gone.

I don't blame her. If I wasn't used to my life here, I might not want to stick around very long either. I head over to the door and pull it open to look down the hall. It's already empty. No, she didn't want to waste any time here.

I shake my head with a soft chuckle and close the door again, securing the lock. It's time to get the hell out of here. I head over to the back and into the stairwell to the roof above, locking this door as well. Can't be too secure now that someone thinks it's okay to share my address with the damned public. I'll deal with that later. Paying jobs first.

I can already feel the chill of autumn blowing through the doorway at the top of the stairs and I wrap my scarf around my neck to ward it off. Avery's left the upper door open, letting in the bright glare of daylight. I hate day, but at least it's not as bright here as it is in the countryside. A sheen of smoke from the industrial section mixes with clouds that roll in off the sea and coat the city in grey. It's impossible to tell where one stops and the other begins. But the sun's glare reflects off the bottom of the muck is headache-inducing. If my goggles didn't have a tint to them, it would be next to impossible to see anything while in the air. As it is, when the smog ceiling's too low, obscuring visibility, flying simply doesn't happen. At least today the skies are clear enough for relatively smooth sailing.

I slide my goggles down to keep out worst of grey light and pull the door closed behind me. I never thought of myself as a hero, but that's exactly what I'm doing for Samantha and Wisen. This job isn't like my usual gigs. Samantha's concerns add a human touch that isn't often part of industrial espionage.

I'm usually the neutral party who acts as a means to an end. Since the rise of industry and the end of the most recent war, the needs of nations were over-taken by the needs of business. And business is worse than war. Every industrial mogul is looking for the next big thing to make him even bigger, and his enemy undoubtedly owns that thing. That sparked the rise of smugglers. Men good at getting into places they shouldn't be, finding what didn't belong to them, and delivering it to the wrong hands. I never claimed to be moral. But then, who is?

The method of my madness sits on the rooftop, waiting for me. The war still haunts me when I'm on the ground, but I can forget all that when I'm flying. I'm happy when I'm with my airship, Airika. I'd like to think that if an airship could feel anything, she would be happy to see me too. Okay. Even I know how sick that sounds. I need to get out more.

Thankfully, Avery doesn't judge me. While most of the tenants are hard-luck cases with nowhere else to go, one of them stands out from the rest. My old friend, Avery Nickols. He's more like an employee than a resident. Or maybe I'm more like his guinea pig. I usually end up testing out his ideas, whether I realize it or not. He had converted one of the lower floors to a workshop for his various mechanical projects. I let him stay rent-free in return for his building and work on Airika. He's the only person I trust to come through my apartment to get to the roof access where she sits.

After the war, he went to work building and maintaining airships for a number of different interests. He made good money at it, but he's as happy to do it for free. Or at least in exchange for having a roof over his head. Innovation lives and breathes in Avery's veins. He built Airika and he takes every opportunity to add to her. Some of his ideas aren't that great, but most of them are amazing. And I sure as hell wouldn't be where I am if it wasn't for him.

As I approach Airika, I hear hammering coming from the far engine. The tracks through my apartment had been telling the truth. Avery is here, tinkering again. Damn I hope she's ready to go.

I don't bother to yell at him. He doesn't hear anything when he's working. I move around the other side of the airship to find him half-way inside the right engine, pounding on…something. Standing next to him, I reach out and tap on the engine compartment to get his attention. "Av." He continues to hammer. His backside is wiggling back and forth as he appears to be dancing to some kind of tune in his head. I tap again, this time a little louder. "Avery. I need to get out of here. Please tell me she's ready to fly?"

"Huh?" Avery pulls his head out from under the engine cover. He's wearing a pair of goggles not much different than mine, and a set of large ear covers meant to block out the sound of his work. He turns his head toward me and starts slightly. "Oh, hey Colt. Didn't hear you there." He reaches up, pulls off the headset, and grins. His face and most of his balding head are covered in coal dust. Somewhere under that mess are a few strands of stubborn red hair mixed with streaks of grey, but I haven't seen the real color of it in years.

Obviously he didn't hear me. Avery usually lives in his own world, but I'm used to it. It's why I don't mind him. He keeps to himself and he keeps me flying. "Yeah. Looks like you've been busy. Is she in any condition to fly? I got a job and I need to take care of it right away."

"Oh. Um…" Avery looks hesitant in a way that worries me. He's clearly in the middle of something that may or may not actually be beneficial. "Er…hold on a minute, 'kay?" He grins and pushes the headset back on before the top half of him disappears back into the engine compartment.

To be fair, I usually give him a little more notice than this. It's easier when I meet with people outside the building because I can warn him before I ever take a job. I stand there for a while, listening to the clank, clank, clank of his hammer echoing in the compartment.

As I wait, I can't help but wonder what Avery is doing to the old girl. He's always changing something, improving something else, not that she needs it. As far as I'm concerned, Airika is perfect. I'm usually not too concerned about Avery's tweaks most days, but Samantha's in a hurry, which means I'm in a hurry.

Avery comes back up for air a minute later. He backs away from the engine and slams the compartment closed. "All done. You should be good now. I was making a few tweaks to the vent system. You should be able to take her a little further now, maybe a bit faster too. I'm actually kind of anxious to see what she'll do. Report everything back to me, okay? This may be the next revolutionary break!"

Yeah. Right. At the end of the day, she's Avery's baby. He built her, he maintains her, but I call her mine and I'd kill anyone who'd harm her. It's a little like being married to Avery's daughter. Every time he improves her, I wonder if he's secretly plotting against me, using her as the means. Still, he hasn't killed me yet. "Yeah, I'll do what I can." I move toward the cockpit as I speak, Avery following after me like a puppy. "I'll be gone for a while. Maybe as much as a week. I'm heading out into the countryside, a couple hundred miles or so. Watch the place, will you? If the woman comes back before I do…"

"A woman?" Avery jumps, tripping over his own feet as he does. "You sly dog! How'd you even…? You were passed out on the couch when I came through this morning!" He reaches over, clapping me on the shoulder, leaving a black handprint on the leather of my flight jacket.

With a grunt, I try to wipe off the mess, only managing to smear it further and coat my own hand in gunk. "Great. Thanks, Av." I wipe it off the best I can on my pant leg and climb up into Airika's pilot's seat. "It's not like that. She's the one who hired me. Just showed up and said here's a job."

Cargo airships are built roughly the same, no matter who's hands have been on them. From follows function after all. The main body is built kind of like a fish, with a hatch that swings open to reveal the cargo hold. The frame is mostly hollow iron bars with thin wooden planks to make up the body. The wings have the same metal ribs, with canvas stretched across the surface for lift. At the front of the airship, is an open cockpit, with a simple seat and controls. Levers connect to critical areas through the airship to control elevation, heat output from the engines, and wheel breaks.

The engines are the real marvel of modern technology. I can't claim to know everything about them, but they're set inside barrels suspended from the wings, and reinforced with beams to the body. They run on steam, and the hotter the stokers, the faster the airship will go. Avery's made sure Airika is a work of perfection. My old militia airship could never compare.

"Ah, yeah, I got you. A looker, eh? Here's a job, don't ask questions, off you go." Avery winks, and all I can do is roll my eyes, letting him believe what he wants. He's not far from the truth. Then his expression changes, growing more serious. "Colton. What if she's a cop? Or worse, a Reddie?"

A Reddie? I blink. Officers from the Republic Department of Investigation were notorious for showing up in the middle of jobs, putting a quick end to lucrative work. I've seen some good guys go to prison for life because they weren't expecting an RDI agent. But, she couldn't be. Nothing about her screams authority. I shake my head and smile as I strap myself into the pilot's seat. "I doubt it. I'll be fine. She already paid half. If she was a Reddie, she would have slapped cuffs on me the moment I said I'd take the job."

Avery considers it for a moment. I can see the hamsters working their asses off in his head. Finally he shrugs and backs away from Airika. "Well, I won't keep you any more then. Get going already!"

"All right, I'm going. Remember, a week. Don't start worrying until then." I doubt I'll be gone that long, and I never actually knew Avery to worry about anything not mechanical, but at least someone knows I have a plan.

Avery moves back as I start the engines. In the old days, airships needed someone to give them a push to get them started, but that's no longer the case. Now the engines are generally powerful enough to get them rolling. As soon as the steam engines are hot, I open the vents and start toward the edge of the roof. The gaps between the buildings leave enough room for a clean take off. The engines take a few minutes to warm up, but soon Airika picks up speed toward the end of the make-shift runway. Before I know it, we're off into the air. Like that, the job has begun.

Chapter 2

Even before industry started taking over, the sky was filthy. Now that industry is king, the air's even worse. No sooner does my airship dip off the edge of the building and rise up through the various structures of the city, than I am coated with a film of black scum to match the marks left by Avery's hand. Every few minutes I'm forced to smear the soot off my goggles the best I can with my scarf. The scarf was white once, and I try to get it back to that state every so often. But after years of use, its permanent color is now a dull gray, with splotches of darker stains.

I'm also not alone in the dirty sky. While it takes a lot to own an airship, there are still plenty in urban areas like New Foundis. Some of them belong to the wealthy who can afford to waste their time on leisure, but more of them belong to legitimate businesses that try to spread their cargo as far as they can. Flying isn't exactly new, but the laws in place are hard to enforce. Mostly, we try not to crash into other airships and buildings. Many pilots take advantage of the lack of laws and oversight. They like to think they own the air and won't hesitate to let others know about their flying prowess. I've had more than a few close calls from jerks suddenly appearing around the curve of a smokestack.

I take the most expedient path out of the city to get away from the worst of the crap as quickly as possible. My building is on the south side of town, not far from the railroad tracks and a rise of bluffs that look down over the ocean to the east. I keep Airika pointed south on top of the roof to make my escape from the city easier. I still have to fight through the air traffic hauling cargo from the train yards, but journey is shorter than going any other way. The cargo pilots are also more careful than the joy riders, not wanting to risk their loads and livelihoods.

A few minutes after take-off, I'm out of the city, sweeping around to the west. Beyond the edge of New Foundis, the air shifts from sludgy coal smoke to cleaner countryside air. Like a curtain lifting, visibility goes from feet to miles. It doesn't hurt to breathe it and my scarf can rest for a little while. Free from the worst of the dangers and out of the cloud of gunk, piloting becomes secondary to being in the air. The open land passes below and it isn't much to look at, so the mind starts to wander.

My thoughts are occupied by Samantha. I had gone through so many different impressions of her and Wisen as she revealed more about the both of them. First, I saw her as a good looking young woman who magically found her way to my door. She's got to be about 20 years younger than me. She would have been born around the time I got out of the militia, and that alone should put her off limits. It didn't stop me from thinking she was the victim in all this, and Wisen was some brutish thug who was pushing her around. Then I find out she's actually a concerned assistant to a failing old man. And here I am, flying out into the hinterlands, risking my life, to bring them both a little bit of happiness. Who would have thought I'd be the guy to help them? I'm nothing but a former street punk and soldier, doing my best to scratch by.

I push those thoughts away for now and focus on what I was hired to do. A lot of my jobs are within the bounds of New Foundis, making this location intriguing. I've flown out here in the wild before, but it's usually to get away from the city. When someone builds a complex out in the countryside where the ground has been stripped bare and it's too far from the city for even the farmers to bother with, that means they have something to hide. If there's something worth hiding, then it's usually something worth protecting. ReGen Corps sounds like a decent corporation, as far as those go, but placing the compound out in the wilds is just inviting people to take advantage of the secrecy, as Wisen apparently found out. Most smugglers wouldn't risk the kind of danger found in secret locations.

    Good thing I'm not most smugglers. I have a reputation for success, which has a tendency to irk the competition. I try to keep my building relatively unremarkable. Sure, there's an airship parked on top, but it's not the only one in the city, and doesn't have any particular identifying marks that could be seen from the air. If someone is leaking where I live, that's a security breach I'd rather not have. Especially if it's a competitor. If anything, that gives me an uneasy feeling about all this. Sending random jobs my way is one thing. At least it's a little scratch in my pocket if I succeed. I'm more concerned about such a person sending something lethal at me. I'll have to look into exactly how this happened after I get back.

    As my thoughts tumble around in my head, I draw near a line of bare, rocky hills that cut off the horizon. Once these were forested steppes, and maybe one day they would be again, unless the city begins to expand further west. For now, it's mostly rough scrub grass and old stumps left over from heavy logging. It adds an eerie feeling to the empty expanse. The compound I'm looking for is beyond these hills, which will be the best choice for landing if I have any chance of taking off again once I get what I'm after. I'll be back here again soon to scout out a good landing spot.

On the other side of the hills, the target comes into view. The complex is bigger than I expect. I thought it might cover a few acres. Living in a city warps perspectives on stuff like that because the large buildings can hold hundreds of people and everything is near at hand. Out here, it's vast expanses of nothing and farms. Just about anyone can get away with building massive, sprawling complexes into old abandoned mines that go unseen by the general public.

As Samantha had said, the complex is mostly underground. The large perimeter wall stretches around at least two square miles of land. In the middle of the solid stone wall are small square buildings that poke up out of the soil to allow in light and fresh air for whatever is going on down below. At the cardinal points of the campus, smokestacks rise up, shadowing over the buildings, but there is no smoke or steam billowing from them.

The place looks dead. Then I notice the wall. I can't see any guards along the top, or down below on the ground. Samantha had said there would be guards. If anyone was on duty, they'd be watching me now, and maybe even shooting at Airika. It's almost as if the whole place has been put here to decorate the landscape and left to rot.

I drop lower, buzzing over the top of the wall to make sure there isn't anyone here. The lack of anything pushes an ill feeling into my gut. Something isn't right here. The way things stand, it will be way too easy to get in. Too easy is never a good thing. That means there's a trap, or something worse waiting inside. Samantha clearly didn't know anything about this place, but I have to wonder if Wisen knew what he was sending me into and choose not to let Samantha in on it. Then again, maybe I'm being paranoid and the place has been shut down since Wisen's been gone. If so, the chance of finding what he wants decreases. Still, I am being paid to take a look, so I should do at least that much. I came here with the intent of casing the place, but if it's going to be this easy to get in, I'm taking the opportunity to get the job done quick. The decision made, I circle around once more and head toward the hills.

The hills are roughly even at their summits. I take a little time to find the highest, smoothest landing spot, not only for a simple landing, but to make taking off easy too. Taking off from a hill isn't as good as a rooftop or cliff, but with enough speed and clear space, it can be done. The hard part would be getting whatever I find back here. If there's too much research, getting it back up to the top of the hill will be a pain in the ass. Too much extra weight in Airika won't make anything easier either. I'd have to worry about that later. First I have to get into the damn compound and hope that things go off without a hitch. I'm expecting all kinds of hitches—guards, scientists, traps, impending doom. That's reality for a smuggler.

I get Airika down a lot smoother than the first few times I had flown. Those days were far behind me. Now I barely think about landing. It's become second nature, maybe even first nature. Once on the ground, I find what I can to blend Airika in with the surrounding scrub. This consists of stacking dead brush up against her hull. Above, the sky is starting to grow dark. It'll be night soon and there's not a single person around, but I don't want to take any chances that someone might accidentally stumble on her. I need her ready to go as soon I get back and it's light enough to fly.

I find a place to settle in and wait for night to come. I hadn't seen any guards on the place, but the darkness would help if they beef up security after normal business hours. The sun finally disappears down over the far off western horizon and the stars come out, dotting the clear sky. Sometimes I forget how peaceful it is out here. It makes me itch in discomfort.

I've seen a lot of things in my time. Not every moment of the war was spent in the air, and most of my time on the ground was forgettable. But as I gather my gear, I start to think back to the time I was shot down over Heavenshrill Forest. It was a forest, not this young scrub and wasteland. A real forest with real trees and real soldiers waiting in the shadows. The crash wasn't bad in itself. I walked away from it with only minor scrapes. It was getting back to base that took its toll. It was kill or be killed, and sometimes at night, the ghosts of that place still haunt me.

My real unease with this part of the world started long before the war. I'm a city boy. I grew up in the light, even when it was night time. Lamps are always burning along the streets. People are always moving around, living life. Out here in the dark countryside, where animal noises and the wind through the grass are the only things to keep me company, I can't help but be a little nervous. If I have to stay out here too long, or the cargo isn't easy to get back to the airship, I'm not going to be happy.

My only sources of light are the kerosene lamps I keep in the cargo hold for emergencies. Avery usually makes sure my gear is ready, and any of the lamps should have enough fuel to get me to the compound and back. For the sake of ease, I only take one along with me. That should be enough. But if no one is actually around, I could always hold up until day break if the lamp runs out.

With Airika hidden, light in hand, and a quick check to make sure the tools of my trade are tucked into my jacket where they usually live, I start off down the western slope of the hill. This side isn't as decimated as the eastern side. It hadn't been hit as hard by the race to industrialization. I don't know much about the natural world, and couldn't give two flying rats' asses about it. All I know is there are various plants sprouting out of the ground and filling in whatever had been taken years ago.

Most of the city-dwelling population doesn't give a damn about whether there is anything growing back here either. People like me don't think about big world problems when it's hard enough to live a day-to-day life. I find I usually do what I can to get by and let someone else worry about whether the world will be here tomorrow. People like ReGen Corps, apparently. With the ever-growing population and the need for more agriculture and coal and iron, the world is doomed anyway. But who actually believes the world is going anywhere any time soon? The inevitable end is about as likely as getting hit by a locomotive while taking a morning bath. It could happen, but the chances are slim. So life goes on, all the while we hope that there's no train lurking in the darkness with its headlamp out.

The walk to the compound takes about an hour. If I was in better shape, it wouldn't take as long, but as it is, I find myself huffing and puffing by the time the high stone wall comes into view. A wall and no obvious access. It had been hard to see the entry point from the air, but as best I can guess, it's on the other side, facing out into the open country to keep it out of sight of anyone coming from the more populated side. It's got to be at least another half-hour's slog to find it, and that's if I manage to go the short way. At least there doesn't appear to be any lights shining off the top of the wall, which suggests no guards. Or that's what they want me to think. If they have some kind of technology to spot trespassers without any light source, I'm screwed. It's bad enough I have my own light showing anyone right where I am.

Even if no one is here, there has to be some kind of security. That's the way it is with places like this. They develop new things all the time that they test before rolling out to the world. I've come across new types of locks that were a challenge for me to open. I've been nearly caught by alarm triggers I didn't anticipate. Somehow I've managed to get around the worst of it. Whether skill or luck, or some combination, I don't know. I've never put much thought into it. I try to focus on the task at hand and laugh about the near misses when it's all over.

I stick to the shadowy side of the wall and walk as careful as I can, keeping the lamp low and close to me. The going is slow but the night is young. After an eternity of sliding against the hard stone, I finally come to an opening. It's nothing more than an iron gate with bars wide enough to slip through. Samantha claimed the place would be thick with guards, but I see no sign of anyone. How long has it been since Wisen had last been here? I hope they haven't cleaned the place out. I told Samantha I'd return to her in about a week, which even in the most difficult situation usually meant around three days, but at this rate, I'd be back by tomorrow morning. With bad news.

Taking my time, since I seem to have plenty of it, I lift the lantern up to check out the bars. Nothing obvious is out of place. No thin wires set to be tripped, no small switches to be triggered. A layer of dust coats the metal. If this gate had been touched any time in the last year, I'd be surprised. Checking out the ground under the gate reveals the same. No tracks, human or otherwise. Nothing to show the gate had been used in ages.

I don't like nothing. Nothing is impossible to work with. I like something that I can get my hands on and manipulate into my favor. Nothing leaves too many questions. Nothing brings a feeling that I shouldn't be here doing this. The only thing that pushes me forward is the thought that I've come too far already and there are people counting on me. Not to mention the other half of my pay. If there's nothing here, then it can't hurt to look around. I might even find a clue to where everything went and follow the trail wherever it leads.

I take a few practice breaths then exhale to make myself small enough to slip through the bars. It's not easy. Somewhere in the last few years I got a little thicker and misjudge the gap enough to have to struggle. Right before panic hits, I manage to pop free on the other side, a little worse off for the experience. I'll have a good set of bruises in the morning. And a few more stains. The disturbed dust tickles my nose, and I blow a quick, much-too-loud sneeze. Damn it. I look around, fearing the appearance of a dozen armed soldiers. Again, nothing.

This is becoming dangerously predictable. I can't let myself start to think that I'm in the clear. I wipe my sleeve across my nose and look around the stretch of flat, hard-packed dirt surrounding me. About 20 feet across from the gate is a square of cinder block that pops up out of the flat surface. To each side of this building, are others in varying widths, none of them tall enough for an entryway.

Only one door is visible, in the building straight across from me. The rest of the buildings have long, narrow slits in their plain, stony faces. They look like windows at first glance, but windows would have glass. These have narrow slats covering them. Vents. Since the only door I can see is right there, I head for it.

I approach the door as cautiously as I made my way around the wall. I feel like my eyes are going everywhere and seeing a whole lot of nothing. Even if someone is here, I have to wonder if I would notice them. All I can hear is wind blowing across the tops of the buildings. It was a cool day earlier and downright freezing now. The wind makes it worse and pushes me to the waiting door with the promise that it will be warmer, and brighter, inside. At this point I'd be happy to see it full of busy scientists running around creating whatever it is they're making down there. That would mean normality, which would make this place feel a hell of a lot less creepy. It'd also add the element of challenge that's helpful in keeping me alert.

I give the door the once over, looking for traps such as unusual catches or triggers, and find nothing but a standard lock. I pull out my lock picking tools with a sigh. I don't want to be standing out here any longer than necessary, but at least a lock is more comforting than if the door had been open. An unlocked door is usually the sign of severe carelessness or a trap, and the way things have been going, I anticipate the trap. A locked door, adds normalcy to the job. Normalcy I'm glad to have.

Over the years I've found that most locks aren't that sophisticated. Function only allows for so many forms, and I've seen nearly all of them. So far I haven't found a lock I couldn't crack. Settled once again, I put the lamp down between my feet, pull out my tools, and turn into the door to focus on my work. Some people slept with weapons under their pillows, others with one eye open, but me? I keep my tools close at hand wherever I go, knowing I always have use for them. Kind of like Airika, these tools are part of me. They've never let me down.

This time is no exception. After a few minutes of working the lock, I hear the click of the tumblers turning and the door clicks open. Light gleams through the gap in the doorway. I flinch, expecting someone to be on the other side, but the door opens into a lit, empty stairwell. If anyone asks, I'll tell them I was cool and collected the entire time. But in truth, I'm relieved more than I'll ever admit when that nothing deadly happens.

I might be all right here, but finding a source of light tells me there has to be people down below. The light comes from gas lamps that are evenly spaced down through the stairwell. They wouldn't waste such a valuable and expensive resource if no one was home. Hell, even lighting an unoccupied stairwell this way seems wasteful, but it isn't my money.

I quickly tuck my tools away, grab the lamp, and whip around inside. Standing in a wash of real light now, I put out the lamp and set it at the top of a newly discovered set of stairs. I would need it heading out again, but for now it's unnecessary. Might as well conserve what little fuel I have for getting back to Airika. These stairs are the beginning of an entire underground campus I'll have to search. If what I see here is any indication, I won't need the lamp down there.

I look down the stairs that lead into the earth. I can't hear anything other than the hiss of the lamps, which seem to be fed by pipes running through the walls. The vents above must keep the gas from building up to dangerous levels. Every so often in New Foundis, people would suffocate or a building would go up in flames because of a leak. Something like that in an underground compound would be worse. At least for any people unlucky enough to be trapped inside. The idea alone sends a shiver down my back. But as far as I can tell, it seems safe. For now.

I pause for a moment, listening to the quiet stairwell. I want to hear something—voices, footsteps, even heavy machinery. If there's anyone down there, I can't tell. I have no idea how many other doors might lead into the heart of the compound, but I only have one option. Down. I've all but forgotten my instinct to leave. It's too late now, and the long passage calls to me. I may be getting old, but I still enjoy a good adventure. I hitch up my big-boy pants and start down the stairs, hoping there's something better than death waiting at the bottom. It's not a very pleasant thought, but somehow it's better than thinking about carrying armloads of research back up all these stairs. That's looking on the bright side.

The stairs switch back and forth, obscuring the bottom from view. I lose track of the flights after a while. Long minutes go by and it feels like I've gone miles into the earth before I finally see an end to the winding. If this compound was built into an old mine site, it had to be a major one. It's not until I reach the bottom that I'm met with another door and nowhere else to go. I look back up between the stair flights but I can't see the top. It's going to be a pain in the ass to climb back out.

I don't know how deep underground I am, but I feel claustrophobia wrapping around me. It's better to focus on the job so I don't have to think about it. I return to the door blocking the way and test it out. Just like the door at the top, this one is locked. At least they're taking security seriously, though I have no idea if there's anything worth protecting. While locking up the fortress is always a good idea, locks have a strange habit of inviting all the mavericks out there who think they can break into any place. I've often thought that when I retire from being a maverick, it might be fun to build a place like this with bigger and better locks and traps as a training ground for the next generation.

This lock is also easy to pick. I slowly push open the door, expecting all hell to break loose. Yeah, I expect alarms to be sounding all over this place by now, but luck seems to be hanging out in my back pocket. The door opens into a brightly lit, sterile hallway. To my right, the hall ends in another normal looking door. The rest of the hall is lined with what I can only guess are more doors. The grey metal blends in with the cement walls, leaving only a slight line around the edges to show any difference. I can't see any knobs or latches. Not even a key hole that would allow me to pick them.

At the far end of the hall is another door like the many blank, knobless ones. I've got two choices; take the easy route and head through the only other door that I can pick, or try to figure out how to open the strange doors. Experience has shown me that if something is worth hiding, it's not going to be easy to get to. So, I turn my attention to the hall full of mystery doors. The research and tick have got to be secreted away behind one of them. And maybe I'll find a few other things worth my time.

The hallway is lit by the same gas lamps that filled the stairway. Even the city streets aren't this bright. But then, the streets of New Foundis are coated in a layer of grime. This place is gleaming and silent. I wish I knew where they were and why they left everything burning. I can't tell how long they've been gone, but if the place is abandoned, they must have left in a hurry. Or they plan to be back. Or they're hiding behind those doors, waiting for me to walk in on them. The thought leaves a hollow feeling in the pit of my stomach, so I try to push it away. Get this job done and get out. That's the best plan.

I move to the middle of the hall to get a better look around. My footsteps echo against the concrete walls and come back, sounding like an army walking with me. I feel like eyes are watching, as if I'm some kind of experiment. A rat in a maze. I have to keep looking around and over my shoulder, to assure myself there isn't a group of scientists following me with clipboards to note every decision I make.

I turn my attention back to the doors. They're spread out about equidistant from one another, all of them closed and none with signs to tell me what's behind them. Nothing so much as a "Records Storage" or "Main Laboratory" to point me the right way. They must have kept their word so secret; they didn't even want to share it with each other. No wonder the researchers got away with building weapons instead of following the corporation's mission.

At the same time, it can't be that hard to find. Wisen would have given a few more details if he thought it would be hard to identify his research. If I understand Samantha, it's just about anything that doesn't have to do with war machinery. In the end, I have to find something. Going back empty-handed would destroy my reputation.

It's time to get these doors open and see what's waiting behind them. I look at the first one on my left. Ten more like it stretch down the hall. Even if I figure out the first one, it's going to take a while to work through them all. I move closer to inspect it, hoping for some sign of a way to crack it. I push on it, first in, then sideways to see if it will slide. It doesn't budge. In one of my brighter moments, I kick the door as hard as I can. The iron-toe of my boot connects with solid metal, sending a sharp "CLANG" echoing down the hall.

My violent impulse does nothing to open the door, but the vibration travels through the walls and the other doors begin to shake with a strange unity. Maybe it has something to do with the structure being built into the ground. One perfect vibration sets off a chain reaction that reaches into the earth itself and sends the whole place into a frenzy. I hope the ceiling doesn't come crashing down. That'll be the end of this job, and I would have no one to blame but myself.

With a cringe and a curse, I press myself into the slight indent of the doorway, hoping to survive whatever happens next. The vibrations move down the hall, rattling door after door until they get to the end, where another door is pressed into the wall. The gas lamps just above my head rattle with the vibration as well. They flicker out with the hard shaking, darkening the area just around me. The vibration travels to the other side of the hall, then down the corridor to meet in the middle at the far door, shaking it harder than all the others. Yep. This place is going to collapse, and I'm going to die in here. Good job, Colt.

I turn to bolt for the open stairwell door, when a new sound hits my ears. The door at the opposite end clicks and I look back to see it slide open, revealing a dark room. I stop and stand there in surprise as the vibrations move through that new opening and settle into silence. A few of the lights have gone out, but nothing's fallen. This place is better built than I had given it credit for. But that's one hell of a way to open a door.

I wait just a few seconds longer, listening for footsteps or voices. This place is too quiet. If anyone were here, they would come running now. Since no one does, I can only guess I'm alone. I convince myself that it's safe and start toward the newly opened door. I came down here to get a job done. I'd be an idiot not to at least take a look. If nothing else, maybe there are switches to open the other doors.

The shaking had knocked out enough lights to dim the hall. Somewhere in the back of my mind I realize they're leaking gas. I'd be worried, but the remaining lights should be able to take up the excess. They're burning a little brighter as they cast strange shadows across the floor, flickering with the vibration that's too low for me to feel or hear any more. I could swear there are people in those ghostly shadows. But no one is here. Except for me, the hall's empty. I push away the feeling of being watched and continue toward the end of the hall.

The corridor looks long, practically endless. But the doors that line each side and the opening at the end assure me it's finite. I pass as quickly as I can by the closed and nameless doors, curious what might be behind them. What form did the military research take? New airships? Artillery? Weapons we've never seen before? I'd wager most of it would make a damn good profit. I get jobs all the time where people are looking to stab each other in the back to make a little scratch from the person with the biggest pocket book. Hell, in the end, that's the real reason I'm down here. Wisen's research might have sentimental value to him, but it's got to be worth something.

It feels like several minutes pass before I'm standing at the threshold of the doorway and gazing into the inky blackness of the room. My biggest fear is another set of stairs I can't see, or worse, a sudden drop off into a bottomless pit. Taking things slow, I plant my hands on each side of the opening and slide my right foot into the darkness. At least my foot is touching what feels like a floor, and the door hasn't slammed closed, cutting off my lower leg. Pressing my luck, I lean in and bring my left foot through the doorway. Luck finally fails as I hear a loud click. I barely have time to react, only able to pull my foot back with a jerk as gears start to turn and rumble deep in the surrounding structure. I'm dead.

Chapter 3

"Horseballs!" I duck down into a crouch and pull my arms over my head. The reflex is useless since I have no idea where the danger is actually coming from. It feels like a natural thing to do. Ducking also does absolutely nothing, except make me look like a jackass, when there turns out to be no danger. It's a good thing no one is around to see me cowering like an abused dog as the machinery turns on another set of gas lamps ringing the room.

It takes a moment for me to unfold, adjust to the new light, and assure myself no one's here. With the lights on, it's easy to see the vast lack of anything useful. The space stretches out a few feet further in a flat, unremarkable cement floor. On the other side is a curved set of large windows that reflect the gas lamps' light back across the room like a dozen flickering spirits. Disappointment fills me as I see nothing I had hoped to find. No boxes, no experiments sitting out on tables, no controls.

But the windows catch my eye. They have to be looking out at something, and I'm too far underground for it to be outside. I take my time to cross over to the windows, not wanting to trigger anything else. The floor is deceptively smooth, but I can't be sure I didn't step on some kind of switch. If there are other triggers, I'd never know until it's too late. I make it to the windows unscathed, but I'm hardly surprised when I hear another click. I lift my foot and look down, but the floor looks the same as it always had. This crazy place seems to be determined to kill me one way another, even if it's giving me a heart attack with all the surprises.

Before my life can flash before my eyes, lights begin to flicker on outside the windows. Like an oncoming locomotive, the lights come on in rows from the back of a massive room toward the front. Tall figures sit in perfect columns, stretching all the way to the back. The figures, human in form, but metal in structure, have to be at least 10 feet tall. It's hard to say though, because they're at least 5 stories below where I stand. The way the lights come up makes the figures appear as if they're moving toward me like an ocean wave and it takes a minute for my eyes to register they aren't actually moving at all.

It's an automaton army. Hundreds of them. And they're armored for war. This is what Samantha had been talking about. When she mentioned war machines, I never imagined I would be seeing anything like this.

Cold shock freezes my spine. A knot forms in the pit of my stomach as I look over them. Samantha had said Wisen hadn't been part of this, but I can't help but wonder how much he knew before he was forced out. How much of his own research wen into these things? The army standing below me is complete and ready war. A big one. One that would be impossible for them to lose. I suddenly wonder if the compound had been evacuated in preparation to let the automatons loose on the world.

My mind is overwhelmed by memories of my time back in the war. All those lives lost for reasons I never understood. Each side looking for newer and better technology to wipe their enemy off the face of the planet. When I was a 16 year old kid, inadvertently joining the militia, I had no idea what I was getting into. Even as a smuggler I try not to think about the things I provide to people who would them for evil. But looking at this? Something in me breaks. What the hell have I been doing all these years?

I shake my head. No. I'm not responsible for those machines. I was hired to find research of a very different nature. Wasting my time staring at these monsters isn't getting that done. I turn to leave, but something stops me. I can't in good conscience leave that army down there to be used at any time, especially with the possibility that someone's about to pull the trigger on this loaded gun. The only way to stop it is to destroy this place. I don't know how much time I've got, but the only thing I can think to do is go get Avery and bring him back here and rig this place up to explode. If they want war, I'll give them a very quick and final one.

But first I need to get as much of Wisen's research out of here as I can carry and that means finding a way to search these other rooms. I start back out into the hall, less concerned about traps since I've always passed this way. That's when it hits me. What, I can't say exactly. It's a feeling somewhere between brain freeze and nausea. I double over, clutching my head as the hallway before me twists and elongates. I don't have time to wonder what's going on as the gas lamps flare and flicker. More are out now, flooding the hallway with their unconsumed fuel. Lamp remains cover the floor, while cooling black marks mar the wall where they had been. How had I not noticed them exploding? Had I been so caught up in the sight of the automaton army? Gas is taking the place of the air. As it does, the remaining lights flare brightly before being smothered by their gluttonous consumption. Shit. I've got to get the hell out of here.

I stumble forward as the hall grows darker. I have the horrible realization that my nausea hadn't been the questions and automatons, but the gas-filled air I had been pulling into my lungs. Each labored step feels like a slog, making me wonder if I'll even be able to get out before I can't breathe any more. While the compound may not have been a trap, it was a mistake to come here, and I feel like I'm inches from death. If I die down here, I won't have been able to stop whatever it is that's happening in this place. Or finish the job I was sent to do. That will be hard enough since I can't search those rooms under these conditions. But if I live, I can come back prepared.

I can't give up. The coughing starts about halfway down the hallway as I stumble from side to side. It feels like I'm running uphill over falling rocks. I can barely breathe and keeping my feet is impossible. The lights are going out around me faster now, exploding with glassy pops. It's all I can do to miss the shards that rain around me. As it is, I can feel them hitting me, burning my face and clothes as I try to run.

I get to the end of the hall where all of this had started. The door I had entered the hall through, is closed. I cough, trying to remember if I had closed it, or if it had just closed because of the vibrations. Not that it matters. I had picked the lock so it should still be accessible. All those stairs are going to be a pain in the ass to climb with my lungs burning so badly though. I grab the knob and try to jerk the door open. It doesn't budge. I push it forward. Still nothing. I run my finger over the knob, searching for a latch to unlock it, but nothing's immediately obvious. With a growl, I twist the knob left and right, shaking the door. "LET ME OUT!" The shouting only results in another fit of coughing.

Damn it. I need to get out of here right now. I turn to the left and the only other normal door in the hall. My head spins with the motion, and I nearly vomit before I catch myself against the metallic surface. Keep it together Colt. If this door isn't unlocked, I'm going to have to pick one of them, and I don't have time for that. I swallow back the nausea and grip the knob. I give it a twist as another light explodes behind me, and something clicks. At least I think it does. I pull back on the door, and it opens, revealing a narrow downward staircase and more gas lamps. The bright glare of the fresh light stabs my eyes.

Stale air puffs against my face, knocking back some of the gas. I pull in a burning breath and decide to go down the stairs. It may not be out, but it's away from immediate danger. I once heard someone say that asphyxiation is a pleasant feeling. That drowning has a peacefulness to it. I can't say I agree. Bright spears of pain cover my body as I gasp in the blending mix of air and gas. I take the first step and try to pull the door closed behind me. My head spins with the gassy intoxication. My feet slip on the stairs and I find myself landing hard on my ass. Then I'm rolling down the uneven surface. It's the worst pain I think I've ever felt, but at the same time it keeps me conscious. Each bump knocks the small amount of air I was able to get, out of me.

I try to stop myself, but there's nothing to hold onto. Who the hell builds a staircase without handrails? I'm just boxed in by walls that push me back and forth across the steps and keep the momentum going. Up above, I hear the shattering of glass as the lamps in the stairwell start to explode. I didn't manage to get the door closed. It won't take long for the gas to fill this area too. Taking this direction is going to prove to be my biggest, and final, mistake.

I keep tumbling for what feels like ages. I have to be going down at least as far as the automatons' room. If I had time or ability to think about it, I would guess these stairs lead right to the blasted things. Right now, I'm only concerned with making it to the bottom in one piece.

And somehow I do. I'm suddenly stopped by the hard, metallic thud of another door. I land against it in a jumbled mess. I can't breathe and everything hurts, but I don't think I have broken any bones. I won't know until I can force myself to get up. I should do that.

All I can do is lie against the door, trying to suck in breaths. I don't have the force of will to do anything else. My strength is gone. A dark realization washes over me. I'm going to die in this place. If anyone does manage to come here later, they'll find my petrified corpse sprawled undignified at the bottom of a dark, gas-filled stairwell. Who would have thought I'd end up like this? I can hear Horner laughing now.

I also hear the bang and crackle of lamps bursting high above. The sound is getting closer, like gunfire taking out my squad members one after another. In the distance I hear pounding. I think at first it's the pounding of my heart, which is working hard under my ribs. That's when I realize it's not me, but something else. Something outside of myself. The pounding sounds like soldiers' marching footsteps, bringing back memories of the war. Explosions. Gunfire. Screaming. So much screaming.

It had been many years since anything brought up the memories of those long distant days. And here in this strange place, I find myself fixated on it all over again. The pain, my desperate attempt to breathe, the darkness, and the sounds meld together and turn into the one thing I spend conscious effort trying not to remember. All the lives I had been responsible for snuffing out. The good men I had seen killed. It's all come back now, fresh in my mind like the smell of baking bread. I can't deny it. I can't ignore it. The horror of war is going to be the last thing I think about in this world. How pathetic.

The worst part is the screaming. Those screams never go away, even though I don't dream about them very often anymore. Now they fill the air again, a cacophony of voices coming from everywhere and echoing in the confines of the stairwell. Some of them are pained, while others are frightened, and still more are shouting desperate orders. That had been the war. One big yelling match. But one scream rises up above the mental din, pulling free from the others.

At first I think it's my own scream in the moments before I give in to terror. But that's impossible. I can't breathe, so I can't scream. It's not me. It's a high-pitched, feminine scream. A scream of pain. It's coming from the other side of the door. Someone is out there. Someone is trying to open the door. Someone is trying to help me and it's causing her pain.

The scream hurts. Deep down in my heart where nothing had hurt for a very long time. It's enough to snap me back to the present. But there's still nothing I can do. I can't move. I'm pretty sure I'll lose consciousness soon and her pain will be for nothing. Despite my wish for her to stop trying, she doesn't and that's a good thing.

Chapter 3

The door jerks open, flooding the stairwell with more bright light. I fall through the doorway, rolling a short distance and come to a stop on my back. Laid out on the ground, my body does what I can't think to do, start gasping for large breaths of air. It hurts my lungs and burns my throat, but at least I can breathe. I hear the slam of the door behind me and realize the screaming had stopped right about the time I tumbled through.

I cough and shake, feeling my head pound and a terrible, acrid taste on my tongue. I hear the soft sound of whimpering and I look up. Everything is hazy in the bright room. Somewhere above I can see rich greens and browns that seem familiar but I can't quite place them. My thoughts are still hung up on the war. I feel like I'm back there. I had just crashed my airship. I had been thrown free of the wreckage. I'm lying injured in a foreign forest, waiting for someone, a friend or an enemy, to find me.

As I lay there trying to recover, a shadow falls over me. I narrow my eyes to focus on the face that appears over my own. What I see makes no sense. Glowing red eyes. Limp strands of dirty, blonde hair, framing a face that's part flesh, part mechanical. This is no soldier. I'm not sure what exactly it is. Had this thing freed me from certain death? Or had it come to finish the job?

Then it speaks in a small, wavering mechanical voice. "You're not supposed to be here."

Chapter 4

"You're not supposed to be here," she says with a slight hint of curiosity mixed with hesitation. But her words are secondary to the sudden appearance of her face. For the first time I realize I'm not completely alone in this strange place. I've been caught by something. What, exactly, I'm not sure.

I gasp, which turns into a hoarse cough. The red eyes of the creature blink and she takes a step back like a cautious animal. My initial thought of being busted by some kind of security device, fades and is replaced by a curiosity over what exactly she is. I fight back the coughing and force myself to look at her again. She's holding her hands against her tattered and dirty yellow dress. While she's some kind of mix of monster and human, I also realized she couldn't be much more than 5 years old. Just a kid. Nothing about her screams that she's a threat. Getting the door opened had hurt her somehow and she stands there shivering and sniffling like and abused dog.

I slowly sit up, checking myself for severe injuries as I do. I can't stay here in this place long. Not with the gas building up on the other side of that door. I'm worse for wear, but I'm still mobile, so I push myself up to my feet. The entire time, I can feel the girl's red eyes watching me. I don't know how the hell she sees with those things. I'm not sure I want to know. But I'm certain she can see a lot more that I could guess.

I turn around to face her again, cringing. She stares at me with those mechanical red eyes, and her left arm and leg are coated in some kind of metal casing. Even the left side of her face and forehead are covered in metal. I reach up to touch the scar on my left cheek, feeling the unusually smooth skin. Most of her alterations are on the left, just like my wound. I'm nowhere near as messed up as she is, but at the same time I feel a kinship with her.

She's not all mechanical construct. She has some flesh. From what I can see of her hands, they seem to be normal and the location of her pain. The right side of her face, nose, mouth and chin all appear to be human. I don't know if she's a machine like that army, or if she was once flesh and blood like me. If she was, who would do this to a child? And then leave her alone in this strange place? A shiver runs down my back. I had been abandoned around her age. I remember what it's like.

A sickening realization washes over me. Or maybe it's the lingering effects of the gas. I spin around a little too face, expecting to be faced with the waiting army. Instead, I come face to face with a stand of trees. No, not just a stand. A whole damned forest. I know I couldn't possibly gotten outside. I fell down the stairs, not up them. And on the other side of me is a solid, gray wall. A forest is growing underground. I blink and gasp again, setting off another round of coughs. I double over, then crouch, trying to get ahold of myself.

The uneven step, thud of the kid's feet move a little closer to me. "You're not supposed to be here," she says again, as if I didn't hear her the first time. "You're not one of them."

Them? I get the coughing under control and turn slowly to look at her. "Them?" I ask, not trusting my words to come out in one piece. "Them who? The researchers?" Or the automatons? I'm afraid she'll pick the latter.

The girl shakes her head though, shrugging her shoulders. "Them," she says again, as if that answers the question.

It doesn't. I frown and look her over. If she had anything to do with the automaton army, she would have a better answer than that. A sudden realization washes over me. "Tick?" I ask, hoping to high hell I'm wrong. If this is the result of Wisen's research, I'm not that keen to hand her over to him. The automaton army was bad enough, but this child? Only a monster would do this to a kid. I don't care what Samantha said, something about this smells all wrong.

"Tick?" She cocks her head in question but her voice still shivers in pain. I have to admit to a sense of revolution in looking at her, but at the same time I feel sympathy for her. It's not her fault she's been made into this and still left to feel pain.

With her questioning tone, I relax a little. Part of me hopes she isn't what I was sent here to get. That Wisen really isn't the asshat I'm so ready to believe he is. I crouch down to eye level with the girl, watching her flinch back as I do. "Do you know what Tick is?" Maybe I still have a chance to find some of Wisen's research before this whole place becomes a deathtrap. That will only happen if she can help me.

The girl nods. "I am Tick." Damn it. Of course she is. So much for any faith I might have had in humanity, which isn't much to be honest. Not after what I had seen in the war, or even in my life before and since then.

I bite my lip, not wanting to ask the next question. "And Dr.

Wisen? Do you know him too?" I hope she can confirm one way or another if I can trust Samantha and Wisen. I want to believe I'm here, doing the right thing. For once in my life.

I'm ready for her to say yes and show some kind of fear or hatred for the man. I'm ready for her to want to run and get as far away from me as she can. She does neither of these things. Instead, Tick's eye flicker for a moment, then she nods. "There are two records available. Dr. Harris Wisen, head researcher for ReGen Corps. Dr. Darla Veital-Wisen, head of botany research and development for ReGen Corps."

"Whoa, hold on," I say, stopping her mechanical rote. This is new and unexpected information. "Two Wisens? Did you know either of them?"

Tick nods, her eyes flickering once more. "I helped Dr. Veital-Wisen with the woods."

This stops me. "The woods," I mutter, remembering the sight hiding behind me. I stand and turn back around to look into the expansive forest. Samantha had said ReGen Corps was supposed to be researching patching up the land. This is apparently how they're doing it, but it baffles the mind. Trees don't just grow underground, and little half-mechanical kids don't take care of them. This is another added piece of weirdness to my day I didn't need. But it does answer one thing; the Wisen's seem to be on the right side of things. Sort of.

The kid is still staring at me when I turn back around to face her. "The woods," she says in a matter-of-fact way that makes me feel like a dope. She nods an even gives me the briefest smile. This forest at least makes her happen, despite whatever other misery surrounds her existence.

"Great. Thanks kid." I cringe as I hear myself. I know I shouldn't be frustrated with her, but my people skills were always a little lacking. I sigh and bring her back to more important things. "So, you helped with this place? How long ago? What happened to Veital-Wisen? What happened to Dr. Harris Wisen?" I want to believe Samantha was telling me the truth, but Tick's appearance raises doubts.

Tick shakes her head this time. "I do not know." I glance around, thinking that time can't mean much down here. I'm not even sure how much time I've been down here, but it's too long. I glance to the closed door, imaging the rising gas levels starting to leak through. Whether I can trust Wisen or not, I can't leave her down here.

First, I need to get her to trust me. My eyes draw down to her hands again. She couldn't be comfortable like that. I crouch down again, reaching out toward her. "Let me take a look at your hands."

She hesitates, shivering slightly as she looks at my hands. After a moment, she relents and unfolds her arms, opening her charred palms to me. The small action is huge for her. She had no reason to trust me or anyone. I'll bet no one had ever even touched her in a kind way. I still can't be sure if there's anything human in her, but if there is, I don't want to see her in pain any longer. It's obvious that she can feel something, and that's enough for me to call her alive.

While most of my time in the militia was spent as a pilot, I had basic training in field dressing wounds. Sometimes there was need for a medic but none were around. That's about all I can do for her now. Even that won't be perfect given the lack of materials. I take her hands gently, seeing this is no minor injury. The palms are burned open, blackened with singed skin and blood. Under that skin is a network of tiny clockwork gears, also burned. Some of them had stopped moving, gummed up by the charred mess. "Ugh…monkey tits. How'd this happen?"

Tick cants her head to the side and I'm certain she's going to ask about monkey tits. I'm not about to explain that to her. She surprises me again by saying, "The door."

I look to the door standing silently behind her. It looks the same as any other door; made of metal with a regular looking knob. Though the knob is smudged with black from the girl's hands. I look back at them with a frown. Did someone purposely build the doors to hurt her? What possible end could it serve? "Right. Let's get your hands wrapped up."

At least the wounds aren't bleeding. She flinches with each slight movement and damn it if my hands aren't shaking like a fresh caught fish. I didn't come here expecting to play the medic, which means I don't have anything but the clothes on my back to wrap up injuries. The girl's dress, while tattered, is too dirty to use as dressing, so I sacrifice my scarf. It's not the cleanest thing I've got, but it's better than her dress and it'll do for now. I pull it off my neck and start ripping it into strips to coil around her hands.

I make quick work of wrapping her hands, her eyes watching me intently the entire time. It's kind of creepy really, those bright glowing eyes peering out of her small head. I want to imagine her with real eyes, but then my brain goes in a different direction forcing an image of what had been an innocent gaze being plucked free of her head to be replaced by cold mechanics. Could Wisen have done this to her? Or was it someone else? A shiver runs down my back at the thought, making me stand a little too quickly. My head swims with the motion, and I stumble back far enough to land against a tree.

"Are you well?" Her voice echoes through the forest, making me wonder how big this place is. She remains standing there, holding out her wrapped hands even though I let go of them.

I nod and try to smile confidently, though I'm not sure if it comes across that way. Or if she even could see it or understand. I guess it makes me feel a little better at least. My head is pounding and I feel like my legs won't hold me a second longer. I need to get it together if we're going to make it out of here. So I take a deep breath to steady myself. "Yeah. Colton. You can call me Colton, okay?" It seems fair that I give her my name since I know hers. As much of a name as Tick is.

She nods and lowers her hands finally, seeming satisfied with the lackluster bandaging. "Colton," she repeats back, flashing a smile a little bigger than she had used before.

I can't help but smile back. I don't know about turning her over to Samantha and Wisen, but there's no way in hell I'm leaving her here. "Now, do you know a way out of this place?"

The question hangs in the air for only a second. Just long enough for me to realize it's the wrong thing to ask. Anyone who had such obvious answers to my previous questions is going to have one for the next. And the girl doesn't disappoint. "The same way you came in," she says with no hint of humor or impishness. That is simply the answer. To illustrate her point, she motions toward the door I had fallen through only moments before.

"You're a lot of help, you know?" The sarcasm is far over the girl's head, but I can't say I give a damn at this point. We don't have time to stand here playing games.

"Thank you, Colton." She stares into my very center and grins like I had given her the greatest compliment in the world. From the look of her dirt-covered, tattered little body, maybe I had. I can't help but remember when I wasn't so much different from her. Just another street kid with nowhere to go and no one who cared if I lived or died. Looking at her, except for the metal and light that had been stuck on her body, is like looking at a ghost of myself. I feel sorry for this kid even if she's mostly mechanical and wouldn't understand my sympathy anyway.

Despite her looks, and whatever lingering pain she has, she seems to be happy. She's also the only one here who might know another way out. I've gotten comfortable with the idea that the rest of this place is abandoned, though the reason is eating at me. That will be something else to question this kid about, but it could wait. "We can't go that way, kid. Is there another?"

Tick looks down at her hands for a moment, flexing her fingers around the freshly placed bandages. Her red eyes dim slightly before brightening again. She looks up and starts walking. "This way," she says, moving past me and heading into the trees.

All right. I raise a brow and watch her go a little way. Tick doesn't look back to see if I'm following her. She walks with a limp to her more mechanical side. Her whole left seems to weigh her down, making her lean that way, but it doesn't slow her. I have no idea how long she's been like that, but she's gotten used to it. I take a breath to clear out the last of the crap in my lungs and start after her.

Tick leads me deep into the forest. I'm surprised just how much of it there seems to be. It couldn't go on forever, but it seems like this place has already broken several natural laws. It's disorienting. I have no idea where I am under the compound that I had seen from above. It's almost like the work they were doing down here stretched beyond the walls and out into the wild. If this is an old mining operation, that's not such a hard thing to believe. Miners follow the coal and iron as far as it will go. It had to be coal. That would explain the abundance of gas running through this place. My real question is how this forest can possibly thrive down here. "What the hell were they doing here?"

Tick glances back at my question. "The trees live here," she responds.

I chuckle slightly and shake my head. This is kid is literal. I'll have to be careful how I say things around her. But she also knows more about ReGen Corps than I do. "No, I mean, how is this even possible? We're underground. Trees shouldn't be growing underground."

Tick goes silent. The only sounds are the metallic clicking of her body and my soft footsteps on the grass. A few feet further along she finally speaks again. "Underground?" Tick asks, glancing back with a frown. She looks down at her feet and shakes her head. "The ground is under us." Then she looks up to the light filtering through the branches and leaves. "We are under the trees and the sky."

Her words break my heart. This kid has never been outside these walls. At least not that she knows. She has no idea what's out there. But at least it means she doesn't know about the automatons either. Whatever might have been going on down here, the Wisens or someone apparently protected her from it, even if it means using the doors to keep her here. Maybe it was for her own good, but that's no way to live. I need to get her out of this place.

While I know it's the right thing to do, part of me thinks it'll be a shame to destroy this strange forest. It's so lush, unlike the sparse land above. I'm having a hard time getting my head around it. "How is it possible?" I mutter to myself before breaking into a yawn. Now that I've slowed down, the lateness and activity have caught up to me.

"It is time to sleep," Tick says in response to my yawn. "The sun should not be up."

I look toward her with a raised brow. "You know about the sun?"

The girl looks up to the tree boughs and nods. "I tell the sun when to rise and set. I tell the rain when to fall."

"You what?" I ask, looking up along with her. The gas had made my head spin before, but it was nothing compared to my confusion now. My brain refused to understand any of this. I'm certain we're at least a mile underground, if not more, and the bright lights indicated a ceiling somewhere overhead. I can't have been down here long enough for it to be the middle of the day. "How...?" I question aloud again, not expecting an answer.

"Like this," Tick says. With a series of clicks, the lights flicker out.

I find myself covered in near pitch blackness, and I stumble to a stop. If not for Tick's glowing red eyes, I wouldn't be able to see anything. As I watch her eyes bobbing away from me, I hear another series of clicks. Drops of water start falling from above, tapping off the leaves and falling on my helmet in wet splashes. I hold my hands up, feeling the rain drops in shocked amazement. "Uh…okay Tick. I get it." I don't, but if she gets any further away I won't be able to find my way out of this blackened maze. "You can turn the sun on and the rain off, all right."

Another series of clicks echoes from above. The lights come on before the rain stops completely. By the time my eyes adjust to the renewed light, Tick is disappearing around a stand of trees. Damn it. I sigh and start to run after her. "Hey, wait for me!"

Tick doesn't respond, but when I catch up to her, I find her standing at the edge of the forest, staring back at me. She's just as damp from the sudden rain as I am, making her look even more pathetic. Just behind her is the wall of the compound and another door. This one is like the one she had hurt herself on. She stands a few feet away from it, her bandaged hands folded together. "They come in here sometimes," she says quietly.

I jog to a stop and look at the door. "Do you know where it goes?"

Tick shakes her head and turns to look at the door. "I'm not allowed," she says in her mechanical, child-like voice. Tick sounds so sad and wanting, which makes her feel more like the child she resembles.

I wonder if she saw others leave this way and never come back. And if the other door hurt her, this one might too. How could she follow anyone if she knows about the pain it would cause? I'm lucky she decided to help me in spite of it. But what if there's something that prevents her from actually going through? Damn them. They were treating her like some kind of pet. It makes my blood boil just thinking about it.

My rising anger causes another round of coughing. If nothing else, it serves as a warning that we can't afford to stand here any longer. The only option is to carry her through the door, hoping that maybe my body will protect her from anything serious. First, I have to get the thing open. I move around her toward the door. "Is it locked?"

Tick shakes her head and holds up her hands. "I don't know. I am not allowed."

I frown, shaking my head slowly. "Right. I'm sorry. Why did you help me? Did you know that would happen?"

She looks at me a moment, cocking her head to the side like a strange little bird. Her eyes flicker slightly before she answers. "I thought..." she stops and shakes her head. "You're not supposed to be here. You should leave now."

I look at her, not sure what to say. Somewhere on the other side of this forest, gas is slowly leaking out of a doorway. This place wouldn't be safe soon, and I sure as hell don't want to leave her alone. I sigh and smile to her. "Yeah, but you're coming with me."

Tick's red eyes blink and she shakes her head. "But I'm not..."

I don't know jack about kids, but instinct directs me to crouch down to eye-level and hold out a hand, inviting her to take it, so that's what I do. "Look kid, I'm allowing you, okay? We got to get out of here before something happens. Give me a minute to get the door open, then I'm going to carry you through, all right? If this doesn't work…" What? Start trying to tunnel into the walls? Find another way? "Well, we'll figure something out."

Tick reaches out tentatively and touches my wet hand. For all the metal on her, the touch is light. She pulls her hand back quickly and nods. "Okay."

I nod and stand up again. "Right. Do you know how the others opened this door? Will it hurt me if I try?"

She cradles her abused hands together and stares at the door. "It burns." It's not a great answer, but I can't expect her to know. She backs away as if she expects the door to jump out and bite her.

My instinct is to help her, but the best way to do that is get the hell out of here, so I turn to the door, crouching down to inspect the simple knob. This is the kind of job where I need to crack my knuckles and pretend to look like a confident professional, despite my strong desire not to experience the burning pain Tick had suffered. Everything about the door looks normal. I can't see any pins or breaks in the doorknob that would explain the pain mechanism.

Only trying will tell me anything about it, so I pull out my tools and get to work. Anticipation is a terrible burden. It heightens any worry that might be there, and usually ends up making mistakes happen. But when that anticipation is proven wrong, it's one of the best feelings in the world. Instead of touching the metal with my fingers, I use my lock pick to poke at it.

When nothing happens, I slip the pick into place and there's not as much as a jolt or feeling of warmth. I glance back at the girl to see her watching silently while she clutches her hands to her chest. I can't tell what she's thinking behind those mechanical eyes, but she waits in silent apprehension.

The door isn't difficult to pick. I don't get so much as a crackle or burn as I start to work the lock. While it could mean this door isn't trapped, it could also mean they were made specifically to keep Tick in here. I just hope freedom for both of us is waiting on the other side.

With a little work, the lock clicks open. I stand and open the door, holding my breath. I expect something horrible to be waiting for us. More stairs going further down, a room full of researchers who had been watching the whole time. Or the room full of automatons, waiting to tear up anyone who comes through. Instead, I find a stairway leading blissfully upward. Like the others, this one is lit with gas lamps, hissing away undisturbed.

I turn and smile to Tick. "Looks like the right way. You ready, kid?"

She glances back toward the trees and bites her lower lip. "But...the forest."

This place is all she knows. It's her home and she clearly cares about it. I nod, moving back to put my hand on her shoulder. "It'll be all right. I promise." I hate lying to such an innocent kid. Especially one who's been through so much. But I have to convince her to go.

Tick looks between the woods and me, thinking about it. Finally she nods and gazes at the waiting door. "Yes."

"Good. I'm going to pick you up now, okay?" I try to appear confident, but I don't know if it works until Tick agrees with a soft nod of her dirty blond head. I nod back and scoop her up as carefully as I can, only to realize there's still some glass stuck in my jacket. Sharp pains cut into me, and I almost drop her, but now isn't the time to be weak, so I grin and bear it. "You ready?"

She nods again, curling her arms around my neck. I can feel her hands avoiding contact. I take that as all the confirmation I need. Like pulling out a rotten tooth, the best way to do it is act too fast to think about it. Some people liked to count, as if reaching the magical number 3 makes everything all right. All it does is give them a chance to second guess whatever it is they're doing.

Without so much as a breath of warning, I turn and pull the girl through the open doorway, wincing as I go. All the clockwork that makes up the bulk of her is heavy, and my body is about worn out. I'm going to pay for this adventure tomorrow.

She yelps, but not because of any effect of some invisible barrier. It's out of fear. Fear that I have to admit feeling myself. We make it through relatively unscathed, and once on the other side, both of us let out a sigh of relief.

I let her down gently and look up at the long flight of stairs ahead of us. "All right, I think we're going to make it. Hope you don't mind a few stairs." I hate them. Especially going up, though I think I've developed a new distaste for down as well.

Tick follows my gaze upward and shakes her head, seemingly emboldened now that she's through the door. I give her a smile, trying to be strong if only for myself. I can only hope these stairs end with an exit outside. Tick glances back out through the open door and the lights click off in the forest, returning it to black. "The trees will sleep until we come back," she says before turning back to the stairs.

She starts the upward climb, and I nod. "Yeah. Good idea." I close the door and head up after her. If the researchers do come back, they're going to be plenty surprised when the sun doesn't rise in the morning.

Chapter 5

By the time we reach the top of the stairs, I can barely walk. The girl, however, is tireless. She bounds ahead of me, stopping at the door and stands looking at it until I join her on the landing. I come to a stop behind her, frowning slightly. Is this door going to be a challenge too? What about outside? I'm certain she's never seen outside, and it's going to scare the crap out of her. "Are you going to be okay?" I pant, leaning against the wall to rest.

She looks up at me with her red-glowing eyes. "Okay?"

It occurs to me that no one has ever asked her that before. I doubt anyone has actually cared enough to worry about her well-being. I don't know what kind of relationship she had with Dr. Veital-Wisen, but I'd put donuts to dollars it was all business. Tick is a tool, not so different from my picks or Airika. The exhaustion, pain, and pent up anger at the people in Tick's life up until now, bubble out in a low growl. "Those monsters. Let's get the hell out of here." I just hope this new door doesn't lead into another endless part of the compound.

"Monsters?" Her inquisitive voice echoes in the tight stairwell. She continues to look at me, her bandaged hands curled together. She had held them tight against her body the whole climb, which I would have found awkward, but it didn't seem to bother her a bit.

I sigh and sit down on one of the steps. It's a mistake. I'm not sure if I'll be able to get back up again any time soon. My legs scream in blissful relief, clearly telling me they're done for now. I close my eyes, trying to focus on something else. "What do you know about ReGen

Corps?" I ask Tick. I suspect the answer is not much. Why would a tool know anything about the work it's made to accomplish?

Tick approaches me on the small landing, and puts her hand very lightly on my shoulder. It's almost like I had put mine her shoulder just a little while ago and I find it strangely comforting. "ReGen Corps grows the trees," she says, telling me nothing I hadn't already known.

I frown and look up at her. "But what about Dr. Harris Wisen? You said he was the head researcher. Was he involved with the trees? Do you know what he did here?"

Tick's eyes flicker once more. I've always been able to read faces. I know when people are hiding something or trying to think of the right thing to say in any given moment. Her face is half-obscured, making that difficult, but her eyes tell me everything I need to know. When they blink like that, she's thinking. I would guess she can do more than just give the plants down there light and water. She seems to have information as well and I hope it's something useful.

After a moment, Tick shakes her head. "I do not know," she says quietly.

"Horseballs," I grumble. That doesn't help me one way or another in deciding whether to trust Wisen. All I have to go on is Samantha's belief he was working on the right side of this fiasco, and the proof of the forest. My experience tells me not to take anything at face value though. I start to stand up, feeling every muscle in my body protest. It's time to get going.

"Are you going to be okay?" Tick's voice echoes through the

stairwell, mimicking the same question I had asked her, but I don't hear any mock in her tone. I would say she is actually concerned, but I think it's closer to repeating what seems like the right thing to say. She remains standing there, pulling her hands back to herself.

I nod and try to smile confidently, though I'm not sure if it comes across that way. Or if she even could see it or understand. I guess it makes me feel a little better at least. My head is pounding and I feel like my legs wobble under me, but I manage to stand. I take a deep breath to steady myself. "Yeah. Let's see where this door leads."

Tick steps out of the way as step up to the door. My knees give loud, protesting pops as I crouch down to inspect the door. Damn I'm getting old. Retirement's sounding better all the time. With the other half of the payment for this job, I might just be in the right place to step away. I snort at the door and shake my head. I'm not sure I want to hand Tick over to Wisen. Not without knowing his part in this. If I don't hand her over, I won't get the other half of the payment.

I glance back at Tick, who is standing silently, watching me. 5, maybe 6 on the outside? At her age, I'd have been fit to bursting to get out of here. My mother, the only relative I had, died when I was about Tick's age. I had to rely on the kindness of other people who had nothing to spare. It hadn't been easy, but somehow I made through those early days. I hadn't been nearly as put together as Tick is now, and I'd argue she's been through more.

Returning my focus to the door, I again make quick work of the lock. ReGen doesn't seem to be too concerned about thieves sneaking around the compound. Good for me. The door unlocked, I push myself back up, using the wall for a little help. I don't even want to think about the walk back to Airika. In the dark. Horseballs. I left the lantern back at the top of the other stairs.

No job goes 100 percent perfect. I'd be dubious if one did. I look back at Tick and try to give her a confident smile. "You ready to see what's waiting for us?" She gives me a curious look, then nods.

I nod back and take a deep breath. Truth is, I'm not exactly ready. But I want to be done with this place, so I slowly open the door. As I do, a puff of cool, fresh air wraps around me. I smile, thinking something at least has gone right. We've found our way out of the underground deathtrap.

I push the door open further, scanning the night for signs of anyone being around. Like the rest of this place, no one is here. I sigh and step out to get a better idea of where the hell we've ended up. As I do, another cold breeze blows around me, chilling the sweat and remaining rain water on my skin. I frown. This door has come out on top of the wall and there's about a 20-foot drop on either side.

"I hate this place," I grumble, turning back to look at Tick. She peeks out through the open doorway. "I hate it all. ReGen, Wisen, everything."

Tick stops and looks up at me, her glowing eyes cutting through the night. "You hate the trees? You hate me?"

"I..." I stop, shaking my head and smiling. "No, I don't hate the trees or you. I'm just..." I look around, trying to figure out the best way out of here. "I'm just frustrated. We need to find a way down off this wall that doesn't involve going back down into the compound. I'm not climbing another goddamned stair."

Moving fully out of the door, Tick points to a spot behind me on the wall. "Will you climb a goddamned ladder?"

Her voice is so innocent and unassuming; it's funny to hear her repeating my bad habits. I laugh softly and turn around to look in the direction she points. I have to squint to pick up any details in the dark, but she's right. Ladders are placed at regular intervals along the wall. They lead to the inside of the compound, but that's better than being stuck up here. "Well, I'll be…" I shake my head and start toward the waiting escape route. "I definitely will. Can you climb down the ladder?" Her hands might be a problem. If I have to, I'll carry her again.

Tick is right behind me. I can hear the clink of her metallic foot against the cement of the wall. It's a damn good thing no one is here, or they would come running at all noise she makes. "Yes," she says behind me. "The trees have ladders."

I raise a brow and glance back at her. I suppose that makes some kind of sense, if they needed to get up into the higher branches. But it still sounds weird. And she also did that climbing when her hands were fine. I keep my reservations to myself for now. I'll just have her test out her hands on the railings before I go down.

When we get to the ladder, I move past, and motion to it. "Try to grab onto the railing. If you can't hold on, I'm going to carry you down."

Tick pauses and looks at the parallel metal loops that stick up over the side of the wall. She raises her hands and looks at the dirty white cloth wrapped around them. Her fingers twitch back and forth a little, then she looks back at me. "I can't."

As I had thought, the damage is too much. She's lost the normal movement of her hands, making it impossible to hold on to the railing. Carrying her down isn't going to be easy, but I'm not leaving her here. "It's okay," I tell her, leaning down. "I'll get you down, and maybe my friend, Avery can patch you up. He's real good at that kind of thing." Not that Tick is exactly an airship or a gadget, but if anyone can get her hands working, it's going to be Avery.

Tick nods and smiles again. "Okay." She lifts her arms up to me, ready to be carried down the ladder. On the outside, she's a monstrosity. Just about anyone out in the world would run screaming from her. But I find myself growing attached to Tick's sweet and innocent personality. I hope there's something more to her story than some poor kid who's been abused and abandoned by everyone she's ever known.

I laugh and pick her up again, grunting under the weight. If I'm not careful, she'll be dragging my sorry ass back to Airika. I have enough strength to maneuver onto the ladder and carefully start edging my way down. Tick clings to me, one of my arms bearing the brunt while my other hand slides slowly along the railing. I take my time, making each foot placement as careful as I can. If Tick has any problem with the height, she doesn't make as much as a peep.

20 feet is a long way down. Or at least it feels like it. But finally my foot touches solid ground. I bring the other one to meet it and step

back from the ladder. "That wasn't so bad, was it?" I lie.

Tick shakes her head, looking as though she enjoyed the journey. "Where do we go now?" she asks, gazing around the compound.

Good question. I had spotted the gate from wall. It isn't that far away, but the view from the ground obscures everything. I know if we head toward the west wall we'll eventually find the gate, so I set Tick down and point that way. "I think the gate's over there." I glance up at the starlit sky. "And it's late. We should hurry. You think you can run?" I'm certain I can't, and I hope she says no. I've never felt like this much crap in my life, and I've been through a lot.

"Yes," she says with a soft nod. Then before I can respond or let her know where to go, she starts running.

Horseballs. Well, at least I can rest when we get back to Airika. I sigh and start trotting behind her, using her eyes to light the way. Because that's not creepy or anything. Tick rounds the corner of the wall and continues on at the same pace, getting further ahead all the time. I cringe and force myself to run faster. If I don't catch up to her soon, she'll keep running around the inside of the compound.

"Tick! Out the gate!" I shout as she gets close, hoping she'll hear and understand. As if I am steering her with invisible wires, she turns and slips out through the bars like there is nothing there. Thank goodness. But now she's going to run off into the wilderness. I shout again, getting near the gate. "To the right!" I get to the bars just in time to see her red eyes shift and turn to the right.

Maybe this is going to be easy after all. I can't help but smile as I muscle my way through the bars and head off after her. At the corner of the complex wall, I shout again for her to turn to the right, which puts her in the general direction of Airika. Now if I can keep up with her. I hate running. Okay, I hate anything that even remotely resembles exercise. But Tick doesn't complain one bit, and I find myself struggling to keep her in sight. Jogging through the dark and uneven landscape, she runs as smooth a deer. She's so different from the street kids I see all the time, screaming at one another day in and day out and struggling to survive. She keeps quiet, seeming happy to be out in the open air and running free across the barren landscape.

I try to ignore the throbbing pains throughout my body and the creeping exhaustion that threatens to trip me up. I focus on questions swirling around in my head like a black pony on a merry-go-round. What the hell am I going to do now? I don't want to just hand her over without knowing the full story. What does Wisen plan to do with her? Why did Samantha seem so edgy when she first appeared at my door? I can only think she knows more than she admits. Damn, there's a lot of large, black horses on this ride.

I look ahead to Tick, who's almost at the edge of my vision. She didn't seem to have any answers for me, though I don't exactly expect her to. Poor kid's a victim in this and she doesn't even seem to know it. I wonder if Samantha does. If Wisen is responsible or would admit to using her like some kind of tool. If either one of them have said a single honest word.

I settle on watching Tick. She has no idea where we're going, but she moves straight on as if the destination's been clear the whole time. I feel completely wiped and I have a headache wedged into my brain, but Tick acts as if this is as much her home as the forest. I suspect she could keep going on forever. I'm both inspired by and jealous of her. She's young and tireless and unburdened by worries. She's the perfect guardian for something like the forest. As far as the compound went, the forest part isn't that bad. Too bad it will have to be destroyed with those damned machines. It could have been a worse place to be trapped.

Except for the whole being trapped part. The freedom she's experiencing now makes me wonder if she knew she had been trapped. I remember when I got out prison after a failed job. Everything seemed fresh and new despite being in the middle of the stinking, filthy city. I wanted to experience my favorite foods again, feel the touch of a woman, get back to a comfortable life, and live by my own rules. Tick doesn't as much as marvel at the scrub grass, small trees, or wide-open land. I'd guess she's jaded by the wonder of her forest, but if that's the case, why doesn't she seem to miss it? Did she have any truly independent thoughts? I don't know or understand anything about this kid.

The trip back to Airika feels as if it takes longer than it had to get to the compound. I blame the fatigue. Once we finally arrive, part of me wants to crash out in the cargo hold and sleep until dawn. It's not like flying at night is the safest thing anyway. It's hard to see other knuckleheads in the air and landing is even more difficult. Besides, I have a week. What could one night hurt?

Tick is still running when we get to the hills where Airika is badly hidden. I find myself dropping further behind as my legs refuse to move as quickly. How long had I been running already? A mile? Maybe more? And that doesn't count the damned stairs. She keeps running while I stumble and trip over the bramble and rocks. I manage to add more than a few new scrapes to my collection, and about half-way up, I find it's too dark to see anything. I trip over a rock and hit the ground. "Damn it," I mutter as I find myself on ground in utter darkness. I can see the glow from Tick's eyes ahead, but it's too far to be any help. "Tick! Hold on! Come back!"

She doesn't hear me. I can see the bob of faint red moving further away. "Horseballs. Damn kid." I push myself up with a grunt, finding movement harder this time. I'm not sure I'm going to make it, and she's going to go running all the way back to New Foundis. I grunt and push on, too tired to try yelling again.

I feel my way up the hill, being extra careful with each footstep and occasionally using brush to keep myself from falling. For a long time it's just me, the night, and a lot of cuts and bruises. Then I'm surprised to see a red glow somewhere ahead. I narrow my eyes, unsure if I'm seeing what I think I do. Soon enough it becomes clear. I'm actually catching up to Tick.

I approach slowly, more because I'm too tired to go any faster. When I finally get to her, I find her motionless, her hands pressing against the brush-covered fuselage of my airship. "She's so pretty," Tick says in soft awe. This is the first time I've seen her interested in something beyond the forest. What's more, she doesn't seem to mind the bandages or whatever pain might be in her hands. I wish I could share in her joy, but all I can do is stand there and pant.

Tick turns her red eyes toward me and I realize how bright they are. I can't imagine how she sees the world, but it's clear she doesn't need a lamp. She smiles, the expression more than a little eerie with the red glow covering her face. It's like a kid holding a light under their chin at night to tell a scary story, only this glow is coming from a different angle. It's a little spooky. But then she speaks again, breaking the illusion of horror. "What is she?"

She? I blink. It's common to consider an airship as a woman. I did it. Avery did it. Nearly every pilot I can think of, did it. We named our airships after women and treated them like lovers. But that Tick knows, or at least somehow senses it, adds more questions to the pile. Had she seen an airship before? Did she know anything about them? Once I catch my breath, I move over to start pulling brush away from the cargo doors. "Airika. She's an airship. She's going to get us back to the city."

"An airship?" Tick looks back to Airika, reaching out to touch her again. "How?"

She had to ask that. I sigh and reach up to scratch my chin, forgetting that my hands are dirty and bloody at this point. Avery's the expert. He could tell her everything about Airika, down to the tiniest bolt. The best I can give her is a simplistic explanation and hope she isn't any more curious than that. "Well, she flies. Like the birds."

Tick pauses for a moment, once more appearing to do some mental calculation. Her expression goes blank while she thinks, but after a moment her smile returns and she nods. "Like the birds. Can we fly now?" She looks at me eagerly as she asks.

An unintentional bout of laughter breaks free from my lips. I have days like that too, when I can't wait to get up in the air. Days where all the rest of the world could burn for all I care, so long as I have my airship and the open sky. But now isn't the time. "Sorry kid. It's dark, and I'm about to collapse. I don't know what you do for sleep, but I need to get some. There's room in the cargo hold. And in the morning, we can get going back to the city."

She gives me a look of disappointment. At least, I think that's what it is. It might be me projecting. I can't tell what she's thinking behind the gizmos pasted to her face. But she turns her red eyes to the sky, frowning slightly. "The sun will not come up."

"Huh?" I'm confused for a minute and look toward the horizon. As it is, there's a slight glow in the distance, signaling the coming of another day far sooner than I'd like. Then my brain remembers her trick in the compound. Lights on, sun's up. Lights off, sun's down. I shake my head, laughing softly again. "Nah. You can't do that out here. Sun's got to do its own thing."

"Oh." Tick frowns and looks back at Airika. I can almost see her thinking that she's going to have to wait to go up in the air. Even then, she's going to be disappointed. The only space for her is in the cargo hold, so she won't be able to see anything. It's almost a shame, and I feel the disappointment right along with her. I've been feeling it for her all along.

"Ah, look, we'll fly in the morning, okay?" She doesn't need to know that she won't be able to enjoy it. I finish pulling away the brush and open the cargo compartment. "Come on, inside. It'll be warmer." I had only started to notice how cold the night had gotten. Most of that has to do with the thick layer of sweat coating every inch of me. "Don't worry. It'll be morning soon." Too soon.

Tick looks into the nearly empty compartment. I keep a few supplies in here, mostly survival gear in case I get stuck out in the wild. Not that it has happened since the war, but I've learned to be cautious. I try to keep enough room to carry three or four large crates, and a few miscellaneous bits. It's a good thing I didn't need to steal one of those automatons. Even one wouldn't fit in here. Those soldiers had to be ten feet tall, if not more, and Airika is only about that long in total. Being mostly empty now, the kid has plenty of room to get a little sleep. She's dubious though.

"You okay? Look," I step into the compartment and look back at her. "It's safe. And I won't hurt you. It's just for a little while, all right?"

She takes a tentative step forward, stopping to look up at the airship. "It won't hurt her?"

I blink again, not sure how to answer that. I know she means Airika, but it had never occurred to me that the airship would care one way or another about people in the cargo hold. "Er...no. It shouldn't. She's made to hold stuff in here. She likes it." Okay, that's not strictly true. I know Airika doesn't feel a damned thing, but I'm not about to burst Tick's bubble.

Consideration flashes across her face, then she nods and steps inside. I head back out and reach for the doors. It's better if I stay outside to keep watch for the rest of the night. "I'm going to close these to keep some of the cold out. You okay with that?" So far I had seen her thrive in large open areas like the forest and out here, but I wonder if she has ever been trapped in a smaller space and how she'll react.

Tick looks at the doors and nods. "It's okay." And then she proceeds to move toward the back of the hold and settle in between a box of tools and small crate of emergency rations. "I'll wait for the sun here."

"Uh, yeah. All right." I turn and close the cargo doors, thinking Tick is a strange, but special kid. I smile and settle in on the ground next to Airika, looking off toward the city to wait out the night.

Chapter 6

I wake as the sun comes up over the edge of the distant city. Somewhere between darkness and dawn I had managed to get some sleep, but not without the return of the dreams. This time they're punctuated with visions of the automaton army, which chases me through the air. Somehow the false soldiers can fly without airships. They shoot at me, trying to knock me out of the sky. I can feel the heat of their ammunition all around me. Then my airship catches fire, and I know I'm going down for the last time.

As I'm about to crash, I shake myself awake. My back screams in pain from having been propped up against Airika for the last few hours. I could have slept in the pilot's chair, but the ground is a hell of a lot more comfortable. Airika may be the best airship out there, but she's a bitch to sleep with.

I stand and stretch, feeling every joint in my body pop in protest. I had taken a hell of a beating last night and it's finally caught up. I don't have a mirror, but I bet I look like a giant, walking bruise. My throat's raw from the exposure to the gas and yelling directions to Tick. I might have to spend the rest of this week sleeping. But first I have to get us back to New Foundis.

I move the pathetic brush away from the rest of Airika and knock lightly on the cargo hold door before opening it up. I expect Tick to be sitting there in the same position, staring at me as soon as the morning light comes streaming through the door. To my surprise, she's curled up between some supply crates, sleeping. She makes the strangest squeaking sound as she breathes. A smile touches my lips. It's a shame to have to disturb her, but once I get Airika going, I doubt she could stay asleep. Explaining what's happening will keep her from being too scared. I hope.

I walk up to her as quietly as I can and crouch down next to her sleeping form. If I had any doubt about her humanity before, it's gone now. She had seemed so alert and awake in the forest, I didn't even think about her needing sleep, but clearly she did. What does she dream about? The forest? Whatever happened there? How she came to be? At the moment she seems peaceful, so at least she couldn't have been dreaming about terrible things. I'd woken up from those kind of dreams enough to know the look of them.

I reach over and touch her shoulder gently. "Hey, Tick. Wake up." My voice sounds harsh and I cringe. That's got to be the worst thing to wake up to. Seeing my mug couldn't be much better either, but it's too late for me to rethink what I'm doing.

Tick shifts and the red glow of her eyes flicker to life as she looks up at me. She cocks her head to the side one way then the other and the glow dims slightly before returning to its normal brightness. "I cannot raise the sun," she says finally. "But, there is light?"

I glance back at the open cargo door. A dim blue washes over the area outside, casting enough light in here to see. I look back at her and smile again. "You're outside now, kid. The world takes care of raising the sun. If you want step out and get some air, now's your chance. We got to be heading back to the city soon."

Tick gives me another curious look before pushing herself up. She moves around me and I stand and turn to watch her. Her steps are cautious, like a timid animal, as she approaches the open cargo door. A pang of sadness hits me. She's never seen the outside world before, at least not in daylight. It hadn't been much to look at last night. I'm still not sure how she sees anything, but she must be able to tell the difference between light and dark.

I follow her out as she steps down to the rough grass. For the first time I realize she isn't wearing shoes. Her left foot is metallic and her right is flesh, but she doesn't flinch at the hard surface as she steps on it. Tick cranes her head back to look at the slowly brightening sky. I come out of the cargo hold and point toward the thin gray line of New Foundis. "See that over there? That's the city where I live. I'm going to take you there in Airika. The sun ought to be fully up by the time we get there."

"Fully up?" Tick asks curiously, looking toward the city.

I laugh softly, dropping my hand. She really has no idea about the outside world. "Yeah. Out here, things are…different. Trust me, by the time we get to New Foundis, the sun will be high and everything will be bright." Well, relatively speaking. The smog makes daylight hazy at best, but she'll see that for herself.

"I want to watch it!" Tick exclaims with the excitement only a child could muster.

I don't have a good reason not to let her. At the same time, I'm itching to sleep on my own sofa in the middle of my own stuff. We'll be lucky if I don't crash the damned airship somewhere between here and the city. I also plan to make certain Tick can see other sunrises to her heart's content. So I smile and put my hand on her small shoulder. "Another time, all right? We need to get back to New Foundis. I'm afraid you're going to have to ride in the cargo hold." I point to the open hold that's shadowy dark in the early morning. It's not the most inviting or comfortable way to travel.

Tick follows my point again, taking a moment to process what I said. Another bright grin crosses her face. She nods and jumps toward the cargo hold. "Yes! Let's go! She's ready to go home!"

I laugh and scratch my head as Tick runs back into the hold. She? Well, I don't know about Airika, but I'm more than ready to get home myself. I walk over to the open doors and nod to Tick as she settles in. "Make sure you hold on tight. I don't know what it's like to ride in there, but it could be rough."

Tick nods, wedging herself between a couple of boxes. "She will keep me safe. We are friends."

"Well, all right then." I have no idea what to say to that. Actually, I feel a little jealous that she had become "friends" with Airika so quickly, though I know how ridiculous that is. At least I shouldn't have worry about Tick being scared. "Take it easy then, and we'll be back in the city soon."

I move to close the cargo hold, but Tick's expression changes to one of curiosity. "Take what? Where is easy?"

"What?" It takes me a minute to realize she has no idea what an expression is. I shake my head and laugh. "Uh, never mind. You just sit there, okay?" Tick nods with renewed enthusiasm and I close up the cargo door. Avery's going to get a kick out of this kid once I get back. I wonder if he'll be able to do anything about her hands. And resist the urge to take her apart.

Getting back is going to take a little more work. Taking off from the top of a building is one thing. As far as flying goes, a rooftop take off is pretty simple. Hit the edge and the air is right there. Taking off from the ground is another matter. I chose this hill to give Airika a little leverage. The idea is to point the airship downhill in a relatively clear area and let her go. Once enough speed builds up, lift is supposed to happen. Hopefully it all goes right before she hits the bottom. If not, then the airship has to be pushed back up the hill for another try. At least Tick is light as far as cargo goes, so she shouldn't make a lot of difference in terms of successfully getting in the air.

I head up to the pilot's seat and climb aboard. It's quiet out here in the early morning. Quiet in an unsettling way. I want to get back to the normal sounds of the city as soon as I can. At least once the engines get going, I won't be able to hear much of anything. So, I wait for Tick to settle, then start the burners. In order to preserve coal, I usually let the fires go cold when I'm not flying for a while. Avery had the burners stoked and ready to go when I left the building, but now it would take a little while for the coals to get hot enough to turn the propellers. I'll never know how he manages to work around such hot machinery.

Waiting is the hardest part, though it only takes a few minutes once the fires are ignited to get to full burn. The coals take in the heat quickly and before long, steam is turning the engines. I release the wheel breaks when the engines are hot enough and Airika starts rolling across the top of the hill. The hilltop is relatively smooth. She avoids or bounces over the few rocks that stick up out of the ground, and soon she's picking up speed. I hope Tick is ready for this. I turn the nose down the hill, ready to make the first launch attempt.

The slope is a lot rougher than it looks, making Airika bounce heavily as the wheels smack against buried stumps and boulders. It's all I can do to hold on and hope my straps don't break. As Airika picks up speed, the bouncing becomes less noticeable. But we're approaching the bottom. This isn't going to work. I'm going to have to push Airika back to the top and try again.

"Come on, baby," I chant to her, desperately hoping my words will do some good. At the last minute, the air catches under her wings. Finally, she lifts off of the rugged ground, pulling into the sky. I let out a startled and relieved whoop as we rise up and the bumpy world changes to smooth air.

The old familiar sensations of flying take over and I practically forget about Tick. As much as she has occupied my life over the past few hours, flying is my first and only love. Overhead, the sun stretches up into the sky, brightening the day. Before long I can see other airships moving north and south from New Foundis on their way to other eastern cities. Those are the more normal travel routes. Few people fly west simply because there isn't much out here.

Eventually we fly in over the farms and wealthy landowners' properties that sit outside the city. It's easy to envy those who escape the smoke and grime, but I wouldn't change my situation for all the money in the world. Hell, I own an entire building with a private airstrip on the roof, and that's better than most people. Sure it's in the heart of the slums and landings are tricky because of the surrounding smokestacks, but that makes it a deterrent to anyone else. So far it's worked out in my favor.

As I break the barrier of the city, smog swarms in around Airika and the stench I've come to know and love, wraps around my head like a second helmet. Reality hits me as we approach my building. I have a mechanical child in the back of my airship, and no idea what to do with her. The obvious choice is to take her to Samantha and Wisen straight away, but that doesn't sit well in my stomach. Not after what I've seen. I decide instead that she needs to be taken somewhere safe while I figure this out.

That somewhere safe is a small town south of here, called Portsmaw. Several years ago, I set up a safe hold outside the town. It's just a cave overlooking the ocean, but it's protected and taking her there will give me time to sort out a few things with Wisen, namely whether I should finish this job. I'll take Avery along to so he can look at Tick's hands and watch after while I'm away. It's not the best plan, but it's all I've got at the moment.

The busy day is in full swing by the time I reach my building, but most of the traffic is closer to the outskirts, so landing is easy enough. Airika touches down on the roof with a lot less rattling than at take-off. I pull her around to her usual resting spot and dampen the fires, letting the propellers slow to a stop. Avery appears out of the tool shed where he had been waiting. It's like the guy has some kind of extra sense to know when I'm coming back.

Avery wanders over to the right engine compartment and pops it open. Sometimes I think he likes burning himself, though I can't say I've ever noticed him with a serious injury. His voices floats up to me as I unbuckle my harness. "How'd she handle?" he asked, not even questioning the fact that I'm back early. He's already half-way into the engine, muffling his words. "How far did you go?"

I hop down out of the cockpit and move around to the engine so I don't have to shout. "Av, we don't have time to screw around. Top her off and get ready to go. We're heading for Portsmaw."

Avery doesn't hear me. I can barely hear him as he tinkers under the reinforced engine cover. He's mumbling something about the coal and heat dispensation. I wouldn't understand it even if I heard him. Finally he backs out of the compartment again. Somehow he's already covered in coal sludge. He opens his mouth to say something else, but he stops and looks at me a moment. "What the hell happened to you?" He looks back at Airika, giving her a quick visual once over. "You didn't crash her, did you? You look like you flew through razor blades or some damn thing. What the hell were you doing?"

I look down at myself. My jacket is filthy and covered in slashes from the glass shards. The deeper cuts have blood crusted on the edges. I'd sacrificed my scarf to Tick, so my goggles are smudged beyond much use. I look like shit and feel even worse. "The job took an unexpected turn. Don't worry, Airika is fine. This happened on the ground."

Avery reached up to scratch his balding head. If it hadn't already been covered in a layer of black, he would have wiped more through his remaining red hair. "So, what now? We need to go to Plan F?"

Plan F. Failure. Not every job goes smooth, and sometimes employers aren't too happy about that. That's what the bolt hole in Portsmaw is for. We'd cleared a landing strip on the cliff top above the cave, but kept it surrounded by the natural features of the area to keep most people away. The entrance of the cave can be reached by a ladder from the cliff, or by boat if the tide is high enough.

And that is exactly where we're going. I nod slightly. "Well, it wasn't exactly a failure, but yeah. I want to get moving as soon as we can. Make sure we have enough fuel and pack up anything you think we'll need. Plan for a couple weeks." I pause and look toward the cargo hold. He's going to find Tick as soon as he starts loading things. "And three people. I found what they wanted, and it's…She's in the hold."

Avery doesn't spend much time being confused. Usually he's in his own world and takes things as they come. For the first time in the 20-some odd years I've known him, he looks dumbfounded. "She?"

"She." I head over to the cargo doors, patting my hand on the fuselage to warn Tick that we're coming in. "They wanted research, and something called Tick. I found Tick. Turns out Tick's a kid. But not an ordinary one. And I'm not inclined to turn her over without some damned good explanations." I'm getting angry in my exhaustion and that's not going to do anyone any good. I shake my head and stop at the doors. "Sorry. None of that matters right now. Anyway, I don't think I can explain her, so I've just got to show you."

Some of the confusion has left Avery's face, replaced now with frustration at my delaying. I trust Avery with my life and I'm still worried about introducing him to Tick. I can picture him pulling a set of tools out of thin air and attacking her like another gadget. At the same time, we're not going get out of here without him knowing about her.

I'm going to have to suck it up and let him do what he will. Maybe I should grab a hammer first. I take a deep breath and pull open the cargo doors. A puff of cool air rushes out and I curse under my breath. I'd forgotten how cold it can get in there. It's not like she has much in the way of clothes. My stomach sinks as my brain screams at me that I've frozen the person I had been trying to save.

"You all right?" Avery asks. He moves a little closer, trying to get a glance into the cargo hold.

I can only imagine the look on my face. Am I pale? Is my jaw hanging open? I shake my head, trying to get my focus back. I have no idea if Tick is okay, and I can't go in assuming the worst. I clear my throat and look at him. "Yeah. I think so." I hope so. It all depends on if Tick is still alive. If "alive" can even be applied to her.

I can't see her from the doorway. I move into the cargo hold, walking slowly because part of me doesn't want to know the answer. Avery comes around the edge of the door. His bulk blocks out the daylight and I swear it gets colder in here. "What's going on, Colt? What kind of shit you got yourself into this time?"

I get to the boxes that she had put herself between and find her curled up in a ball. Cringing, I kneel down next to her and carefully touch her shoulder. She makes a soft moan and shifts away from my hands. Tick is asleep. She moves a little and I can see the dim red glow of her eyes, barely visible in the shadows of the cargo hold. I suck in a breath of relief and pull one of the covers off a box of tools to drape around her.

"The hell?" Avery's standing behind me. I look up to see his eyes locked on Tick's half-mechanical face. "Who did that to her?"

Good old Avery. Most people would have asked what the hell she is first. Some of them might even run screaming. But not Avery. He's a big ball of compassion for a kid who isn't even aware he's standing over her. I stand again and sigh. "Don't know for sure. I thought it might be Wisen at first, but it's not adding up."

Avery shrugs. He doesn't know who Wisen is, or Samantha, or anyone else involved with this. "So how's running away supposed to help?" he asks, finally looking at me.

"We're not running," I growl. It's enough to make him hold up his hands in mock surrender. Yeah, I need a serious nap. For about a month. I take a breath to calm myself. "We're not running. That woman who came to the door compromised us. She knows where I live. There could be people watching. I need to figure stuff out, but first I want to get Tick to a safe place." I look back down at her. She hasn't moved since I put the cover over her. "She was injured down in the compound. I don't know if you can do anything for her, but I'm not sure who could."

Avery lets out a deep laugh that startles me. What the hell could be funny about this? "So, I'm going along as the medic? Can't say I've ever heard that before. You must have hit your head. Want a bandage?"

I cringe. It does sound a little on the crazy side. "That's not...I mean, look at her face. The rest of her is like that too. More machine than person. I don't think a regular doctor's going to help." I start back for the doors. "Don't worry about it right now. Get Airika fueled and loaded. We'll deal with Tick's injuries when we get to Portsmaw."

"You got it," Avery chuckles, following after me. He's not upset. I've never seen him upset, but I get the feeling if he ever went that direction, the whole world would know. Avery's the kind of guy who has to be holding it all inside and when he finally blows, that'll be the end of everything.

We part ways and Avery goes into the shed to get Airika ready. I can hear him chuckling behind me as I head to the stairwell and I can't help but smile a little myself. I have a lot of questions, but maybe things aren't as serious as my tired brain wants to make them. We'll get out of here, I'll do a little poking around, and those questions will be answered. Everything will work out, and Tick will be all right. I have to admit, the kid's grown on me. Hell, I don't even care about Wisen's money any more. He can keep the other half. I must be going soft.

I'm still smiling when I put my hand on the stairwell doorknob. Suddenly the door pushes open on its own. I start and jump back only to see the door hasn't come to life. Someone is on the other side. And not just someone. Samantha. She rushes through as I watch helplessly, and pulls the door closed behind her. She leans against it, her eyes wild and staring at me. I stare back. Only one thing comes to mind. "You're not

A.K. Child   Steamroller
                                                     Chapter 6

supposed to be here."

Chapter 7

The words hang in the air between Samantha and me. *You're not supposed to be here.* Just like Tick had said to me down in the compound. That had led to a wild adventure up way too many stairs, and a lot of questions. Questions this woman could potentially answer. The look on her face says she's in no condition to try.

Her once well-coifed hair is loose and plastered against her fair-skinned face, which is more of a crimson now. The flesh rosy with effort. She must have run up the stairs, maybe all the way from the bottom floor. Samantha's clothes, once elite and proper, are disheveled. Her skirts slightly torn. Something has happened and I know in my gut it's not a good thing. All I can do is stare at her, telling her she shouldn't be here.

"I..." she opens her mouth, letting that single sound escape, then looks back over her shoulder to the closed door behind her.

"Look, never mind." I can see the urgency in her features as my voice brings her eyes back to me. Those rich, dark eyes. A hint of red snakes its way across the whites of her eyes, and I see now that her makeup has trails streaked through it. She's been crying. I have to know what's going on. I need to calm her down. "What are you doing here? What's happened?" For a brief second I wonder how she even got up here. I swear I had locked the apartment door before I left. But then, Avery might have been through and forgot.

Samantha takes a long, shuddering breath and jumps toward me. Her fingers latch painfully onto my shoulders. "Did you get her?" she hisses. "Is she safe?"

I wince at the grip. It's not the pressure of her hands, but the cuts and bruises under it. Her hands hit all the wrong places. I reach up to pull her hands away, then her words hit me and I stop. Her? She? Samantha must be talking about Tick. I'm not ready yet to answer those questions though. "Samantha. I need you calm down. Why are you here? I said I'd be in touch in about a week."

Samantha looks at me, searching my face. What is she looking for? The answers to her questions? Or something else? I suddenly feel like I'm under a microscope. Her hands drop from my shoulders, leaving a burning itch from the relaxed pressure. She drops her forehead against my chest and shakes her head slightly. "They were watching," she mutters against my jacket.

"They?" I look down in to her mass of dark brown hair and draw in a nose-full of her panicked scent. I want to curl up in a corner with her and forget about everything else. I want to make it all okay. But her words have me worried. If someone is watching her, how safe are any of us here? "Who's they? Tell me what happened."

"Colt?" Avery's voice calls out behind me. "You all right?"

I don't know if he means me or Samantha, but I answer. "Yeah. Get Airika ready. I'll handle this."

Samantha leans to the side to peer around me. Her eyes are filled with suspicion as she looks at Avery. "Who is that? Get ready for what? Are you going back to the compound?" She looks back up at me. I hadn't realized how much taller than her I am until she is pressed up against me like this. "You didn't find the research? Tick?"

An overwhelming mass of questions pound my brain. Not just from Samantha, but in my own head. She knows Tick is a "her," does that mean she knows a lot more than she initially told me? How did she get back into my apartment? Up here to the roof? Who is the "they" she's talking about, and why did they send her running back here?

I want to ask her all these things, but before I can, I hear Avery saying something behind me. He's talking about Airika and wanting to wait, but his words aren't sticking. They're being carried off in the wind before they can settle in my brain with the questions. I'm on the verge of figuring out something, but it's about an inch outside my understanding. I'm missing too much information and I'm too damned tired to draw conclusions with what I've got.

"…we don't have time," Samantha said. I look down to find her still glaring at Avery. He's behind me now, trying his best to argue calmly with her.

I step away from Samantha and turn to look at both of them. "Stop. Just stop." My eyes shift to Avery, whose face is starting to look a little like his hair. Here comes the explosion. "What were you saying about waiting?"

Avery turns and points off toward the ocean. A line of dark clouds is visible through the smog. During the fall it's not unusual for storms to roll in off the water as evening sets in. "Storm's coming. We won't make it all the way to…" he stops, looking at Samantha. "To our destination before it starts raining."

It's a good reason, actually. Flying in the rain is a terrible idea. The rain water has a tendency to soak into the engine compartments. If it doesn't put out the fires completely, it cools the steam coils to a point where the airship loses speed and eventually crashes. I can't tell how far off the storm is, but Avery could be right about not having enough time to get to Portsmaw before it rolls in. "We'll have to settle in for the night and head out tomorrow morning." And hope whoever was watching Samantha would stay away. After all, they couldn't possibly know that Tick is safe in Airika's hold.

Samantha looks between us, her jaw hanging slightly open. "You don't understand." She turns and looks at the stairwell door. As she does, she pulls a handkerchief out of her handbag and uses it to dab at her swollen eyes. "They were waiting when I left the building. They followed me back to Wisen's home. They…they…" She shook her head and sniffled before pressing the handkerchief to her face.

It's going to be my downfall someday, but I hate to see a woman cry. My mother used to cry every night because of the sickness. I was barely five years old when she left this world. I couldn't comfort her. I couldn't make it better. I refuse to fail someone like that again. So I step back to Samantha and pull her into my arms. Avery's standing there, watching silent, forgotten. "Shhh…you're safe here. I promise. Who were they? What did they want?"

She shakes her head, pressing her wet face against my jacket again. She's going to end up as dirty as Avery at this rate. "I don't know," she mumbles against me. "I don't know who they are. But they want Tick. They forced Dr. Wisen to give them the location of the compound. You have to get her before they do." She looks up once more, her face predictably smudged with grime from my jacket. "They murdered Dr. Wisen. I only barely escaped. And when I got here…they had broken into your apartment and searched through your things. I ran up here when I heard you landing and hoped they hadn't gotten here first."

Damn it. This confirms it. We have been compromised. I flash Avery a look that he knows all too well. "We can't stay here." Samantha is the cause of this. She had brought me one of the most interesting jobs I've ever done, and now she's led these people right to us. I'm tempted to leave her behind, but I know she's acting on Wisen's request. She couldn't have known all of this would happen.

Avery nods and looks a little less like he's about to blow up now. "Where you want to go, boss?"

"Back to the compound," Samantha squeaks. "You have to get Tick before they do. Who knows what kind of horrible things they have in mind for her."

Her again. Samantha's words remind me that I still have some questions, but now isn't the time. I can't leave Samantha here, and if I'm taking her with us, she'll be in the hold with Tick. I have to tip my hand. "That's…not a problem," I say carefully.

"Really?" Samantha blinks her bloodshot and puffy eyes at me, before looking at Avery. Avery gives her a snort and folds his arms together in return. "You'll go back to the compound? What if they're already there?"

I shake my head this time. "It doesn't matter. We don't have to go there. They won't find her, because I already did."

The look on Samantha's face is somewhere between shock and excitement. Even though she's a mess, that look makes me smile. I made her day. Avery isn't so pleased. He steps forward, breaking up the staring contest I'm having with Samantha. "That doesn't answer where you want to go."

"Hmm?" I pull my eyes away from Samantha and look out toward the ocean. I can't see the water from here, but I can make out the dark line of storm clouds. The options are limited. Head inland and find a place to camp out for the night, or head for Portsmaw and the bolt hole, where there's shelter, beds, and very little chance we'll be found. "You said you suped her up, right?"

Avery nods, his grin finally reemerging from wherever it had been hiding. We're talking about Airika now. "Yep, that's right. Made her faster, more efficient. Least that's the idea. Still got to test her out."

"Well, here's your chance." I try to give a reassuring smile to Samantha who still looks stunned. "We'll take the risk of heading south. It'll be safe there."

Avery snorts and starts to turn. "I hope you know what you're doing, Colt." But I know if he thinks I'm wrong, he'll say so. We've known one another too long not to have a little faith in each other's skills.

I turn my attention back to Samantha. She watches Avery stalk back toward Airika, but I don't understand her expression. Her face has a mix of distrust and anger, but I have no idea why she would feel either of those things toward Avery. He's harmless. "I'm sorry about all this. You'll be able to get some rest on the ride. You ever been in an airship before?"

She looks up at me. It feels nice to have her in my arms. Too nice. I have to remind myself she's half my age and a client. "No," she says with a shake of her head. "We're taking Tick too?"

I nod and turn to escort her toward Airika. "That's right. She's in the hold, sleeping. It's going to be dark in there, and the ride might be a little rough. It'll take a couple hours, but Avery will make sure you're all right."

Samantha narrows her eyes for the briefest second, but nods silent and walks along with me toward Airika. She worries the handkerchief in her hands. So much has happened in the last 24 hours, this must be difficult for her. At the mention of Avery, her eyes dart toward him as he loads coal into the stokers. Her lips press into a thin line and she quickly looks away again. "Yes. Well, thank you, Mr. Reed. It seems plans have changed. Even though Dr. Wisen is…well, you'll still be paid the other half. I'll see to it. But, I'm not sure how I'm going to repay you for helping us now."

"That's easy." I rest my hand on her back, guiding her toward the airship. "Give me a few more answers. But that'll wait until we get to…"

BANG! The stairwell door flies open, slapping against the outside wall of the frame. I look back in time to see two men burst through, each of them carrying what look like revolvers. Horseballs. These must be the guys who had followed Samantha. Time has run out.

Samantha makes a movement next to me, but I'm too focused on the situation to see what she's doing. I shove her toward the cargo hold.

"Get in the hold." But I'm already looking for Avery as I head toward the cockpit. "AVERY! BUTTON HER UP AND GET STOWED! WE'RE GOING NOW!"

I hear "Shit," come from multiple directions. It sounds like everyone has roughly the same opinion. Everything happens at once—the slamming of the engine compartment on the other side of Airika, Samantha saying something I don't quite catch, and the gunmen yelling. I scramble up into the pilot's seat as the first bullet pings against the left engine barrel.

"GO!GO!GO!" Avery yells from the back of Airika. He doesn't have to tell me three times. I've already got the engines heating. It's a good thing she hadn't been sitting here long enough to cool off, though I have no idea if Avery managed to fill the right-hand stoker. A sick feeling settles in my stomach, convincing me he didn't, but another bullet reminds me I can't worry about that right now.

The bullet ricochets off the right propeller, which is turning with enough force to send the bullet flying off in another direction. Just like in the war, more pilots were killed by their own airships bouncing stray ammo around, than by direct enemy fire. I'm damned lucky this isn't my time.

As the props spin faster, they drown out the rest of the noise on the roof. I have no idea if Avery and Samantha are safe in the hold, but the gunmen are getting close. It's now or never. I lift the brakes and Airika starts rolling forward. Now the bullets really start to fly. These guys mean to stop us no matter what it takes. One of the shots is too close, glancing off my leather helmet with a soft thump. Whether everyone is secure or not, it's time to go.

I jam the throttle forward, opening up the heat vents all the way. Even at full blast, water takes time to evaporate into steam, but I don't have a minute to wait. The gunmen are running after Airika as she rolls, taking shots at the engines and me. I duck down as much as I can, pressing against the fuselage, but I'm only going to stay safe for so long if they keep shooting.

About the time they run out of ammo, the edge of the building is right in front of me. "Come on, baby," I whisper to Airika. She's never failed me before, and this would be the worst time for her to decide she doesn't like me anymore. Airika jumps out over the edge. My heart stops for a few seconds as she hangs in the air above the filthy city. It's not just my heart. Everything stops. The wind, the noises of the engines, I'm pretty sure that startled bird right in front of me freezes in place too.

And then, like that, the world starts moving again. The bird swoops up and to the right, the propellers turn, and I wrench the yoke back to bring Airika soaring into the air. I let out a great whoop of joy as I realize we've made it. Gaining altitude to lift outside the range of a standard revolver, I circle back around to make sure I didn't leave anyone important behind. Down on the roof the gunmen glare back up at me, one of them taking another useless shot. But there's no sign of Avery or Samantha. I hope they made it on board.

Satisfied that we're as safe as it gets in the air, I swing back around to the south and start down the coast. Off over the ocean, the dark line of clouds is clearer, but not much closer than it was a few minutes ago. Sometimes storms, like the one brewing out there, stay off shore. If we're lucky, this will be one of them. All I can do now is settle back and push Airika as fast she'll go. What happens now is up to fate.

Chapter 8

Breaking free of New Foundis' smoggy border, I push the attack out of my head. It isn't much of a leap to guess that anyone who knows about Tick would want to get their hands on her. She's something special, and though I don't completely know why, I do know I need to keep her safe. I wish Samantha had been free to tell me the truth. Maybe it would have saved us a lot of trouble. Or at least I could have been aware that trouble was coming.None of that matters now. We're relatively safe and on our way to Portsmaw. So long as that storm holds off, we ought to arrive early evening. I shift my focus to getting us there in one piece.

Every time I go up, I think of the first time I flew. I had been a fresh, reluctant, recruit in the Invenio Militia, fighting against Lanceprorov and their allies in a war that had no reason. The whole world had been involved, which meant every able body fit into the picture somewhere. Sometimes as the wind rushes around my helmet, I can still hear the wing commander's voice yelling my name off the roster.

I had been pretty damned scared. All of us were. Except Vann Horner. I don't think he has the sense to be scared of much. Airship technology had been new to us. It was a technology stolen from the enemy and put to use against them. It didn't give us much of an advantage since the enemy had more experience using it.

The new recruits selected for flying attended ground school for about a week, not enough time before being thrown into an airship, right into enemy fire. It felt like a death sentence. What amazes me is that I love to fly even after that. After ground school, we were thrown right out into the middle of battle. The sounds of gunfire and the smell of burning wreckage died away when I made that first leap. I felt like it was the greatest experience in my life, but I wanted to puke at the same time. I still feel like that when I hit the edge of my building for take-off. Will this be another successful flight, or the last one I ever have? I was damned sure the first time would be my last flight, but I managed to make it through. However, it was only because I turned tail and ran like hell.

It's not easy to admit to being a chicken-shit. And I did try to do my duty. I got in that damned airship and I flew the hell out of her. Then I started thinking. Having a conscience is one of my weaknesses. I couldn't help but wonder if the enemy had a family, a home to go back to. It made me hesitate, then Horner swooped in and made the kill I wasn't willing to take.

That had been enough for me to turn around and quit the war I didn't want to be part of to begin with. It was also my first landing, and I got down without causing much damage. The wing commander had been livid when I swooped in over his head, and put the airship down on the hilltop we had all taken off from. When he was done yelling at me, I was put in lock-down for a couple hours. They didn't go too hard on me, because the real punishment had been making me stay in the militia. After that, I flew countless times and ended up killing more men than I want to remember. I was glad to finally get out with my life intact.

Not that the life I had was all that easy. Like many of the guys who survived the war, I came back lost. I had no idea how to hold a real job or live an ordinary life. So I fell back into the criminal world, running odd jobs for shady people. Avery didn't approve of it at first, and I don't blame him. I'm certain he stuck with me to watch my back, and he built Airika to get me away from the worst of that life. Avery's a good guy and I owe him a lot. That's the kind of thing neither of us would talk about aloud, though. Not without a lot of whiskey.

My choice of career also puts me in direct competition with Horner. Though Vann Horner and I served in the same unit during the war, I don't know much about him. He's older than me, but most of the guys were. And he's one of those pretty-boys who thinks the world owes him something. He always had cronies around him back in the war. He made himself untouchable by forcing his lackeys to cover his ass. We had more than a few scuffles, and I'd like to think I gave as good as I got. I fight the street way – dirty.

I was shocked when I found out he was running the same kind of jobs as me. I would have figured the guy came from the right side of the tracks and would have a cushy business job waiting for him to come home. Smuggling takes a lot of work, and Horner is the kind of guy who avoids a challenge by making someone else do it. Then again, for all I know, he has other guys run his jobs for him. I know he's out there, but I can't say I've run into him. I'm glad Samantha didn't go to him first.

But someone's been hired to get in the way. The gunmen were proof of that. This is an added complication none of us need. It's something else I'm going to have to deal with after I get Samantha and Tick settled at the hideout. And then I'm going to have to find out a lot more from Samantha. Maybe she has more a clue to who came after her than she thinks she does. Another one of the researchers, or maybe this mysterious Veital-Wisen. Could there have been some kind of falling out between the doctors?

I come out of my thoughts to realize two things. First, I had been drifting into an exhausted doze. Second, the sky has become dark and I hear the tap-tap-tap of raindrops plinking against my helmet. Horseballs. I look up, much more awake now, to see a dark roil of clouds just overhead. And by just overhead, I mean, I can almost reach up and touch them if I want to. I don't want to. I don't want to be anywhere near this storm.

I look back down to try to get a lay of the land. Maybe we'll be near enough Portsmaw to make a safe landing before the engines give up. A good airship like Airika can stand up to the weather for a while, but even the best of them eventually become soaked by the rain. Once water begins to seep into the steam engines, it's over.

I don't see anything that looks like the fishing village. At my best guess, we're still about an hour away and the rain is coming down hard. I push further inland, hedging my bets that the storm hasn't moved in too fast. I'm less familiar with this part of the world, and if I lose sight of the ocean, I may not be able to find Portsmaw at all. It's a delicate balance between trying to stay safe and not getting lost. I do manage to find a line of lighter rain, and I stick to it as best I can.

The light rain doesn't last long enough. I start looking for a place to set down safely when I spot lights in the distance. It's got to be Portsmaw. And if it's not, well, it'll do for tonight. I swing back toward the ocean and heavier weather, aiming roughly for civilization. Now to find the landing strip on a bluff outside the town before the rain overcomes the engines. Or something that will do as well.

"Come on baby, just a little further," I mutter to myself. Avery built this old girl solid, but I can already see smoky trails rising up from the engine compartments. It could be the rain burning off the surface, or it could mean something worse. I don't want to stay up in the air long enough to find out which.

Back in the war, our unit had a slogan, "A Wing and a Prayer," plastered over every free surface. A lot of the guys had gone with the prayer, leaving behind nothing but broken wings. My search for the landing strip is covered with mental images of the ruined airships that had littered the battlefield. All I have now is a wing and a prayer, and who knows how long the wings will last. I trust Avery's craftsmanship, but I've never tested Airika in conditions like this, so I'm praying pretty damn hard that her wings are strong enough.

I sweep in closer, trying to get a better look at land. I've been here a few times, and from what I see, it looks like we've arrived at Portsmaw. The village is just like I remember it, and the high bluffs just south rise up like they always have. I start searching for the landing strip, which I hope hasn't become overgrown since my last visit. I hadn't been down here in a couple years. Not enough time for the trees to overgrow the strip, but any tire ruts would be hard to make out on a rainy night.

The bluffs are rocky and forested, unlike the land outside of New Foundis, which has been stripped of resources and is much more open to landing an airship. No, this place still has a lot of wild, and some seriously strong winds blowing crossways. I fight Airika to keep her straight as I scan the surface for a good landing spot. I don't find anything I feel comfortable about. I start to pull up and circle around again for another look, when I realize the propellers have stopped. I don't know if I've run out of fuel or if the rain has finally seeped in, putting out the fires. Either way, we're screwed.

In my panic—and I fully admit to losing my ever-loving shit in the middle of this—Airika dips and scrapes across the tops of the trees. It's only by luck that the boughs don't rip up the cargo hold, but Airika is thrown to the side, forcing her into a roll. She doesn't get all the way over before being bounced back the other way by the tree tops. Being strapped in tightly keeps me from falling out of the open cockpit, but it doesn't stop my stomach from losing whatever contents are left in there. Fortunately, it's been hours since I ate anything, so there isn't much to lose. My passengers can't be doing any better. They don't have much to hold them down back there.

I wrestle Airika through the trees, trying to keep her right side up. The thick boughs bounce her left and right, ripping through the structure as they do. A thin layer of wood separates the pilot's seat and cargo hold, but I'm pretty sure I can hear screams. In a way that's good. Screams mean my passengers are still alive. I can't let myself get distracted by thinking about what could be happening to them back there as sharp gusts of wind push Airika into yet more trees.

While the body is sturdy, the wing canvas isn't so fortunate. Out of the corner of my eye, I can already see the material ripping and fluttering in the wind. As I dip again into the trees, the right-hand wing cracks loudly, threatening to rip free. The fixed wheels catch and pull at the treetops. I'll be impressed if I have them by the time I get her down. Only the forest keep Airika from falling into a death roll, but there's no way I can manage even a decent landing now. I'll be good to keep any of us alive.

I guide Airika toward the bluff's upper edge. If I remember correctly, the bluff ends in a plateaued surface before diving down to the ocean below. If I've lost as much speed as I think I have, I should have room to set her down. I hope the wheel bars are strong enough to keep the cargo hold from smashing into the rocky dirt. If the whole thing breaks apart, that will be the end of my passengers.

I jerk the yoke back, pulling it to the left to try and keep Airika straight. I've lost all control on the right and over-compensation is too easy. As the trees run out shortly before the end of the bluff, Airika jerks sideways again. She dips and threatens to roll to the left, but the full force of the wind whips into us, keeping us from going over. This is my only chance. I can't be sure, but if my estimation is right, I have maybe a couple hundred feet before the edge. I jam the yoke forward while Airika is still relatively straight and push the nose, and me, toward the ground. I might not make it out of this, but if I do this right, maybe the others will.

And then the ground is there, right under my feet, as Airika dives into the earth. I can feel the grind of the wood and metal hull against ground, sending a shock of vibrations up through me. All I can think is, *don't flip over, don't flip over!* The unmoving propellers bite into the terrain, splintering and spreading shards of wood and dirt in every direction. Rocks fly up too, some of them barely missing my damned fool head.

I can still hear screaming somewhere behind and below me. Somehow I manage to keep Airika from flipping over and crushing me. She does keep sliding forward several more feet, shedding paneling as she plows across the bluff's top. Then she comes to a sudden, painful stop. My straps tighten as my body slams forward, squeezing the breath out of me. I find myself gazing out over the edge of the bluff to the storm-wild ocean. The straps are going to leave deep bruises, but at least they're still holding me in place.

I only hear two sounds, the pounding of my heart and the howl of the wind. Everything else is devastatingly quiet. And then laughter. I don't know where it's coming from, but I definitely hear laughter. It's the kind of sound an insane person might make, full of hatred and anger. I feel my body shaking and I look down at my hands. They wobble with each gasp of giggles that exit my throat. I'm alive. I don't know about anyone else. But I'm alive.

My vision swims at the sight of the churning waves beyond my fingers. The laughter is carried off by the wind. I drop my hands into my lap, the exhaustion returning to me as heavy as an anvil. I slump forward and close my eyes. A quick nap can't hurt, right? Not now that we're safe on the ground. Just a few winks. Just for a little while.

"Nice flying, Reed!" Vann Horner bursts in through the door to the barracks, surrounded by a cluster of toadying airmen. They laugh, one or two of them clapping Horner on the back, others high-fiving each other. They squeeze in through the doorway like a sausage going into a casing and I feel their eyes on me. For a moment the light outside creates a silhouette of their bodies, obscuring their individual faces and making them look like a single monster. But I don't need to see them to know who's there. The voice is high-pitched and nasally and it pierces the atmosphere like a needle through my eyeball. I cringe. Vann Horner is a dick.

I don't bother looking up from polishing my uncomfortable boots as Horner makes fun of my flying skills. He's talking about the incident earlier in the day, where I ran from the first flight I had ever made. It isn't that I'm a bad flier, I realized that my life is more important to me than taking someone else's. I'm not the first guy who's had that happen to him, and I'm not going to be the last.

My inattention lets him get close and I feel the breeze of his motion waft over me. "Maybe you should keep your ass on the ground, you little chicken-shit," Horner says, leaning down. The boot polish has a foul smell, acrid and burning. Horner smells worse, like stale smoke and piss-pot whiskey. His cronies circle around the bench I work on, waiting to see how I'll react.

My first instinct is to shove the polish in his long-nosed, snooty face. But the five guys stationed around me make that a bad choice. They would be on me in an instant if I fight back against their boss. I had seen it happen before. Most of the guys in our unit are decent and good people, but also under Horner's thumb like ants. If he sets his sights on a target, that target doesn't last long. He had pushed out some good men. Men who would never be the same again. And that was all before we got off the ground.

I have no interest in being intimidated by this jerk, and I'm not in the best mood anyway after the day I had. I still don't look at him as I speak. "What? And not be around when you crash and burn?" I may not have had the best day, but I've got this flying thing down. Horner is brash and reckless and only interested in the kill. While being ready to kill helps in battle, it also gets him in the way of the guys on our side. He's got a few air jockeys to kiss his ass, but he doesn't have any real friends. The thugs who hang on him figure they'll get something out of their loyalty. Killed, most likely.

While most of the other guys keep out of Horner's business, I have a few friends I know will back me up. Avery Nickols is one of them. He's a goofy grease monkey, but he's not afraid of anyone as far as I can tell. If anything, Horner might be a little intimidated by him because of both his mechanical genius and his constant filth. I bathe once a month or so, but I don't think Avery would know a bar of soap if he saw one. The higher-ups keep Avery with our unit, the rest of whom are pilots, to have someone handy to work on the airships.

Horner snorts at my taunt. "Better watch what you say, Reed. You might be the next one to wipe." His men step in a little closer and I know this is going to turn ugly. Fast.

The few other guys in the barracks are watching now, including

Avery who had been lurking somewhere around his bunk, tinkering with some device. Their eyes feel as heavy as the presence of the thugs around me. Most of them aren't going to act though. They're going to watch the show, maybe even be a little entertained by it. None of them want to face-off against Horner or his crew, not because he has the power here, but because self-defense is the manly thing. I'm on my own unless Avery decides to step in. He doesn't give a damn about public opinion.

I need to respond, but everything that comes to mind seems lame. Finally, I settle on cold, calm rationality, knowing that it's unlikely to work. "Look, we're all on the same side. We have enemies crawling up our asses out there. Why bring the fight in here?"

What I consider to be rational means nothing to guys like Horner. He's a bully. A pathetic grown-up bully. Bullies have one-track minds. They find their targets and don't let up, no matter where the argument might go. Today, I'm Horner's target and I'm not going to get out of this so easily. He leans back at least, giving me a little more breathing room, and starts to laugh in his nasally, over-confident way. "You are a chicken-shit, aren't you? I've seen women with bigger balls than you."

I don't want trouble with these guys. At least not any more than I already have. But he gives me such a good opening, the perfect response is ready before I can think about it. This is the first in a long line of lessons where I should have learned to keep my damned mouth shut. I never seem to learn. I look up at him, pausing in mid-shine and without missing a beat, "Oh, you mean like your mom?"

Now, I don't know much about Horner's background, but

somewhere deep down under that asshole veneer, I think he's a mamma's boy looking to please the family back home. Whatever the case, the insult has an instant effect. Before I can think better of what I said, his fist is rushing toward my face and my hand with the boot shine comes up to block him. His fist connects with the polish tin, spilling the thick liquid all over both of us before I'm falling back off the bench with the impact.

The guys in the barracks gather around and start shouting encouragements to violence. Some of them are making bets. Avery tries to jump in and pull us apart, but Horner's guys hold him back. I've got flecks of polish in my eyes, half-blinding me, but I don't think Horner is doing much better. Most of his flimsy punches don't connect, and his pale skin and blonde hair is streaked with black.

Horner is the kind of guy who's all talk. He's older and bigger than I am, but I've been in my share of fights and I know how to get the upper hand. I take the advantage and slam Horner's pretty-boy face into the wooden floor. There's a crack and a splat of blood is left on the surface as he jerks back, pushing me away from him.

The small crowd of onlookers moves like shifting sand as we roll and struggle across the floor. It seems like more people join the group with each passing moment, but it's hard to tell if that's actually the case. Over the cheers, I can hear Avery yelling for us to stop, but there's no stopping this fight now that it's in full swing.

Another roll and I find myself on top again. I don't know how he does it, but a knife appears in Horner's polish- and blood-covered hand. My eyes widen when I see it. He means to kill me. Death may get me out of the war and there's something to be said about whatever justice would fall on Horner's formerly well-coifed head, but in a moment like this, self-preservation kicks in. I wasn't ready to die earlier today, that hasn't changed now.

Horner snarls and takes a swing at me with the knife. I pull back reflexively and he's on the move in an instant, barreling into me and knocking me flat on my ass. Less than a second passes and he's pushing the knife into my face. I jerk, pulling my head to the side, moving enough that the blade bites into my left cheek and the tip sticks in the floor. The dull thud of the blade is startling and I turn my head to look at it. A close call. I have to end this.

I can see Horner flexing to pull the knife free of the wood and I push the heel of my hand into his chin, slamming him backward. He yelps and falls away. I hope the jackwad bit his tongue. I hope I've added a broken jaw to his already mangled nose. Whatever damage is done, he falls back, releasing his grip on the knife.

Without thinking, I grab the handle and pull the knife free, then roll forward to try to get to my feet. If that dick thinks he's going to get away with this, he has another thing coming. A taste of his own medicine is what I have in mind. I'm barely to my feet when I see him sitting on his ass, stunned and holding his pointy chin. His eyes look dazed and I doubt he sees me coming. I don't give a damn.

But someone out there is looking out for this jerk. Before I can make a move, strong hands grab my arms and pull me back, nearly knocking me off my feet again. I struggle, desperate to get to Horner while he's still down.

"That's enough, Colt. Drop the knife." It's Avery. Once they saw their boss in trouble, Horner's cronies let Avery go. I can smell the coal and grease rising off him and mingling with his sweat and the polish that cover me.

I look down at the knife in my hand, then back to Horner. He's looking back at me with an expression of confused hatred. I want to kill him. If I don't, he'll keep coming back. If I do, then I would spend the rest of my life in lock-up. Part of me thinks it might be worth it. But that's not who I am. I drop the knife, letting it clatter to the floor. The fight is over. For now.

Chapter 9

When I wake up again, the world around me is warm. I don't expect this. I expect wind and rain and pain. But I get none of that. Instead, I get warm and comfortable. It's enough to make me want to roll over and go back to sleep, even though I know the dreams are waiting for me. The most recent one, a nightmare about Horner. I hate that guy.

But at least it's just a dream. A relived memory that I can push right back into place and forget about it again for a while. The warmth helps. As much as I'd like to go back to sleep, I'm awake now for a reason and I should see what it is. I yawn, stretch, and open my eyes on a small, dim room that reminds me of the barracks. Maybe that wasn't a dream. I reach up to run my hand along the scar on my cheek, half expecting to feel tacky, congealed blood as if the fight had just happened.

All I feel is a couple days' worth of stubble and the smooth line of scar where hair refuses to grow. I couldn't still be in the militia. I could barely grow more than peach fuzz back then, even by the time I got out. A lifetime of memories flood back into my head, reminding me of the old fart I've become. This couldn't be the barracks anyway. The ceiling is rocky and the place smells like the ocean. I snort a laugh and slowly sit up, feeling every bone in my body ache in complaint. I need is a drink.

"Mr. Reed?" A light voice touches my ears and I turn my head to see Samantha sitting in a nearby chair. She's cleaned up, wearing a fresh, but ill-fitting dress. She still looks worse for wear. Her face shows scratches and bruises I can only guess cover the rest of her. I can't image I look any better. But she smiles softly as she sees me awake and alert. "Are you all right?"

I nod, though I'm not sure that's the truth. I've seen better days. "I'll survive. What about the others? Avery? Tick?" This is also the place most people would ask, *where am I*, and *what happened*? But I know the answers to both of those. We crashed. I crashed. And now, somehow, we're here in the bolt hole. My guess is Avery made it through and brought us here, but I want to hear Samantha confirm it.

"Your friend," she says in a heavy tone I don't understand. I don't think she likes Avery much, but he's not exactly known to be a ladies' man. In the twenty-some odd years I've known him, I can't remember him caring one wit for a woman. Maybe women are simply repelled by his existence. "He held onto Tick and me as the airship went down. We only suffered minor injuries. Tick was out the entire time. She still is." She glances toward a screen that gives the room a little privacy. The hideout isn't much, but it serves its purpose. "He's been trying to…fix her."

I shift to get out of the cot, drawing Samantha's attention back to me in time for me to realize that I'm not wearing much. I flinch and pull the blanket across me. "Ugh, sorry…I didn't…"

Samantha shakes her head and points to a pile of folded clothing sitting on a chair. "You were drenched through and a mess. Mr. Nickols saw to your well-being. He hasn't rested since we arrived."

Mr. Nickols? Her formality with me is one thing, she's employing me and it's only right to keep a certain distance. But Avery? He's not the kind of guy anyone feels the need to be formal with. And from everything she's said so far, he's saved the day. All I hear in her voice is distrust. I smile and reach for the pile. "He's a bulldog. Once he gets his mind set on something, he doesn't let go until it's finished. He's also a genius. Don't you worry about Tick. He'll have her up and running around again in no time."

Samantha stands and turns her back to me while I dress. "He has had very little luck so far," she says quietly, folding her hands together. I wish I could say it surprises me. Avery can work wonders with airships and gadgets, but Tick is more than that. She has flesh and bone parts that need healing, and she would need a medical doctor for that. If she can be healed at all. I have no idea how much is human and how much is mechanical. Or how much damage she's taken.

I pull on the trousers and stand up. Damn. Everything hurts. The sleep had done me wonders, but I still have a way to go before I'm recovered. "We'll figure something out. I promise. Maybe go into Portsmaw to find a medic. We're going to need some supplies anyway. How long was I unconscious?"

"Two days," Samantha says, cautiously turning around once more. "I've already gone into town for a few things." She motions to her dress, which looks like it's made out of a burlap sack. Places like Portsmaw aren't exactly known for high fashion. "But Mr. Nickols was mumbling something about parts for your airship. I wouldn't know the first thing about getting what he needs."

I pause in buttoning up the shirt and look at her. No, she wouldn't know anything about fixing Airika, but I think she knows more than a few things about Tick. Many of my questions come back to me and now seems like as good a time as any to ask. "But you do know more about Tick than you've told me, don't you? With all that's happened, I understand your caution, but it'd be nice to hear the truth for a change."

Samantha looks at me a moment like she has been slapped across the face. Okay, the question is blunt, but I did try to soften the blow a little. Maybe I should have led with understanding. Before I can apologize, she closes her eyes and looks down at her folded hands. "She is…was…my niece." Okay. I had not been expecting that. Now I feel like I've been slapped. "My brother, her father, well, Wisen had taken in both of us when we were young. My brother was something of an apprentice to Wisen, and became a brilliant researcher. He knew all kinds of things about radio waves and frequencies." Her voice softens as she talks, but she looks back up at me. I can already see the sheen of tears forming in her eyes. So far she hasn't said anything that seems upsetting. I can only guess that something went terribly wrong.

"So, what happened?" I ask, trying to encourage her. A conversation from the recent past swirls up in my head. Tick had said there were two Wisens, and she had worked with one of them. I still can't imagine who would turn her into such a monster and then go on as if everything is fine. And what did radio frequencies have to do with forests and war machines? "Did they do that to her? On purpose?"

Samantha shakes her head. She sits back down again, pressing her face into her hands as the tears come. "No. No, of course not." She looks up again. I wish I could offer her a tissue or handkerchief, but there aren't any. "My brother loved his daughter. He loved his wife. And Dr. Wisen is…was, like family to us. But there had been an accident. Or maybe it was intentional. I'm not sure. As I told you already, some of the researchers were more interested in making tools of war than finding ways to make the world better."

I sit back down on the cot to listen to her. "So, you think someone in the compound may have injured Tick on purpose? Who keeps a kid in a place like that anyway?"

Samantha presses her hands into fists, the tears stopping for a moment as she cringes in pain. She takes a breath and nods slightly. "Tick, and her mother. My brother. A few others. There was an explosion. Tick…her name was Patricia, before. But she was there because my brother and his wife were always there. As was Dr. Wisen. Dr. Wisen did what he could to save her life. She was the only one he could help." Her voice chokes slightly at this and she wears a far-away look as she remembers.

I'm still missing something. Her story isn't making any sense, so I try to add a little more of the information I already know into the conversation. It will either trip Samantha up, or she'll be able to fill in the holes. "Tick mentioned another Wisen. Dianne, or Darlene…"

Samantha takes a sharp breath and purses her lips together. "Dr. Wisen's wife." She nods, but doesn't offer up the woman's name. "She was killed as well. Dr. Wisen tired not to talk about her much, and I guess I got used to saying nothing. We've been through so much."

"I see. I'm sorry." She doesn't have to tell me this. Her brother, Tick, both the Wisens now, Samantha's lost everyone she knows. She already looks like she's on the edge of breaking, so I change the subject slightly to something less painful. "Look, there was no one down in the compound. Just the forest. And the war machines you told me about. I thought they'd be vehicles. But they were more like metal soldiers. But there were no researchers. No guards. Where would everyone have gone?"

"I'm not sure." Samantha's face screws up in a puzzled way. "I only worked at his estate, as a personal assistant. Sometimes I would see research papers, but I can't claim to understand everything I saw. Dr. Wisen kept Tick away from the other researchers. They knew about her; they had to. But he made sure they couldn't find her by teaching her not to trust them. He didn't trust them, so that was easy. How were you able to find her so easily?"

The question startles me. I shrug slightly and laugh. "It wasn't easy. I got a little stuck and she actually helped me. Risked her well-being to do it. I wouldn't call that afraid or distrusting."

Samantha glances around the small alcove and shakes her head. "I...that was very fortunate. I guess she knew you weren't one of them." She takes a slow breath, looking up at me once more. "Are you sure there was no one else there? Just the machines and the forest? You didn't find anything else?"

I raise a brow. What the hell did she expect? She only sent me to get research and Tick, but she sounds as if she wanted me to find something else. "That's it. Why don't we start at the beginning? Tell me how all this happened."

Samantha takes a deep breath and closes her eyes. She looks down at her hands, twining her fingers together. "I believe my brother was tricked into helping build the war machines. Or maybe coerced. After the accident that killed his wife and injured Tick, he started asking questions. He was the one who alerted Dr. Wisen to the research that was going on. He was killed for his efforts. Dr. Wisen tried to shut it down through the Corporation, but ReGen Corps was far more invested in the machines. They tried to scare Dr. Wisen into silence by killing his wife." She continues speaking softly, playing with her fingers as she reveals each detail.

"When Dr. Wisen realized that the other researchers were getting ready to sell the war machines, he tried to sabotage them," she says so quiet I can barely hear her. "He failed, and had to flee the compound. He was injured. He couldn't retrieve Tick before leaving and was in no condition to go back. That's when we hired you."

I let Samantha's words settle for a moment, then nod. Her story passes the sniff test. Someone is always trying to find a way to make money, and get rid of anyone who wants to stop them. The only real mystery that remains is where the other researchers had gone, but she doesn't have an answer for that. I lean back, rubbing my chin as one final thing eats at me. "So, the men who were after you. You said they wanted Tick. If she was the result of an accident, what value could she have to someone else?"

Samantha shakes her head and stands up once more to begin pacing the small enclosure. "I'm not sure," she says, her voice shaking slightly. "Yes, her current condition is the result of the explosion and trying to save her. But I think they wanted to use her for more. Dr. Wisen spoke of her being a key to the war machines. That's why he wanted to get her away from the compound. I'm certain someone else might have known more about that."

"Huh," I grunt as I stand. I finish buttoning up my shirt and move toward the screen. "One or more of the researchers wanted to get their hands on Tick, but couldn't for some reason. If the Wisens wanted to keep her away from the others, they did a pretty good job. The doors were rigged to keep her from opening them, and she had the whole damned forest to hide in." I stop at the screen, and turn to look at Samantha, who is watching me silently. "I want to know one last thing. Why didn't you tell me what you knew before? It would've saved me a hell of a lot of trouble."

Samantha looks toward the screen and purses her lips. I notice for the first time that she isn't wearing any make-up, as she had been when I first met her. She's still as beautiful, even with the occasional bruise and scratch and that sad look in her eyes. "I'm sorry, Mr. Reed," she says in a whisper. "We didn't know if we could trust you, or who might be listening. Dr. Wisen asked me to keep the information at a minimum."

I nod and push the screen open. "Well, all right. But from now on we stop keeping useful information from one another, right?" I still need to find out how she managed to find my apartment, but that could wait. After all, the damage has been done. She nods back to me and I give her my best comforting smile. "Now let's go see if Avery needs anything from town."

Chapter 9

The inside of the hide out isn't much to look at. The opening faces out toward the ocean, but it's far enough up the cliff that it's safe from most flooding. Sometimes the water does come up higher than expected, especially during storms. Avery built a barrier to keep out the water and prevent any random fishing boats from getting too curious. It's up now across the cavern opening. I can't see any spray smashing against it, so if the water had been high earlier, it's down again now.

The cave is a little bigger than my apartment, with natural alcoves. We put in a series of privacy screens built from driftwood and discarded sail canvas on the larger nooks to create rooms, but the central area is open. It's large enough to hold Airika, but getting her down here is a special pain in the ass neither of us are willing to attempt. So the open space is empty except for an old table. Tick is on the table, lying motionless and Avery hovers over her, picking at one of her damaged hands.

Samantha follows me as I head over to the table. "Av," I say, trying not to startle him. He doesn't look up from his work, forcing me to get closer and raise my voice. "Avery."

Avery jerks up, dropping Tick's hand, which makes a painful thud on the table. Avery mutters a curse under his breath and looks over at me. "Oh…hey boss. We were wondering when you'd wake up." He glances at Samantha, nodding to her. "Ma'am," then returns to his focused attention on Tick's hand. "You messed her up pretty good, Colt."

I sigh and go around the other side of the table to lean on it. Samantha stops at the end, frowning as she looks over Tick. "I didn't do this," I say with a shake of my head. "They had some kind of security on the doors down in the compound. She tried to open one and it burned her hands. Think you can fix her?" 'Fix' sounds so cold, as if she's a toy or some kind gadget that's destined for the trash bin if she can't be repaired.

Avery snorts and glances up at me. "I meant Airika." He lowers Tick's hand to the table more gently this time and frowns at me. "Even if I could get the parts I need in this backwater village, it'd take me weeks to get her airworthy again."

Oh. Right. Airika. Why do I feel like he slugged me in the gut? I take a step back, and rub my stomach. "Yeah, sorry. I did the best I could. At least I got the three of you here alive." I look at each of them in turn, stopping on Tick. Had I gotten her here alive? She doesn't seem to be breathing, but then I'm not sure if she actually needs to breathe anyway. "We'll worry about Airika later. We're safe here for now, and she's our priority," I nod at Tick and look back at Avery. "What do you think?"

Avery shakes his head and looks back down at Tick. "This is some pretty advanced stuff." He looks over at Samantha and narrows his eyes. "What the hell were these people working on anyway?" Ah, good ol' Avery. Always out to impress the ladies with his verbal skills.

Samantha keeps her eyes locked on Tick as if looking at Avery causes her some kind of pain. How did these two manage to tolerate each other over the past couple of days? It's as if they have some kind of hate at first sight. They seem to grate on each other's' nerves without even trying. But she answers him, keeping her words short and sweet. "Radio frequencies mostly. Something about kanik motion?"

Avery's face springs to life. "Kinetic motion?" He blinks and gives Tick's arm a shake. "I wonder…"

"What is it?" I ask, watching the largely motionless girl. She doesn't respond to the shaking, but I have no idea if that was Avery's intent. "Is there something you think you can do?"

"Yes. No." Avery paces away from the table. He runs a dirty hand through his coal-stained hair as he thinks. I can almost see smoke coming out of his ears. Whatever he's hit on, it's something big. "Radio and kinetic. I'd love to get my hands on their research." I wince, scolding myself for not getting any of the research.

Samantha frowns and shake her head. "He kept some at the estate, maybe not enough to be helpful. The bulk of it is at the compound." She glances at me. "You would have to go back and get it before the men who were after me get there."

I smirk and shake my head. "They'd have a hell of a time doing that. There were…complications," I say, watching Avery pace back and forth. "But we're kind of stuck here anyway. Airika being out of commission limits our options. Is there anything you can do without the paperwork?"

Avery stops his mad movement and shrugs. "Tinker," which is his way of saying take a wild guess and hope something works. "The stuff that's showing might be all right. She's got a lot of little, intricate parts, but most of the damage is a matter of cleaning. It's the internal working parts that'll be more difficult."

I glance at Samantha, who looks about as clueless as I feel. Then back at Avery. "Internal working parts?"

Avery snorts and gives me a look that says I don't understand anything. He's right, at least when it comes to mechanics and technology. That's why I keep him around. He comes back over to Tick and presses his hands down on the table, looking her over. "I can fix the stuff on the outside, right? That shouldn't be a problem. But this...kid? She's got flesh and bone, and I'm going to bet she has more mechanics buried under that." He looks up at me, frowning. "Like I said before, I ain't a medic. I'm not about to cut into her to see what I can find. And we have no idea if that'll help anyway. She might be..."

"What if we find a medic to assist you?" Samantha says quietly. Her voice cracks as she speaks, and I think I know how she feels. We're grasping at straws without knowing if anything will work.

"That's your call, lady," Avery says with a huff. He turns his attention back to me. "I'll fix what I can, if that's what you want. But I ain't making any promises."

If it's what I want? I almost laugh. I had seen the light on his face when he heard the technology involved. Nothing's going to keep Avery from playing around with it. If we had gone through all this and lose Tick, well, there'd have to be something seriously wrong with the world. "Yeah, do what you can. Samantha and I were talking about heading into town. We can look for a medic. Anything else you need?"

Avery grunts and I realize he's back to poking at Tick's hand. He has a pair of tweezers and he's pulling out black flecks of gunk. I guess that answers that question. If he needs anything we'll go back later.

Portsmaw isn't that far away. I motion to Samantha and turn to head out of the cave. Avery's always worked better without an audience anyway.

Chapter 10

We chose this cave to hide in because it's hard to get to. A rope ladder leads down from the bluff, but access from the sides is cut off by rocky outcroppings that prevent anyone from simply strolling by. Any number of fishermen from the village could reach the cave by boat during high tide, but so far no one has. They're more concerned about their work. I had found the spot on a fly-by some years back and knew this would be the perfect place to bug out if we needed to. Since then, I come by every couple of years to clean up the airstrip and make sure everything is untouched. Guess I should have come here a little more recently. Not that trying to land at night in a storm would have changed much if the strip had been recently cleaned. I'm good, but not that good.

In order to get to the town of Portsmaw, which is something I don't do that often, we have to climb up the ladder to the bluff, then walk back down to the village. The rope ladder blends into the rocky bluff, obscuring it from view. It's also not an easy climb. How Avery had managed to carry Tick and me down after the crash, boggles the mind. I owe him a hell of a lot, and I'm not sure I'll be able to repay it. Knowing him, he won't ask either, but I'll have to think of something to make it up.

I'm a little surprised Samantha had made it there on her own while I was out, but she's full of surprises. She's stronger in character than many of the women I've met over the years. Though, that hasn't been a lot to be honest. I don't deal with very many people at all, and most of those I do, are men. I head up the ladder first so I don't get accused of looking up her skirts, even though I wouldn't mind a peek. That's the last thing I need after the fiasco that is this job.

When I get to the top of the cliff, I know exactly how I'm going to make things up to Avery. Airika. She came to a stop a short distance away from the ladder. A string of broken parts stretches out behind her and a serious groove runs through the rocky surface. Her right wing is nearly torn off, sitting at a strange angle to the rest of her body. My baby is in rough shape, and I can only imagine her condition has Avery weeping inside. I'll do all the heavy work on her, so he can focus on the intricate mechanical parts.

But Airika would have to wait for now. I help Samantha up over the edge of the cliff and we start down toward the town. The conversation is light, almost non-existent. We chat about the day, which is warm for autumn, and how quiet this part of the world is. I find that Samantha has never been further outside of New Foundis than the Wisen estate, and even that is only a few miles north of the city. I tell her she isn't missing much. The larger world is a messy place full of war. Or at least that's the world I've seen. Give me my lonely street corner where I only have to worry about own sorry hide and not the lives of total strangers.

As we near the town, Samantha finally brings up the elephant tagging along behind us. "Your friend, Avery. He doesn't seem to like me much. Did I do something wrong?"

I raise a brow. She didn't seem to like him either, which makes the question surprising. I can't think of what might have caused their mutual distrust. Unless being a woman counts. Even that's just a guess. I have a hard time believing Avery would have a strong dislike for the fairer half of the population. "Wrong?" I shake my head. "I think he doesn't trust you. You came in at a bad time. I had told him that you were a security breach, and..."

"A what?" Samantha says, narrowing her eyes at me.

Well, crap. I sound like I don't trust her either, but after all we've discussed, that can't be further from the truth. I sigh, doing my best to back-peddle. "I didn't know as much then. And you did just show up at my door. Which means someone told you where to go. I can't have people out there giving away all my secrets." I laugh slightly, trying to put her at ease. "He even thought you could be a Reddie. He's got an active imagination."

Samantha gives a soft, nervous laugh, shaking her head. "A Reddie? Someone like me? That's just silly. But, I guess I understand. It would seem strange to me too. I guess he's just trying to protect you. He must be a very good friend."

I nod, though I don't know for certain what might be going on in Avery's head. "He's kind of like an older brother to me. We met during the war and had each other's backs in the worst of times. So if I say there's a problem, he agrees. He hasn't had a chance to hear your side of things. Unless you talked during the flight? Or while I was out."

She shakes her head again slowly, looking at the ground. "No. I tried to talk a little once things smoothed out, but he was focused on Tick. Do you think he can get her back on her feet?"

I nod, having every confidence in Avery's abilities. "If anyone can, it's him. But he's going to need help." I look ahead to the approaching town. It's a quiet place with a handful of residents. But fishing is a dangerous life with lots of accidents. They would need a good medic to keep the fishermen running. I don't want to take their healer away if there's only one in town, and yet I want an answer, one way or another, that Tick can be fixed. "We should be able to find someone here, if he's not scared off by the patient."

Samantha frowns slightly at that. I don't know if she is simply bristling at the idea that Tick is horrifying, or if it's about what was done to the poor girl in the first place. "Did she frighten you when you first saw her?"

I snort a laugh, thinking back to a few days ago. It feels like forever now, but the memories are still fresh. "She scared the hell out of me. But not because of her looks, if that's what you mean. If anything I felt sorry for her. No, at first I didn't know what to think. Was she human? Machine? Something else? But the more I talked with her, the more I thought she was an unfortunate human. I feel like she was some kind of prototype to those other war machines. That just pissed me off."

"I think, in way, she was," Samantha says softly, looking down at the ground. "Dr. Wisen could only help her using the same kind of technology to make those machines. None of them would have wanted to do that without reason, but she became an experiment the moment the accident happened. If Dr. Wisen hadn't helped her with good intentions, one of the other researchers would have done it simply to exploit her."

"Well, she's safe now," I tell her, trying to be comforting. I can only imagine how difficult it must be for her to see Tick in such a condition. I've grown fond of the kid myself, and I hate to think she might be beyond repair.

"You...really, care about her, don't you?" Samantha asks.

I nod without hesitation. "I guess so. She kind of reminds me of myself when I was a kid. I know how tough it can be if you don't have someone watching your back. I want to make sure she doesn't have to suffer any more." Samantha smiles at my words in a way that warms my entire body. Even if I'm not the typical hero, I've made myself seem like one in her eyes. "And once we get her and Airika up and running again, I'm going back to that compound and putting an end to the research there. The world doesn't need any more war."

Samantha pauses, stumbling a step. I reach out to catch her, but she rights herself and waves me off. "I'm all right. You just...well, how do you mean to put an end to it?"

My mind shifts back to the hallway filled with gas. If those guys who had been following Samantha head there, they're going to be in for a pretty big surprise. The compound has to be saturated by now. Even if they went days ago, it would have had enough gas to be dangerous. They wouldn't find Tick, or anything else alive. I'm banking on them not being able to get far before getting pushed out again. Sure they could leave a few doors open, but it would take more than that to air out the place. If I'm right, it will be a simple matter to add a little fire and let it do its work. "Oh, I have an idea. I plan to take out the whole damned place. It'll be a shame to lose the forest too, but it's that or let someone else eventually find the war machines and use them."

Samantha catches her breath and purses her lips together. "All that research," she says softly, shaking her head. "It's a good thing Dr. Wisen isn't…"

I can see the glassy start of tears in her eyes, and I curse myself for even bringing up the subject. I reach over and put my arm around her shoulders, hoping to soothe some of the hard feelings. "I'm sorry. This must be very hard for you. But at least you have Tick, and soon she'll be good as…well, as good as she can be. She's going to need you here in the outside world."

"Yes, you're right," Samantha replies, sniffling a little. She reaches up to brush the beginning of the tears away. "No more crying today. I've done enough of that. Thank you, Mr. Reed."

I drop my arm again, not wanting it to become awkward, and smile. "It's all right. You hired me to help you, so that's what I'm going to do. And call me Colton, or Colt. We've been through too much to be formal." I get a vague nod from her as we cross into the village. "Now, let's see about finding a doctor."

Dr. Leah Kepling is easy enough to find. Most of the population is out to sea on a day like this, leaving the merchants, fishwives, a small number of children, and service people on dry land. A group of kids race by us as we enter town, and I manage to stop one with the promise of a few coins for information. The boy is happy enough to point us to the little house near the docks where Kepling keeps shop. I pay him with some loose change I had stuffed in my pocket before leaving the cave, and we head toward the doctor's house.

It makes sense for the medic to be located near the docks, since most of the injuries would be coming off the ocean. The house looks like it's been repurposed from some kind of shipping office into a dwelling. It has two stories; the bottom part from the street is boarded up for the privacy of patients, and the top part looks like a normal house.

The door shows that we've come to the right place. A placard is nailed to the weather-worn wood, stating, "Doctor Leah R. Kelping, Medicine and Surgery." Below this is another sign reading, "Open. Please knock for assistance." I smile and look at Samantha. "Looks like we're in luck. The doctor's in."

Samantha smiles and nods, looking at the door. "I hope she's willing to help us. Where will we go if she doesn't?"

I shake my head and raise my hand to knock on the door. "We'll figure that out if we have to." I hope to high hell we don't have to. With Airika down, this is really the only option. The next closest town is still miles away and I have a feeling the longer we take, the less chance Tick has. If she's even alive now.

I knock twice and strain to listen for the sound of footsteps on the other side. Instead of movement, a voice calls out. "Come in!" Those two simple words are both warm and matronly, but they carry a sense of someone who is busy beyond her capabilities. I cringe slightly and look at Samantha, silently asking if we should accept the invite.

Samantha nods and I take a deep breath before opening the door. I remind myself this is for Tick. The kid deserves a break for once in her short life. I step in and I'm hit with the smell of antiseptic that reminds me I haven't had a drink in days now. I'd have to fix that soon. But first things, first.

The downstairs portion of the building is split in half. A desk sits against the left hand wall and several supply cabinets are against the right side. In the center is a low table, with a fisherman sitting on it. A middle aged woman is stitching up a long gash across the fisherman's forehead. She doesn't look up from her work as we enter. "Be with you in a minute," she snorts softly, focusing on the stitch work. "Stop fidgeting, Walter, less you want me to poke your eye out."

"Er…no, ma'am. I mean, yes, ma'am," the fisherman answers. I can see even from half-way across the room, his knuckles are turning white as he grips the edge of the table.

"Dear lord!" Dr. Kepling hisses at him. "You been eating raw fish? Your breath smells like a tuna boat."

"It's Thomas' fault, ma'am," the fisherman complains. "'E started it. Whacked me upside the head wif a bait ball. It 'ad hooks in it!"

I'm trying not to laugh at the conversation. Even Samantha has her hand to her lips, holding back her lovely smile. This woman has some moxie. I guess she would need it to deal with a bunch of salty fishermen day in and day out.

The doctor gives her patient another snort, and finishes up her stitching. "Well be sure you clean yourself up before going home. The last thing Martha needs is you bringing more sickness into the house."

The fisherman reaches up and touches the wound lightly. He's frowning, but I don't know if it's from the pain, or something else. He drops his hand again and nods. "Yes, ma'am." He hops down from the table as Keplin goes to wash up from a basin sitting on one of the counters. "An' fank you, ma'am. I'll be sending payment at the end o' the monf. Just like I promised."

"Yes, yes," Kepling says with a wave of one of her wet hands. "Now, go on. The day's burning and I'm sure Thomas is itching to get back out on the water."

"Aye," Walter responds. He looks at us curiously as he heads out the door. In a place like this, everyone knows everyone, and we're obvious strangers. He makes a large path around us, as if getting too close would infect him with strangerism. Samantha smiles at him and I do my best not to laugh.

"And what brings the two of you here today?" Kepling's voice comes from the other side of the room. She comes along with it, walking toward us as she dries off her hands. "Can't say I've seen the likes of you around here. We don't often get new folks or visitors."

The amusement of the floor show fades away and I step forward, holding out my hand to the woman. "We're sorry to bother you, doctor. My name is Colton Reed, and this is…" I look back at Samantha, not sure exactly how to introduce her. She's too young to be my wife. She could pass as a daughter, but that would be a stretch. So I settle on the most likely thing. "My assistant, Ms. Samantha Loral."

Kepling looks at my hand suspiciously. In New Foundis it's not that unusual to find a woman practicing medicine. Women seemed to be inclined to healing, especially when it came to helping birth children. But in places like this, where it's more common to treat injuries like the one that just walked out the door, men often took the lead. I can only guess she's giving me that look because she isn't sure if I'm secretly judging her. Finally, she takes my hand and gives it a shake. "Mr. Reed. Ms. Loral." She drops my hand and nods to each of us. "Though you both seem a little worse for wear, you appear to be relatively unharmed. And I doubt this is a social visit. What can I do for you?"

I glance at Samantha, who has gone very quiet. She's leaving the conversation up to me, but I'm not sure what, or how much to say. I understand how Samantha must have felt when she first came to me. Tick's a delicate subject and has to be handled with the right lack of information. Looking back at Dr. Kepling, I clear my throat slightly. "Er…yes, well, we could use your help. There's a patient, a young girl, who could use your skills."

Kepling raises a gray eyebrow up almost to the poof of white hair that's gathered on her head. "And where is this young girl? Are you keeping her in your pockets? I certainly don't see her here."

Yeah, I like this old bitch. But Samantha harrumphs beside me. She crosses her arms together. "With all due respect, ma'am, we couldn't bring her with us. As my…" she looks at me and narrows her eyes, "Colleague mentioned, she needs your help. We didn't want to risk hurting her more by bringing her here." Ouch. Apparently 'assistant' was the wrong choice. But she's right. We couldn't bring Tick through here unless we wrapped her in a blanket. Even then, getting her up the cliff would be a pain.

Kepling's eyebrows remain glued to her forehead as she looks over Samantha. "And how far away is this child? What is the problem?"

Here comes the fun part. Well, one of the fun parts. I'm not going to believe she's going to help until she actually sees Tick, but getting her to come with us is going to be a challenge. "She's in a sea cave, out on that bluff, south of here. She's been injured, and may need surgery." I hope that's enough for her.

Kepling looks at us for a moment. I feel her eyes boring into me like gun fire. I should have thought about it before. A cave. It's hardly the sanitary location that Kepling's house is. How the hell am I going to convince her to go there? A long pause later and she clears her throat. "Let me see if I understand this. You would like me to leave my practice, in the middle of the day, to help an injured child? While it would be altruistic on my part, how am I to know you aren't up to something? Am I also to presume you've left this poor child all by herself in a cave?"

I cringe. I hadn't thought of that angle. I guess I had hoped she would have an assistant or someone to look after things here while she helps us. At least I can soothe her fears about the last part. "She's not alone," I say, the words sounding weak as they come out. "I have someone tending to her right now, but he doesn't have the same skills you have. You'll have to believe me that this isn't a trick."

Dr. Kepling turns then, and makes her way back over to the cabinets. I'm certain she's about to throw us out. I think I might at this point. I'm about to turn and try to make a quiet exit with Samantha, when

Kepling speaks again. "It does sound intriguing."

Expecting the worse, I nod and start to turn. "I understand. We're sorry we wasted..." Samantha elbows me softly, pulling my attention to her. She gives me a look like I'm the biggest idiot in the world, and finally Kepling's words sink in. I turn back to her, cocking my head. "Wait, are you willing to help?"

Kepling sighs and pulls a satchel out from under one of the cabinets. "I did not say that. Not at all. I simply said it sounds intriguing." She turns and looks at us once more. "You do understand, I cannot simply leave the practice in the middle of the day. The people here depend on me day and night, and they do take a certain priority over strangers who come waltzing in, demanding my services."

"We haven't demanded anything," Samantha says softly, approaching the woman. I watch her, waiting for the tears to start. Samantha can convince anyone with those tears. Her voice remains steady as she pleads our case. "We're only asking. But we're desperate and there isn't anywhere else to turn. This little girl may die if she isn't tended to by a medic. You've got to help us."

I cringe as Samantha takes the guilt angle. It would have been cruel coming out of my mouth, and I'm not sure it's much different coming out of hers. The worst part is, Tick may already be beyond saving. Dr. Kepling isn't going to be happy if we drag her out there for nothing. I step forward in an attempt to smooth things before the situation blows up. "We will compensate you for your time and services, Doctor. And this will be very different from your typical fisherman."

Kepling shakes her head and starts toward us. "The two of you need to stop talking before I change my mind." She smiles and passes us, opening the door. "Now come along. The less time I'm away, the better." The doctor pulls the sign that claims she is in, off the door and stuffs it into her bag, then she starts walking away from the house.

I glance at Samantha, and we shrug to one another. I'm going to have to keep an eye on Kepling, not because she's crafty, but because she's probably going to be pretty damned entertaining. I smile and follow her out, Samantha behind me. Samantha closes the door and we head off together back toward the cave.

The walk back to the cave is silent. I had thought Dr. Kepling would ask questions about her patient or what we were doing out here, but she keeps whatever questions she might have to herself. Good. I don't feel inclined to give answers. It's going to be hard enough to explain things once she sees Tick. She does make a questioning face when we go passed Airika, followed by a nod of her head. The condition of my airship is enough to explain what happened.

Kepling is spry for her age. If I had to guess, I'd put her somewhere around Avery's age, a few years older than me. But she has the look of someone who's lived a hard, life full. I'd wager she's spent most of that life in this village, watching people from their birth all the way through death. Maybe even those close to her. That has a way of hardening and aging a person.

She has no problem climbing down the ladder to the cave entrance, though she does give me a dirty look before heading down. All I can do is apologize and promise to explain once Tick is taken care of. Kepling accepts that and heads down, fearless of the long drop to the rough ocean below.

When we get inside, Avery is still working on Tick, cleaning out the mechanical features of her face. As if he was working on Airika, he's focused on his task, and doesn't bother to look up as we enter. We head toward the table and I whistle, trying to get his attention. "Oy, Avery. We're back and we found a medic. How's Tick looking?"

Behind me, Kepling stops and whispers something I don't quite catch. It's the kind of reaction I might have had seeing Tick laying there, so I chalk it up to that. Avery remains focused on the kid, but he nods his head slightly. "Good. I don't think there's much more I can do here. Her hands were the worst, and I got those cleaned up." He looks up finally, his eyes coming to rest on the new person in the room, Kepling.

Samantha and I approach the table, and I motion back to Kepling, who's staring at Avery. "This is Dr. Leah Kepling. Dr. Kepling, this is…"

"Avery Nickols," Kepling says, regaining her distant tone. I blink and look between them. They know each other? How could they possibly know each other? It's easy to forget Avery had a life before I met him.

"Doctor?" Avery says, raising a brow. "Kepling? So you married?" I blink as realization dawns on me. They do know each other. After all these years of coming here to maintain the cave, Avery never once went into town. He had no idea an old acquaintance lives here.

Kepling nods curtly, shifting the bag in her hands. "I got tired of waiting." Her eyes shift to the girl on the table and she comes closer. "I do not believe this is the time to bring up the past. I'm here for a purpose."

Samantha frowns and asks the question that's rattling around in my brain. "Is this going to be a problem? Working together, I mean?" She's also looking between Avery and Kepling.

"Not at all," Kepling replies, setting her bag down on the edge of the table. She's looking over Tick already, ignoring Avery whose jaw is hanging open. Though it's hard to tell under the perpetual smudges, I'm pretty sure he's several shades paler than usual. "Now, what is this?"

Avery clears his throat and tries to speak, but nothing comes out. I step in to rescue him. "This is Tick. She's been…well, modified."

"She was normal once," Samantha says, taking over the story. "The mechanical pieces were added after an accident. She's been unconscious for a few days now." She looks at Avery, though I'm not sure if he's listening to a word of this. "Mr. Nickols has been working on the mechanical pieces, but we think there may be more inside. We need you to help with the flesh parts."

"I see." Kepling's voice is cold, and I'm beginning to regret bringing her here. If only we had another choice. Avery's going to kill me once he gets his sense back. Not that I could have possibly known this would happen. She starts to dig into her bag and pulls free various medical tools, laying them next to Tick. "I presume the airship had something to do with this?"

I look down at my hands. Kepling had commented on my minor injuries already, so she has to know we've been through a few things. I look back up at her. "Some of it, yeah. But she was out before that. I'm not sure what might have happened. Her hands were burned by a trap, but I don't know why she's unresponsive."

"Kinetics," Avery croaks out, shaking his head. All eyes turn to him as he comes out of his stupor. "I think something inside has come loose. Something she needs to keep moving. I don't know much about the technology. It's…well, it's really theoretical. But, that's the only explanation I've got."

Kepling nods, poking and prodding Tick's motionless body. "And you need me to open her up properly so you can get at whatever that might be?" She sighs, frowning deeply. "This is not the best environment for major surgery."

"I think you see why we didn't bring her into town," Samantha says, motioning to Tick. "But we must…"

"No, no," Kepling waves her hand in Samantha's direction. "We'll make do." She looks up at me. "We'll need to boil some water, and I'll need a great deal of clean cloth. Can you provide that?"

I nod. "Water's not a problem. I can probably get some cloth, but I may need to go back into town." For the first time in a while I'm feeling hopeful that maybe this woman can actually help Avery fix Tick. What they might find when they get inside remains unknown, but at least they're willing to giving a shot. If I have to go out of my way to help, I'll do it. We've come too far to give up now.

"Very well," Kepling says, looking between Samantha and me. "Get everything ready and I'll operate as soon as I can." She finally turns back to Avery, who recoils slightly as if he's been slapped by her gaze. An odd, impish smile crosses her face. "Just like old times?"

Avery's expression slowly changes from shock to a strange, happy smile. He nods. "Yeah. Old times."

I'm not sure what's happening or what passed between them, but I'm glad it does. I motion to Samantha, and point to one of the closed off nooks. "I'll get the fire started for the water. There's a few linens stored in there. She can use whatever she needs." Samantha nods and heads over to the nook for the cloth while I go to the fire pit near the back edge of the cavern. This is going to be a long day, and it's only just starting.

Chapter 11

I've seen more than enough blood in my life. More than enough death and pain. I've caused more than I'd care to admit. I take it as just another thing when it's my own blood being spilled. I don't need to see Dr. Kepling and Avery work on Tick. Once I get her the water and Samantha fetches the linens, which turn out to be enough for the job, I go my separate way and let the professionals get to work. Samantha stays behind to assist them. I never would have guessed she'd be all right around surgery, but better her than me.

To occupy my time, I head up to Airika. The old girl's going to need a lot of work, if she can be repaired at all. At least time isn't as much of an issue any more. Those goons would be out looking for us, certainly, but I doubt they'll be able to find us way down here. The most they would know is that we headed south, and there's a lot of land between New Foundis and Portsmaw. They could be searching for months, and even then they might not find us.

I don't plan on giving them that much time. I'm not the kind of guy who sits back idly waiting to be found. As soon as I can get Airika sky-worthy again, I plan to head back to the city and find out who's after Tick. I'm not a murderer, but if that's what it takes to put an end to the running, then that's what I'll have to do. Then I'll figure out a way to destroy the compound, so no one else can stumble on it. I'm thinking dynamite air-dropped down the smoke stacks. Could be fun.

But first, Airika. I climb up to the top of the bluff and look over the wreckage. Avery had already pulled her back from the edge to get me out of the pilot's seat. The nice thing about making a machine light enough to fly is that it's also easy to shift. The damage means there's less of her to weigh her down too. Everything has a silver lining, but it still hurts my heart to see Airika in this condition. She's worse off than Tick.

I start my work by inspecting her to see what's missing and broken. Airika held up pretty well through the crash. She lists to the right where the wing and landing gear are broken, but they're in place. The left side is a little scratched up, and some of the wood panels are missing in various places, but structurally, she shouldn't be too hard to put back together. I'll need to get some new planks, and a few metal bindings. With that, I should be able put her back together.

I don't even bother looking over the engines. That's Avery's thing. I will need new propellers, both sides are broken to nubs. And the barrel for the right engine will need to be completely replaced as well. If the mechanics inside have suffered any damage, it will take a while for Avery to rebuild. The nice thing about being near a fishing village, most of the parts used to build and maintain boats will work for airships. Getting parts and equipment will be easy.

Figuring out how to get a lift up here so we can right her and get the wheel and wing back in place, will be another matter. I might need to hire a few guys from town. The chunk of money Samantha threw at me ought to cover the repairs. Almost. What I don't have in available funds, I'll have to cover with bartering and promises. I may even have to do a little late night shopping from the docks when no is looking.

But more drastic measures would have to wait. I don't want to get too far away from the cave until everything is settled with Tick. Once the doctor is finished I'll escort her back to town anyway, so that will be a good time for getting stuff I need. Until then, there are plenty of tasks to keep me occupied out here.

I climb into the cargo hold to dig out the few tools I keep stored away. They're actually Avery's. He keeps them here for emergencies. He doesn't often travel with me, except when coming here to Portsmaw, but he's forward thinking enough to know I could use tools as necessary. Never know when something's going to break off, or at least become loose. This is why I keep Avery around, so he can think of this crap for me.

Because Avery had to pull Airika back from the ledge, the cargo door is closed. It takes me a few minutes and quite a bit of effort to pry it open. It's meant to swing down, like a gaping mouth, but with the airship sitting almost sideways, the hinges on the bottom right side don't want to cooperate. I dig a little of the dirt out of the way with the heel of my boot, then give the door a few more good, hard yanks. Finally it falls open, revealing the mess left inside.

The tie downs hadn't been enough for the rough landing. Samantha had said that Avery held on to her and Tick, but it looks like boxes were flying around. It had to be dangerous back here while we were crashing. They were lucky they weren't more seriously injured. I'm going to have to see about making the cargo hold more secure for passengers. I laugh at myself and shake my head. That would assume I carry passengers more often. Imagine that, an airship that was all about carrying passengers? It would put the trains out of service!

Pushing my musing aside, I start to clean up the cargo hold. Not so much to organize it, but to find the tools. I quickly find they've been scattered throughout the hold and buried under debris and chaos. They used to be jumbled together in a box, but that got broken in the crash.

The first tool I'm able to dig out is a hammer. Though useful in many situations, it's not what I need right now, so I stick it up on a metal strut for later. What I need at the moment is a saw to clean up some of the rough edges, and a wrench and screwdrivers to start pulling stuff apart. Avery once said he could fix the world with a good screwdriver, and I don't doubt it. Hell, I doubt he'd need even that much.

Which is why I have so much faith that he can fix Tick. If she's fixable, Avery's the guy to do it. Dr. Kepling is an unknown though. At least to me. The way Avery had been looking at her, he doesn't just know her. He knows her well. That he didn't immediately reject working with her means he trusts her enough to help, and that's fine by me. But, I am curious. I'd have to pester him about his past once things smooth out.

I finally find a few more tools and busy myself tearing apart the broken pieces still attached to Airika. It's ridiculous, but I cringe with each piece that comes off. I find myself muttering apologies, promising her that she'll be good as new soon, maybe even better. Airika doesn't respond beyond a few creaks and groans as her body settles in the dirt. I wonder if this is how Samantha feels about Tick. Upset that she has be torn apart before she can be put back together and worried that she may never be the same again. The worst part of it all is, I'm at fault for both of them.

I spend the next few hours kicking myself and trying to keep my mind on getting Airika sorted out. We got Dr. Kepling to the cave around early afternoon, but now it's getting closer to evening and the sun is hanging down low over the trees. I ran out of real work to do some time ago, but I don't want to go back down to the others if they're still working on Tick. So I sit on the bluff with a piece of extra wood and start whittling to pass the time. When it gets too dark, I'll have to head down anyway and I dread that quickly approaching time.

I'm about to give up on my avoidance when I hear the sound of grunting coming from the ladder. I look over to see the top of Avery's head peer over the edge. At least I think it's Avery. I blink and stare at him for a moment, then I realize that the old coot is clean. I stand as he pulls himself up over the ledge. "What the hell happened to you?" I laugh a little and put away my whittling knife as I wander over to him.

Avery folds his arms together and looks straight at Airika. "She made me wash up. Said I couldn't get near Tick until I at least washed my hands. Then there was all that blood." He snorts and shakes his head. "What've you been doing out here? Looks like another storm hit."

I glance at Airika and the pieces of her strewn over the hilltop. He's trying to change the subject. I indulge him for a minute, if only to soothe his mind that Airika will be all right. "Just started pulling off the broken pieces to make it easier to put her back together." I look back at him and smile. "Dr. Kepling, huh? What's the deal?" Blunt maybe, but I've known Avery far too long to be subtle.

Avery grumbles something under his breath and reaches down to pick up a piece of broken propeller. "Knew her before the war, that's all. Smartest woman I ever met. She's done good by it." He tosses the piece of wood back on the ground and looks at me. "We managed to get Tick going. She's got a lot more real bits inside then I thought. The important thing's her heart. That was all mechanical. A piece got knocked loose. I put it back in place, got everything moving right, and those eyes of hers lit right up. Leah had to close up fast after that."

I had no idea Avery was this good at avoiding things he doesn't want to talk about. The image of Tick waking up in the middle of surgery is enough to make me wince. As much as I'm curious to know more about Kepling, Tick is the priority here. "Was she in pain? When she woke up?"

Avery shakes his head and starts moving around Airika, inspecting her and the work I've done. "I don't think so. Not really. She didn't so much wake up. It was more like she was alive again. Leah did quick work, but I think Tick is still basically sleeping. She has to recharge, if that makes sense."

Well, no, it doesn't actually, but that's not exactly my area of expertise. If Avery says she needs to recharge, I'm inclined to believe it. "So, what happens now? Do I need to escort Dr. Kepling back to Portsmaw? I still need to figure out a way to pay for her services. This can't have been cheap."

Avery comes to a stop at the right hand engine barrel and frowns at the busted container. "She said she wants to observe Tick for a while. Make sure she's okay." Then he looks up and around the impromptu landing area. "Where's Ms. Loral?"

"Ms...?" I blink, reminding myself that he's talking about Samantha. I look down at the shaped piece of wood in my hands, only to see that I had carved a cameo of her likeness. Had I intended that? I think I may have been considering giving it to her. I close my hand around the smoothed wood and look back at Avery. "Samantha? I...thought she was with you, helping with the surgery."

"She was," Avery says. Somehow he finds the screwdriver and is already picking around inside the engine. "As soon as Tick's eyes lit up, she made some excuse and disappeared. Can't say I was paying much attention. I figured she thought she wasn't needed any more and came out here."

I push the cameo into my pocket and go over to lean against the engine on which Avery tinkers. "I didn't see her come this way. Maybe she's getting some rest." I shrug, deciding it's time to stop skirting around the real issue. "You...don't like her much, do you?"

Something inside the engine goes "clang," and it's followed by Avery cursing under his breath. He pushes himself out of the barrel and looks at me with a grimace. "I...there's something off about her. Don't know what it is. You sure she's not a Reddie?" He's holding his hand that had the screwdriver in it, but the tool is missing and there's a small cut across his palm.

I wince slightly. Haven't I caused enough damage already? "Sorry. Didn't mean to..." I motion to the injury that Avery is already wiping off on his pants. "Anyway, No, I don't think she's any kind of agent, government or otherwise. I thought she was kind of suspicious at first too, but she's explained everything I wondered about. Give her a chance. She's not that bad."

Avery gives me a doubtful look and goes back into the engine to retrieve the screwdriver. His voice echoes out as he starts clunking around again. "I don't know, Colt. You're not thinking straight here. That woman's got you by the balls. Plus, she looks at me like I'm shit she almost stepped in."

I nod slightly. I had seen that look on her face when she first saw Avery. But then, that's the kind of look most people give him. Not that he ever gave a damn. Still, I have some sympathy for him. "Well, I told her you were all right. Maybe that will change now that you've fixed Tick. She's got to appreciate…"

TWANG! I jump back as something hard hits the metal rim of the engine barrel. Avery jumps at the same time, thumping his head on the inside of the compartment. Another line of curses and accusations flow from his mouth. "GODDAMNEDMOTHERFUCKING WHAT THE HELL ARE YOU…!"

But I'm not listening to him. No, I'm looking at the man with the gun leveled at me. And the other two guys on each side of him. They had come up the bluff and stood a couple dozen feet back from Airika. The guys on each side are also armed, but they haven't drawn yet. It's times like these I think I should start carrying a gun.

That is, if I live any longer than today. It's not just any random stranger staring me down. Slicked back, thinning white and blonde hair, crooked nose, narrow eyes, spindly build. No, I haven't seen him in 20-

some years, but I know him. I can't forget him. "Horner." I glance at the small ding in the metal where his bullet had struck. "Glad to see you missed me."

Horner snorts and takes a few steps toward us. His gun remains steady on my face. Age doesn't seem to have taken away from his nerves. "Always the smart ass. Maybe I'll have them put that on your tombstone." He pauses and shrugs. "No, wait. You're not going to have one."

"What the hell are you doing here?" Avery asks, moving around to stand beside me. He rubs the back of his head and glares at Horner. Now that he knows his most recent injury is Horner's doing, I hope he turns a little of that pent up angry on the right person. It must have been fun to watch me smash Horner's nose in the first time. I'd love to see someone else take a whack at him.

Horner raises a brow. He's too far away for me to see if he looks at Avery, but I doubt he does. "Avery Nickols." His voice is low, betraying the usual nasal quality of it. "Thought you died a long time ago." He shrugged and took another step closer. My eyes remain on his gun. "Ah well, today's as good a day as any." He pulls the trigger.

We were soldiers. Our main focus had been flying, but we also learned how to shoot. Even with the advancement of age, some skills are never forgotten. Sure, Avery and I both jump to the side to avoid the bullet, but we're both old farts like Horner is, and moving isn't as easy as it used to be. The bullet whizzes harmlessly between us and past the outer edge of the engine barrel. Horner misses on purpose. He's not ready to kill us yet.

Or, he doesn't want our blood on his hands. The moment he shoots, his cronies pull their own guns free and move toward us. I'd love to read into this, to understand what the hell he's doing, but there's no time. Horner means to kill us, but he's going to do it slow. That's his mistake, because I don't mean to die so easily. If he's going to give me time, I'm going to use it.

Confusion is the name of the game. One of the gun men slams into Avery, as the other rushes toward me. They don't seem to be interested in using their weapons, instead opting to go for hand-to-hand. How considerate of them. Horner hangs back as we wrestle his goons. I can feel a tingle in the back of my mind, questioning Horner's tactics, but I don't have the focus to figure it out right now.

I hear a shot off to my left, but it's not followed by any yelps of pain from either Avery or the guy on him, so I can only guess it was a misfire. I'd look, but the guy I'm fighting is trying a little too hard to smack me in the nose with the butt of his revolver. "Think about what you're doing," I growl at him as I dodge his wild blows. "You're working for an asshat, buddy. He's going to get you killed."

My attempt at diplomacy is met with a shove into Airika's broken wing. The remaining wooden supports crack under my weight and the wing shifts, breaking further and spilling me onto the ground. Before I can even catch my breath, the thug presses his boot down on my chest, crushing out what little remained, and aims his gun at my face. "Don't move."

"Yeah, anything you say," I gasp out. I do my best to look in the direction I think Avery might still be. He's not a fighter, so I don't expect much out of him. What I can see out of my periphery, is him crouching on the ground with his hands over his ears. The gunshot I heard earlier must have discharged right next to him. The other gunman is standing over him, holding the revolver to Avery's reddened head. Great. How the hell are we supposed to get out of this now?

"They're both secured, boss!" the gun man over Avery yells. Secured? So Horner is delaying. But why? Lack of breath and pain in my chest make it hard for me to think.

Horner saves me the trouble. "Good," he says, a little bit of added strain in his voice. I dare to raise my head to see him come around the back end of Airika. He's carrying something lumped over his shoulder, and Samantha is a step or two behind him. She's flushed as if she had exerted a lot of effort, but seems otherwise unharmed. "I wanted him to see this before the end. Get him up."

"You heard him," the gunman grunts, pulling his boot off my chest. I suck in a great gasp of air that burns going down. It's a damned good thing I never took up smoking. "Get up," the man says, waving his gun at me.

"Yeah, all right," I cough out between gasps. It would have been better if he kept his foot there. Now I have to breathe. And move. I grunt and slowly sit up. The wind's been knocked out of me, but it doesn't feel like I've broken anything. I might still have a fighting chance here. As I climb to my feet, I glance at Avery again. He's watching us and he still has a hand over one ear. I nod to him, silently telling him everything is under control. Not that it actually is, but he looks like he could use the lie. I get a nod back in return.

Shifting my focus to Horner, I see now what he has over his shoulder. Tick. And she's still unconscious. Samantha is behind him and she's holding Horner's gun now. She swivels back and forth between Avery and me, but I can see her hands shaking. She's not comfortable with the weapon. Still, it breaks my heart to see her on that side of the field, betraying us. Avery was right.

"You lose, Reed," Horner says, his smarmy, nasally voice returning. "I guess I should thank you for taking care of the hard part, but I'm too annoyed that I had to chase you to the ass end of the world to claim it." He jostles Tick slightly, indicating her.

I narrow my eyes as another piece of the puzzle slips into place. "You…planned this all along? To get Tick? Why?" I want to ask him a lot of other questions. Samantha's story is unraveling in my head and I find I can't believe anything she told me. Not that I'm inclined to believe anything that comes out of Horner's mouth. I want to buy enough time to think of a way out of this mess.

Once again, Horner obliges me. He laughs. "Seeing how you'll be dead soon, I have nothing to hide. She's the key. The key to regaining my fortune. The key to paying back this world for taking it away in the first place. That I get to rid myself of you makes it all the sweeter." He glances over at Avery. "I'm going to take out your friend first. Just to watch you squirm."

I'm more confused now than I had been before. The key? That

keeps coming up, but I still have no idea what it means. I know Tick has information, but what could she possibly do for Horner? If only I had time to ask. Right now, I've got to pull Avery's ass out of the fire. "Wait! Avery hasn't done anything to you. Let him go. Your beef's with me."

Horner flashes the most unpleasant smile I've ever seen. "You're right. I have no interest in the useless buffoon. But this isn't about him. It's about you. I want you to suffer as much as I have over the years. Oh, but don't worry, your suffering won't last nearly as long." Hooray for me. Looks like time is running out and I need to act before it's too late.

And then Horner turns his back. He shifts to look at Samantha. "Take this thing and give me my gun."

Samantha looks at him, screwing up her face in a way that ruins her looks. "But she's bloody heavy. Just let me shoot them." I was unaware that my heart could sink any further. I feel it hit the ground and keep going as her words fill my ears. She's that eager to shoot me? Avery I can understand. They have a rocky relationship at best. But me? I've done damn near everything, including risking my life, for her.

Horner growls loud enough for me to hear him. "You'll do what I tell you, bitch!" Though having Tick on his shoulder makes the motion awkward, Horner pulls back his hand and slaps it across Samantha's face. He knocks her over and the crack echoes over the bluff, startling everyone but Horner himself.

No matter what I feel about Samantha now, what Horner does isn't right. It also gives me the opening I need. The slap snaps me into motion and I dart toward the gunman standing next to me. I grab his gun hand and slam my other fist into his gut. He grunts and doubles over in pain and I push him back against Airika's broken body.

I'm not the only one moving. Avery's on his feet as well, which I only know because I hear a startled scream a short distance away. Not only startled, but pained. Avery's done something to the guy and I'm a little sorry I missed it. Only a little. I still have this guy to take care of. I jam the gunman's arm against Airika, knocking his weapon loose. Then I take a step back and slug him as hard as I can in the jaw, knocking him to the ground.

I turn back to Horner in time to see Samantha sprawled on the ground and Horner running slowly, weighted down by Tick. I can see the flash of metal from his revolver in his other hand. Thinking as fast as I can, I grab the unconscious gunman's weapon and start after Horner. "AVERY! Take care of Samantha! I'm going after him!"

I rush past Samantha's slumped form and take aim at Horner. She reaches out, grabbing my leg before I can shoot. With a startled yelp, I fall. "NO! DON'T!" she shouts, covering the sound of me hitting the ground. I pull the trigger as I hit, sending a bullet off into the woods, nowhere near Horner.

"HORSEBALLS!" I roll over enough to glare at her. "What do you think you're doing, woman?"

"I...I'm sorry..." Samantha says, her voice trembling. She shakes her head and pulls her hands up to her chest.

"He's getting away, Colt," Avery says, moving toward us. I look up to see the crisp white of Horner's clean shirt disappearing into the trees.

I push myself back to my feet, determined to go after him. "He can't get far that way," I say over my shoulder. "He can't have an airship nearby, and there's nothing but Portsmaw and wilderness. He damn sure isn't going to run all the way back to New Foundis with Tick on his shoulder."

"He doesn't need to run," Samantha whispers loud enough to catch my ear. I falter to a stop and turn back to her. She's already getting to her feet and smoothing out her ill-fitting skirts. "They have steam machines. Bicycles with engines."

I narrow my eyes and look at Avery. "Then we have to get there before he does. Avery tie these guys up. Samantha, or whoever she is, too." I look over at the guy Avery had been fighting. The handle of a screwdriver sticks out of the man's ear at a painful angle that makes me cringe. He doesn't need to be tied up.

"Please," Samantha says, moving toward me. "If you go down there, he'll kill you. But I know where he's going. Back to the compound. You can follow from a safe distance and surprise him there."

I look between Samantha and Avery. I'm not that worried about Horner. He's carrying Tick, which slows him down and makes fighting more difficult for him. But then, I could end up injuring Tick further if I go after him. "What do you think, Av?"

"I think your pretty little bird sings an interesting song," he grunts. I never knew Avery to be so poetic, but I understand exactly what he means. One minute she's asking to shoot us, and the next she's offering to help. It doesn't make for easy decisions. He looks at Samantha, glowering.

"What about Leah?"

Samantha winces and looks toward the ladder at the edge of the bluff. "Dr. Kepling? I...had to knock her out," she admits quietly. Avery takes a sharp breath at this news, and steps toward her, his fists balled up tight enough to turn his knuckles white.

Damn it all. The more time we waste here, the further away Horner is going to get. I move between them, looking at Avery. "Av...get that gun man and Samantha tied up, then you can go check on Dr. Kepling. I'm going after Horner."

Avery pauses, looks between Samantha and the cliff's edge, then nods reluctantly. "Yeah. All right."

I nod, and turn. "If I don't get him now, I'll come back. I'm going to need you at the compound." I raise a finger toward Samantha. "And I'm not done with you yet, either. Don't cause any more trouble." Samantha gives a quick nod and I move past her, down toward the woods. I don't know how things went to hell so quickly, but I mean to pull us back out again before someone else I care about gets hurt.

Chapter 12

Horner appeared at the worst time. Evening had already come, and now it's getting darker as I head into the forest. A path leads down the bluff to the village, but Horner doesn't take that path. He goes down through the trees, roughly following the broken branches and boughs I had knocked down while making my spectacular landing. The forest litter makes for difficult going, but it's got to be even worse for Horner. He's carrying Tick, which has got to slow him down.

Tick. The poor kid has no idea what she's going through right now. I can imagine her waking up on Horner's shoulder and wondering what's going on. What would he tell her? Would he try to knock her out again? Something tells me he's not exactly the fatherly type. He's not the kind of guy who would give two shits about her beyond whatever it is he thinks she can do. And that worries me. I've got to stop him before he gets any further along with his plan.

I stick close to the trees, rolling around them as I keep an eye out for Horner. About half-way down the hill, I finally spot him. He's stopped in the middle of a small clearing, and hunched over something. I can't see Tick, so I can only guess he's securing her to his steam machine. I press back against a tree to stay out of sight and call to him. "Horner! Don't do this."

The normal night-time noises die immediately as I speak. The silence is creepy. It reminds me of the moments after the crash when all I could hear was the rain and my own, crazy laughter. Horner doesn't help by taking his time to answer. "Why aren't you dead?" he finally growls.

The first thing that comes to my mind is, *because you're an incompetent ass,* but that would only make things worse. I want to put an end to this with as little bloodshed as possible. "I don't want to kill you, Horner, but I will if I have to. Let the girl go, and we'll go back to being competitors, like nothing ever happened."

His response comes in the form of a shot fired. I duck down, having no idea where the bullet might decide to strike. For all I know, the guy has exceptional hearing and has already pinpointed exactly where I am. I remain crouched for a moment, assuring myself that I'm all right and that he isn't going to fire again. Then I try once more to talk him out of his plans. "I know you're going to the compound. It's not worth it. The place is flooded with gas. You won't be able to get in." I don't know if that's true, but he doesn't need to know that.

"What's the matter, Reed?" Horner taunts back at me. "Don't have the balls to come out here and face me? You're the same chicken-shit you always were. Why don't you do us all a favor and jump off the cliff." He laughs and I can hear the sound of it shift away from me. He's turning his back.

Some guys might let their egos get the better of them. I guess I'm too old for that shit. But I'm not too old to follow through on my own promises. I give him a couple seconds. Long enough to make him think he's right. Then I stand again and move carefully around the tree. It's almost fully dark now, making it hard to see much of anything. The bright white of his shirt is like a ghost, floating in the middle of the field. If I screw up, I could hit Tick and that turns a tight knot in my stomach.

I raise my borrowed gun, my hands shaking with doubt. In the war, I objected to the killing I had been forced to do, because I didn't think most of the enemy deserved it. I don't have that problem with Horner. And still, with the possibility of hitting Tick and a feeling that I don't have the right to decide who should live or die, I find it hard to pull the trigger. *Come on,* I chide myself. *It's now or never. Don't let him get away...*

The forested hillside erupts with the sputtering sound of an engine, and I see a flash of light from Horner's direction. He's on one of the steam machines. Soon he'll be moving and almost impossible to hit. *Pull the damned trigger!* I squeeze my eyes closed and my finger reacts to the mental command, pressing back on the revolver's trigger.

BANG! The gun kicks back, rattling my hands with its force. It's been years since I shot a gun and I'd forgotten what it feels like. I can already feel a deep ache in my hand bones that's going to last the next couple of days. As the gun discharges, I open my eyes again. I imagine Horner's white shirt dropping to the ground and the motorized bicycle falling over. Tick would unfortunately be caught in another accident, but if I'm lucky, she'll be all right.

What I see doesn't match that ideal at all. Instead, the steam machine is moving forward. The light of a kerosene lamp illuminates the trees ahead, and Horner is very much in control of the mechanical beast. Horseballs! Using reflexes I didn't know I had, I take another shot at him. Then a third. But Horner is weaving back and forth across the clearing. He breaks into the line of trees on the other side. For a few seconds I can see the light zipping left then right as he rides around trees. Then he's gone, the sound of the engine fading away behind him.

"RRRAAAAHHHH!!!" I scream out in rage and throw the revolver as hard as I can into the clearing. Damn it all to hell and back again! I think for a minute about grabbing one of the left behind steam machines and going after him, but I don't know how to work the damn things, and it's too dark to try to figure it out. The only option is to wait until tomorrow morning. I kick the tree I had been hiding behind, and turn to head back up the hill. I can't remember the last time I've been in such a pissy mood, but I damn sure know a few people who are going to pay for it.

When I arrive back at the cave, Avery is sleeping. He's huddled in one of the many nooks with Dr. Kepling. The doctor is also asleep, but she looks otherwise fine. I'd be happy for them if I didn't have so many other things on my mind. At the top of the pile is Samantha.

I find her sitting against one of the cavern's stalagmites. She's tied back to back to the surviving gunman with a heavy chain, the rock between them. Avery should have been guarding the two of them, but it doesn't look like either is going anywhere. The rock is too tall for them to stand up and slip the chains over, and the gunman is slumped, still unconscious. I must have whacked him harder than I thought.

Samantha, however, is awake and looking at me. The cavern is lit with lamps scattered around the sides, but I can't read her expression in the dim light. Then again, I'm not sure I could tell what she was thinking even if it was the middle of the day. She watches me as I stalk over to her.

When I get close, I can see her shivering. Even under the locomotive rumble of Avery's snoring, I can hear her unsteady breaths. She's afraid. I don't know if her fear is of me, or what she thinks might happen to her, but she's definitely afraid.

I crouch down and start to unbind her from the unconscious thug. Samantha finally speaks, whispering harshly in my ear. "I'm so sorry, Mr. Reed. I…I had to…" her voice wavers with each word and some sick part of me I didn't know existed, actually enjoys her discomfort. It's someone else's turn to suffer for once. Someone who deserves it.

Not saying a word, I finish undoing her and refastening the chain so the thug can't get away. I haul her up by one of her arms, but she doesn't protest. It's like she's expecting this. We march across the cavern to the entrance and around the barrier. She asks where we're going and what I'm going to do to her, but I stay silent until we come to a stop on the ledge. I let go of her arm a little more violently than I intend and look down at the ocean splashing against the rocks some ten feet below.

After a long moment of listening to the crashing waves, Samantha speaks again. "Mr. Reed? Are you planning to…kill me?"

The thought hadn't even crossed my mind. I had hard enough time shooting at Horner, and that guy's a jackass. But if she wants to believe I could, I decide to let her. "Maybe. If you don't answer my questions truthfully."

Samantha gasps and looks down at the water. She takes a step back to lean up against the barrier as if it will somehow save her from falling over the edge. I turn to face her, just in case she decides to save herself by pushing me over. "I...of course I will. Just please...you have to understand that I had to help him."

I raise a brow. She has to believe that I'm a cold bastard, willing to kill. If I show her any sympathy, it will break the illusion. "You offered to shoot me."

Samantha goes silent again, and starts to fidget. "I truly am sorry, Mr. Reed. Colton?"

"Mr. Reed," I growl back at her. The time for anything more familiar has long since passed.

She takes a step back toward me and I brace myself in case she tries to shove me. If she realizes that her fearful act isn't getting her anywhere, she might turn to desperate. I have to be ready for that. For now, her voice remains low and she doesn't make any sudden movements. "Fine. Mr. Reed. Go ahead and ask your questions. I'll answer what I can."

I nod and take a slow, calming breath. I feel a little like a detective now, sorting through the criminals and the innocents to figure who actually done it. Though I've lost all trust in Samantha, I still hope to high hell she's not the mastermind here. "Let's start with who you are, Ms. Loral. Is that even your real name?"

She surprises me by sitting down on the edge of the cliff. It's a smart move, I'll give her that. I would have a harder time pushing her if she's sitting. Samantha looks out over the dark ocean and the thousand stars gleaming over it. Why couldn't we have flown here on a night like this? "My name really is Samantha Loral," she says quietly, folding her hands in her lap. "But I have nothing to do with Dr. Wisen or Tick. I didn't even know Mr. Horner until a month or so ago."

I had already guessed as much. She had told a convincing story full of tears and drama, but it was all an act. Samantha would have done pretty well on the stage, and I wonder for a moment if that's exactly what she is. A hired actress who played her part. I sigh and sit down next to her, deciding that getting comfortable would probably get me more information. I keep a smart distance from her, just out of arm's reach. "Start at the beginning. Tell me everything. I don't like an answer, you'll know it." I have no idea what that threat means, but it makes her shift uncomfortably away from me.

Samantha pauses, gathering her thoughts. I can see her trying to decide what and how much to tell me. Finally she takes a slow breath and lets the words flow. "Mr. Horner hired me, about a month ago, as I said. He told me everything to say and sent me to your home. He's been tracking me with this." She reaches into her bodice and pulls something free of the material. I should look away, but my first though is she has a gun. I tense, keeping my eyes on her. Why didn't someone search her? She doesn't pull out a weapon, at least not one I've ever seen before. Instead, she holds up a round disk with small wires and coils jutting out of the surface. It can't be comfortable.

"What is that?" I ask, curiosity taking over as I focus on the device. It's the kind of thing Avery would be interested in.

"He called it a trans…transpond…something." She shrugs slightly, lowering her hands to her lap and looking at the device. "I'm not sure. It has to do with radio frequencies. I don't know where he got it or how it works. But it does work. That's how he knew where to find us here. I'm so sorry, Mr. Reed. I should have destroyed it or thrown it in the ocean." She closes her hand around it now and I can see her thinking about doing just that.

I'm torn between letting her do it and stopping her. The stupid thing led Horner right here, but I know that Avery would be more than interested in it. I reach over and put my hand over the device. I'm softening too much, but I feel like her apologies are sincere. She's as much a victim here as any of us. "We'll give it to Avery. Maybe he can find a way to use it against Horner."

Samantha starts at my touch and looks up at me before quickly moving her hand away, leaving the device in my grip. "Do you think he can do that?"

"Don't know," I tell her, putting the device in my shirt pocket. "But it's worth a try." I settle back again and look up at the stars. Why did she have to go and ruin such a great spot? Now there are people who know about it. If we survive getting Tick back, we're going to have to find a new home and a new hideout. "I still have a few questions. What does Horner have planned for Tick? What did he mean by her being the key to everything? And why the hell did he send you to me instead going to get Tick himself? I'd have never known a damn thing if not for that."

Samantha shakes her head then bows it. "I'm afraid I don't know much about his plans. He told me what to say, and that's about it." She looks up again, her eyes focusing on me for the first time since she betrayed me. "I'm certain he meant for you to die. He assumed there were security measures at the compound, and thought you would be able to test them, which would make it easier for him to get inside. He was hoping that might have killed you. But he made plans in case you made it back and had Tick. We waited at your building. When we heard your airship return, I ran up with the story that I was being followed. They meant to kill you and take Tick then."

I snort and shake my head. "Nothing about that surprises me. Horner's a lazy idiot. He's always made other people do his work for him."

"Why does he hate you so?" Samantha asks. Her voice is still quiet, but she seems to have become more confident in the fact that I have no intention of harming her. At least for now. As long as she keeps telling me what sounds like the truth, she'll be fine.

I laugh at her question. "We have a long history and it started off that way. Guess he decided I was a good target. Or maybe it's because I stood up to him when most everyone else laid down." I shake my head and move to stand up. There's nothing more she can tell me that will help and I'm too tired to process any new information anyway. "Come on, it's time to get some sleep. I'm going to have to tie you up again. Sorry, but we can't take any chances. Dr. Kepling can decide what to do with you in the morning after Avery and I leave."

Samantha stands as well and looks down at the rocks below. "I...understand," she says quietly. I turn back, already reaching out in case she decides that death is the better option. Instead of jumping, she asks me a question. "Mr. Reed? Why?"

"Well, you're a security risk," I say with a shrug. "You can't come here, give away our location, let Horner get away, and expect us to blindly trust you."

She looks back at me and shakes her head. "No. Why are you really going after Horner? Is it revenge?"

I stare at her for a moment. Why would she even care about my reasons? "Long story," I tell her. The story's short actually, but she doesn't need to know it. What really matters is that I'm going after him to help Tick and because I'm pretty damn scared of what he's planning. If it has something to do with that automaton army, then there might be a whole heap of trouble brewing.

Samantha reaches up and touches her cheek where Horner had struck her. "I want to go with you," she says quietly. "I want to pay him back for using me."

I nod, not believing a word of it. I watch her as she turns toward me, her hand dropping back down to her side. I mull it over, then shake my head. "You are one hell of an actress, lady. I don't know what you're up to, but I can't take the chance that you'll stab me in the back again. Besides, this'll be dangerous. I don't need you getting in the way."

Samantha balls her hands into fists and looks at me with a slack-jawed expression. "I…I'm not up to anything!" she protests, stepping toward me. "And…well, you could use my help. With Tick. I can keep her safe while you and Mr. Nickols go after Mr. Horner. I won't be in the way at all."

I sigh and rub the bridge of my nose. I'm too tired to think about any of this right now. "We'll…talk about it in the morning. Right now, I need to get some sleep." I go around the barrier, not bothering to see if she follows. She only has a couple of options after all. Try to run and see how far she gets in the dark, jump into the ocean, or come back inside. If she's smart, she'll pick the last one.

It takes her a few minutes to decide. By the time she comes back in, I'm standing by the rock waiting for her. She doesn't look me in the eye as she comes over, and I'm glad. I'm not sure I could face her like this right now. She sits down without argument and I bind her back to the rock and still unconscious gunman. It's not going to be a pleasant night for her, but I doubt it will be for me either. Too many things are bubbling around in my head for me to sleep.

Once Samantha is secured, I go over to check on Avery and Dr. Kepling. They're both still asleep as well, and despite the events of the evening, they look happy snuggled together. I thought I knew everything about Avery, but clearly the old grease-monkey has a few surprises left in him. I hope I'm not about to get him killed.

Satisfied that I've done everything I can tonight, I head back to the sleeping area I had woken up in that morning. It's been a damned long day and I'm more than ready for it to be over. I lay down and close my eyes to try to sleep. I spend the next few hours tossing and turning. Damn. If only I had something to drink.

Chapter 13

At some point I realize that the light filling the cave isn't the flickering yellow of lamps, but the cold blue of dawn. It's too late to try to get any more sleep. Though I had been unconscious for two days after the crash, I'm still exhausted. I push myself up from the old militia cot I use as a bed, and head out through the screen. I hadn't bothered taking off my clothes when I laid down, knowing I'd be up again far too soon. I don't exactly have a lot of clothing options here either. The handful of previous times we had come to the hideout, I had time to pack a few things before making the flight.

I head over to the open nook where Avery and Kepling fell asleep. My stomach gives a loud, angry growl as I walk. When was the last time I had anything to eat? Or drink for that matter? I can't even remember. Breakfast is a priority before we leave. First, I'm not going to be the only one awake this morning. Time to get this cave up and moving.

Avery's snoring loud enough to shake the stone walls. His head is tipped back, mouth agape, and a stalactite is dripping water right on his tongue. I have no idea how that doesn't wake him up, considering his awkward half-upright sleeping position with Dr. Kepling curled against him. For that matter, how the hell does she manage to get any sleep?

I shake my head and tap his boot a couple times with my own foot. "Avery. Wake up." I don't give a damn about being too loud. Dr. Kepling will have to be disturbed when Avery gets up, and the prisoners aren't going to sleep much longer after we're moving around anyway. I'm also not such a big ass to leave them without something to eat or drink. We're going to have to figure out what to do with Samantha and the gunman anyway.

Avery grunts and shifts, disturbing Dr. Kepling, who sleepily raises a hand to thump him on the chest. I can only watch this display with amusement. They hadn't seen each other in twenty years, and they're acting like an old married couple. It's almost a shame to have to disturb them. But I'm going to need Avery at the compound, so I crouch down and grab his booted foot, giving it a hard shake. "Avery, wake up. It's time to get a move on."

In the end, it's not me that actually rouses him. Since he moved, the stalactite is no longer directly over his mouth, and the next drop of water lands squarely on his cheek, splashing across his face. He jumps awake, startling Dr. Kepling, who sits up wide-eyed. They look at one another in confused terror, sputtering random sounds.

"Good morning," I say as casually as I can. It's damn hard not to laugh at them. I stand up and take a step or two back. "Dr. Kepling? I'm sorry about all this trouble. I hope you weren't injured."

Dr. Kepling realizes I'm there for the first time. Avery is glaring at me now, but he moves to stand. Dr. Kepling clears her throat and checks her bound up hair to make sure it's still in place. "Er…no, not really. Thank you, Mr. Reed." She glances to the stalagmite and the two people chained to it, her face souring. "But no thanks to your friend."

I nod and look at Samantha as well. She's slumped over, either pretending to sleep or unconscious. "I am so sorry about that. If I had only…" What? Known that she was a lying traitor? That she would use the first open opportunity to ruin everything? I shake my head and look back at Avery and Dr. Kepling. "I'm sorry. We appreciate your help, and I'm afraid I'm going to have to ask you to watch these two while Avery and I go after the man who has Tick."

"He got away?" Avery growls. He's up now and holding his hand out for Dr. Kepling to help her to her feet. "What the hell happened?"

Any sign of amusement in my face is gone now. "He got away. That's all you need to know. And we're going after him." I look back at Dr. Kepling as she stands. "We're going to need you to keep an eye on those two. I'm sorry for asking. I feel like I already owe you so much."

"I'm going with you," Samantha says from behind me. I wince. She's awake and she remembers the conversation we had. I told her that we would discuss it in the morning, but I had already decided to leave her here.

Next to Samantha, the gunman groans as he comes around. Perfect. I'm actually glad he's all right, but I don't need to deal with him right now. He couldn't have waited until there was food and Avery and I were on our way out? I turn around to look at the two of them. "No. It's going to be hard enough to get Avery and me into the lab." I glance back to Dr. Kepling. "Do you need help getting them back to town?"

Dr. Kepling lets out a short laugh. "I'm not taking these two back to town. Can you imagine that? Marching a pair of bound up strangers through the middle of Portsmaw? I don't think so, Mr. Reed."

Avery scratches his head. "I guess they could stay here, but then you would have to go back and forth between here and your practice." He gives Dr. Kepling a worried look, which I can understand. It isn't exactly an easy stroll, and Dr. Kepling is an older woman with what I can only guess is a heavy workload. She's been away from her house too long already.

"Damn it, you have to take me with you!" Samantha howls, pulling at the ropes. The gunman mutters something, showing a little life, but he doesn't fully come around. It's a good thing Dr. Kepling is here, or he might be dead by now like his friend.

I sigh, not bothering to pay attention to Samantha's ranting. I look at Avery, shrugging slightly. "You know my opinion. What do you think? Dr. Kepling, what can you handle?" I feel like some kind circus ringleader who's been given the task of juggling all the monkeys. All I want is something in my stomach and to get the hell out of here. The further away from Samantha the better. I actually shock myself with that realization. It's not that I think she'll get in the way or slow us down. I don't want her around.

Dr. Kepling looks at Samantha and the gunman thoughtfully, then nods. "Don't you worry about me. Just get that little girl. We've all gone through too much already to let her down. I'll have Constable Barns come collect whomever you decide to leave behind." She looks back at me, furrowing her brow. "This cave will no longer be very useful to you with so many people knowing about it. And Mrs. Barns is known for her mouth. Nearly everything that happens in the constable's office is public knowledge."

I sigh and fold my arms together. "Yeah, I've already thought about that. I don't mind the townsfolk knowing, but if we don't manage to stop Horner, this place is useless anyway. We'll figure that out later. We don't have the time right now."

Avery nods slowly. He's disappointed. He had found Dr. Kepling again after so long apart and now I'm threatening to pull him away. Life can be a bitch at times. Avery looks over at Samantha who is still struggling against the ropes. "I agree with you. I think she should stay here. We don't need to be watching out for her and Horner."

"DAMN IT REED!" she shouts in a high-pitched voice that cuts right through me. "YOU CAN'T LEAVE ME HERE! YOU CAN'T…"

I pinch the bridge of my nose and the headache that's quickly developing there. "That's enough, Samantha," I say, cutting her off. I turn and walk over to the rock. Samantha is glaring at me with fire in her eyes and the gunman looks groggy and pained. "I wish things could have been different. But you know what? Actions have consequences. You've already proved we can't trust you. This is the way it's got to be." She continues to glare and doesn't answer. I'm right and there's no argument against that. I turn back to Avery and Dr. Kepling. "Let's get some food then get out of here."

"How are we going to go after Horner?" Avery asks with a frown. "Airika's still a wreck."

"Horner's steam machines," I reply with a shrug. "He left at least two behind. We can take some of Airika's coal stocks with us for fuel. Maybe that will buy us a little time on him."

"If he didn't sabotage them before leaving," Avery snorts as he heads over to the fire pit to get it going.

I laugh slightly and nod. I don't know how much time Horner had before I caught up with him, but I'm hoping it wasn't long enough to destroy the other bikes. "That's why I'm taking you." I look over at Dr. Kepling, giving her a wink. "Always keep a mechanic handy."

Dr. Kepling snorts and folds her arms together. "Now you tell me."

Though Avery's back is to me, I can imagine him smiling. The small moment of levity isn't much, but it's enough to lighten the mood in the cave. It doesn't spread to Samantha and her compatriot though, and I don't give a damn. Okay, that's not exactly true. I care a little. I want to believe she's one of Horner's victims like she said. But I'm not sure what's truth and what's lie any more.

Samantha keeps quiet the rest of the morning, refusing to even look at me when Avery and I get ready to leave. Dr. Kepling takes care of the prisoners, even going so far as to exam the gunman to make sure he is going to be all right. Once she declares that he'll live, I pack up some spare coal, we eat a meager meal, and I step outside to let Avery say a proper goodbye to Dr. Kepling. I stand on the ledge, looking out over the sun-touched ocean. It's going to be a long day.

A long couple of days to be exact. Horner hadn't bothered with the spare steam machines. We find them in the clearing where I had encountered him the night before. A clear trail etches its way through the grass and dirt. He would be easy enough to find, though I already know where he's heading. It takes Avery a few minutes to figure how the machines work, and another hour for him to teach me how to ride the damned things. Balancing on two wheels is the hardest thing I've ever done in my life. Avery rides without a problem, as if he had pulled the bike out of his back pocket. Sometimes I hate that guy.

Once I'm finally comfortable, we head off after Horner's trail. I thought airships were loud, but this steam machine is even louder. It spews a thick cloud of steam and soot behind us. I make the mistake of getting directly behind Avery, which blocks my view of everything. By the time I get free again, I'm coughing and sputtering so bad I nearly dump the whole contraption over.

The heat on my legs and the vibration that rattles everything keeps me distracted from my thoughts. That's a good thing, since I'd only be dwelling on Samantha, Horner, and Tick. I should be coming up with a plan, but there are so many unknowns. Will Horner actually be at the compound? Will he figure out how to get in and siphon off the gas? Will he set up a trap under the assumption that I'm on my way? Maybe he's already set up a trap and I'm falling right into it. I'd be paralyzed with worry if I didn't have to concentrate on keeping myself upright.

We keep riding until the sun sinks down over the western horizon. Roads don't exist out here. Most long distance travel is done by locomotive, steam ships, or the occasional airship. That makes the going rough for these two-wheeled vehicles. But the steam machines do pretty good on fuel. We don't have to stop as often as I would have thought. I try not to think about the fact that Horner also doesn't have to stop that often. Tick's added weight might make a difference, but I have no way of knowing how much. What I do know is it's getting dark and we haven't caught up with him.

As we top off the coal in the bikes, we debate whether to go on or not. The steam machines have lights, so traveling in the dark is no problem. And, Horner might be desperate to get to compound and do whatever it is he's planning. But a steady drizzle has already started and promises heavier rains. I don't want to see what kind of rider I'll be in poor conditions. I also don't know the land from this angle well enough to trust getting to the compound from here. We finally agree to camp for the night, hoping Horner makes the same decision.

By camping, I mean, we huddle under a rocky overhang and try to stay out of the rain. The drizzle does eventually turn into a downpour and the temperatures drop to near freezing. It's a good thing Avery and I know each other so well, making the effort to stay warm only slightly less awkward. I don't think I've ever been so glad to see dawn come again.

After shaking off and wringing out the wet, we get going again. The plan for now is simple. We ride north until we're outside of New Foundis, then we head west. Everything looks different on the ground. Landmarks that I'd normally spot from the air are obscured by features that seem so much bigger down here. I never appreciated how much open land there is. The frightening thing is I'm starting to get used to all this open, peaceful countryside. I'm actually starting to like it. Though I'd bet it's the rough, noisy machine between my legs that makes it tolerable.

As the day wears on, we start to get into farmland. We come to roaming herds of livestock first, and the steam machines do a good job of scaring them into stampedes. Someone is going to be pissed. Good thing we won't be around long enough for them to know who's responsible. The last thing I need to deal with now is an irate rancher.

The fenceless, rolling pastures give way to smaller, crop-yielding farmland. Harvest season is over by now as the autumn days grow cooler. The fields lay bare, ready to sit fallow for the winter. Fewer farm workers are around than there would be at the height of summer and during the harvest, but there are enough people around to give us odd looks as we race by.

When the farms become more numerous and closer together, I take the lead, directing us toward the west and the compound that waits somewhere out beyond the hills. The lack of roads makes the going hard, and slows us down. It's already mid-day and we still have hours to ride, pending no mechanical failures. I shouldn't even think that, expecting it to happen the moment the thought touches my mind. Scaring myself with the prospect of disaster, I press on harder, willing us to be there already.

Then we get to the hills, the sun already sitting low in the sky. I can actually see the churned up ground where I had taken off in Airika with Tick aboard. It's only been less than a week since I rescued her, but it seems like forever ago. And now she's back at the compound again. Back in danger.

I open the throttle up as far as it will go, but the steam machine sputters on its way up the hill. They don't seem to be meant for this kind of terrain. Somehow I manage to get to the top and come to a stop, waiting for Avery to catch up. His bike has even more trouble with his bulk. I can hear the engine cough with the effort as he catches up to me. He kills his at the top too, giving the machine time to rest from the arduous climb.

"That's it," I say, pointing down to the long grey line of wall.

Avery shields his eyes from the setting sun, and grunts slightly. "So, what's the plan? We knock on the door, and hope Horner'll let us in?"

I laugh slightly and shake my head. "If only. Nah, we'll have to go in the same way I did before. There's a gate on the other side of the compound." I glance at Avery, frowning slightly. "I'll be able to slip through the bars, but I'll have to find a way to open it for you. From there, there's a doorway and stairs that lead down into the compound."

Avery drops his hand and looks at me. "You know more about this infiltration stuff than I do, but it sounds like there's not a lot of cover. Horner's got to have men down there, right?"

I shrug. "Don't know. Probably. If he's got any kind of brain, he should. I sure as hell wouldn't want to go in alone if I had other people available. Then again, I've been down there before." I sigh and narrow my eyes at the compound, thinking it over. Horner hadn't been in there before as far as I know. He didn't know what to expect. He didn't know what he would need. But I had left the damn place wide open for him. "We'll have to watch each other's backs. You up to this?"

Avery thinks about it for a minute then shakes his head. "Nope. But if you say you need me there, I'll go. What do you want me to do once we're inside?"

I take a slow breath as his question hits me. I feel like I knew all along why I needed him here, and the answer sits heavy in my throat. I have no idea how we're going to accomplish what I have in mind, or how we're going to manage to get out once everything is set in place, but I had come here to save Tick and get rid of this place. Avery is here to make sure the second part happens. "I need you to rig that place to blow up. Destroy everything down there."

He looks at me a little too long. I can't read his face. Either it's a horrible plan or he has no idea how to get it done. Then he starts to laugh. "That's the Colt I know. If you can't eat it, piss on it. What the hell's down there anyway?"

"An army," I say, surprised I hadn't told him everything. We had been putting out so many fires, I hadn't told him much about the compound. "An army of mechanical soldiers. They're huge, and there's hundreds of them. Maybe more. I guess Horner wants to use them, or something. I can't imagine he'd have much use for the forest."

"Forest?" Avery asks, raising a thick eyebrow.

I nod, looking back toward the compound. "There's a forest. A massive one. That's where I found Tick. It's probably starting to die with her being gone, and the gas…" I frown, glancing at Avery. "There're gas lines down there too. For the lighting. I managed to break some of the lights in a portion of the underground complex. Nearly killed myself with the gas build-up. You might be able to use that. It sure as hell should slow Horner down. That part of the compound is inaccessible."

"This'll be fun," Avery grunts with a slight laugh. "Well, it's been a great life, I guess. Can't complain too much. Just wish I'd known you were leading us to our death before we left Portsmaw."

"I'd kind of like to survive this, if it's all the same to you," I shoot back at him. I move to start the steam machine up again, when I notice something out of the corner of my eye. The sun is at the edge of the horizon and I spot a strange shimmering in the air near the north end of the compound. I look up and narrow my eyes to see it better. "What is that...?" I ask aloud, though I don't expect an answer.

Avery looks in the same direction, studying the shimmer for a minute. "Looks like some kind of fumes coming from the compound. Gas?"

"Horseballs," I mutter. "Horner must have found a way to vent the gas." Details are hard to see, but from what I had seen before, I can guess the fumes are coming from the inactive smokestacks.

"Well, at least we know someone's home," Avery says. "We aren't going in totally blind."

I nod. "Good bet it's Horner. Tick knows all about that place. She's probably awake and venting the gas for him. We should hurry." I fire up my steam machine once more, drowning out whatever Avery says next to me. Not waiting to see if Avery follows, I start down the hill. I'm coming, Tick. Just hold on.

Chapter 14

We stop again at the northwest corner of the wall, and kill the steam machines. The walk from here to the gate is a hell of a lot shorter than the first time I did this, and with the evening light, everything is easier to see. Bringing lamps along with us is the last thing on my mind. But Avery is usually thinking three steps ahead. He grabs the lamp off the front of his steam machine and holds it up.

"If I'm gonna blow stuff up, I'm gonna need a light. You might want to take one too," he says, looking up to the darkening horizon. "It'll be getting dark soon." Plus, Horner has Tick, which means he has control of the lights once we get down there. I have no idea if she can control the entire compound, but I'm not going to take any chances. If he knows we're coming, he'll use her to his advantage.

"Good idea," I tell him, grabbing the other lamp off of the machine I was riding. "Tick controls the lights in the forest. Maybe other areas too. Horner might have her keep it dark if he thinks we're following him. The first door we come to leads down into this hallway with several rooms. That leads to the army, and is probably were Horner's heading. We can go directly in there, or take a more indirect route through the forest."

Avery shrugs and looks at the stone wall. "You're the expert here. I'll follow your lead." He frowns slightly, turning back to me. "I'm going to need to tap into the gas lines. I'll need tools and access."

I nod, thinking a minute. If they built the compound over an old mine and there is a pool of gas under it, then the equipment to pump it through the buildings would further down. Tools would be harder to come by. The most likely place to keep those would be in one of the rooms along that hallway. And the more time we waste out here, the more likely Horner will succeed. I sigh and start toward the gate. "We'll go in through the hall. I couldn't get most of the doors open, but maybe you'll have more luck. They work on some kind of vibration or noise. Anyway, you should be able to find tools there. Maybe a map of the place."

Avery follows me, dimming his lamp to the point of almost putting it out. "Seems like Horner has all the advantages here."

I shrug, turning my own lamp down. "We have the best advantage. We're smarter than he is." Sure it's been 20 years since I last dealt with him, but some people never change. If Horner's behavior in Portsmaw is any indication, we'll be all right. He had been acting erratic. I'm not sure what kind of shit he's been through in the last 20 years, but something tells me he may have actually snapped. Avery and I have sanity on our side. With a little bit of luck, that's all we need.

"It's days like these I have my doubts about that," Avery grumbles behind me.

I laugh, thinking back to the days when I was a lot more reckless. Before the war, I thought nothing mattered, and I took all kinds of stupid risks. Being in the wrong place at the wrong time had gotten me enlisted in the militia in the first place. And after I came back from the war fields, I thought myself invincible. If I survived there, I could survive anywhere. A stint in prison for a botched job, and a few close calls after that, made me realize how fragile I am. This time, I'm not looking to get myself or anyone else killed.

Steamroller
Chapter 14

"Trust me and follow my lead," I tell Avery. "Once we get through that gate, we'll have to go silent and keep your eyes open. You know what you need to know?"

Avery nods reluctantly. "I've...got an idea. We'll split up once we get down in there. You go after Tick and Horner, and I'll do my thing."

It's a simple plan and the best we've got. I nod and head for the bars of the gate when my own words trigger in my head and stop me. Crap. I had forgotten all about the device Samantha had so willingly handed over to me. I pat myself down, Avery watching curiously, then I pull the device out of one of my pocket and turn back to him. "Here. You might be able to use this." I hold out the device for him to take.

He looks at it a moment, then picks it out of my palm to study it closer. "What is it?"

I shrug, telling him what Samantha told me. "Some kind of transmitter, I guess. Horner used it to keep track of Samantha. That's how he found us."

Avery frowns and closes his meaty hand around the device. "So, he could know we're here right now?"

"I..." I match his frown and look at the compound beyond the gate. Avery might be right. Horner had to know we wouldn't just let him walk off with Tick. What did it really matter if he knew we were here now? He's got to be too busy pushing Tick around anyway to notice. "I'm sorry. It slipped my mind. What do you think?"

Avery opens his hand again and looks at the wire-coated disk. He's silent for a few seconds, then shrugs. "I can get a spark out of it. Use it as a trigger to light the gas. If I can find the right tools. And I'll need something to set it off."

I flash him a grin, following along with that much at least. "Horner's going to have whatever he was using to pick up that thing's signal. Will that work?"

Avery nods back, tucking the device into the breast pocket of his overalls. "Yep. That should do all right."

"I knew I could count on you," I say, clapping Avery on the shoulder. "Come on, let's get down there." He nods with a grunt and I turn to slip through the bars of the gate.

My first time here, I hadn't thought much about the gate. It had been easy enough for Tick and me to slip through, but Avery has a lot more mass. I have to open it if he's going to get down into the compound. I find the controls easily enough. They're set into an unmanned guard box. Like everything else up here, a layer of dust covers the controls. I find a lever marked "gate" and push it forward. It sticks a little, but eventually moves. If I had to guess, this thing hasn't been used in years, but that doesn't make any sense. Could the place have been abandoned for so long?

I watch the gate, waiting for the old metal to roll open. Nothing happens. Avery and I look at one another and shrug. Several other switches rest on the control board, labeled various things like lights, security, alarm, communication, and something called "sub. tran. lf.," whatever that is. I start with the security switch. Maybe the gate is simply locked. I press the lever forward, straining my ears to listen for a click or turning of gears.

Painful seconds pass. The only sounds are the chirp of crickets and light evening breeze through the grass. Then the ground under our feet begins to rumble. This had better be it, or we're screwed. Avery steps back from the gate as a tell-tale click rattles the bars. The gate begins to slide open. Avery takes a quick look around then steps onto the compound grounds.

"Well," I say, breaking the verbal silence as I come back out of the guard box. "I guess if he didn't know we were coming before, he does now. That must have shaken the entire place."

Avery nods slightly, coming to stand next to me. "The kid's worth it, right? You're ready to die for her?"

That's a good question. I hadn't even thought about it. I just assumed that she is. We've rushed over the countryside, survived crashes and attacks and betrayal, only to come back here where the odds against us are so high, it feels like I'm being crushed by a mountain. If she isn't worth it, we've come a hell of a long way for nothing. I nod to him. "Yeah, I guess so. To me at least. If you're having second thoughts, I don't blame you. You can turn back now. No hard feelings."

Avery smiles, brushing away any perceived insult that he would abandon me so easily. He turns, starting toward the doorway that leads down into the compound. "If you're in, I'm with you. Let's get this done before Horner has any more time to get ready for us."

Avery's a good man. I smile and start after him. Maybe we have a chance after all.

Horner went down this way. He left the door open, announcing his trail. Light spills through the doorway from the stairwell. I'm a little surprised the gas didn't leak in here and take out these lights as well. The doors have a better seal on them than I would have expected. My lamp is missing from the landing though. Horner must have decided to pick it up.

I take the lead as we go through. Before we left Portsmaw, I grabbed the gun Samantha held on us. I draw it now, heading down the steps. I'm not comfortable with it, but I can only assume Horner knows we're on our way, so it's better to be ready. Avery sticks close behind me, like some kind of thick, sweaty shadow. I should have told him about all the stairs, but it's too late now. He's not going to be too happy about getting back out of here, especially if we have to run. I had a hard enough time, and I'm in better shape than he is.

For now, we continue down into the belly of the compound. I listen for anything besides the sound of our footsteps and the hiss of the gas lamps. If this place really is built over a gas reserve, it's going to make the impending explosion spectacular. I don't know if we'll make it out before that happens, but if we don't, it'll give new meaning to going out in a blaze of glory. They'll be able to see the fireball all the way in New Foundis.

I've got to stop thinking about dying. It's going to get to me before we reach the bottom of the stairs, and then what? Turn around and forget about everything we've been through? No, I can't scare myself out of helping Tick. Not now. I focus on the flickering gas light. They seem weaker than last time, but I might be imagining that. Still, I'm glad we have lanterns with us, in case the gas being vented steals the remaining light. Or Horner figures out a way to shut them down.

We can't reach the bottom of the stairs fast enough. Maybe a little too fast. My body aches from the long ride and my knees are screaming by the time we get to the bottom. From the look on Avery's face, he doesn't feel much better. If we get out of this alive, I'm going to strongly consider going into retirement. If we don't, I'm going to kick Horner's ass in hell for putting me through all this shit.

Horner left the bottom door open too. Either he's in a real hurry, or he's baiting us, and I'd guess the latter, but I don't know if Horner is thinking that far ahead. If he knows we're right behind him, he'll be rushing to achieve his goal and not bothering with anything else. I don't think I'd even be that careful if the end was so close.

As we approach the door, I can feel the air getting thicker. It makes my lungs hurt, but it's not unbreathable. I hear Avery cough behind me and I glance back. "I ran into trouble here," I whisper to him. "This is where he's venting the gas from. It's gets dangerous here."

Avery snorts and motions for the door. "Let's just get this done. And don't make any sparks." He flashes a grin at me. At least he's in good spirits about this adventure. If I don't retire, I might bring him along on future jobs. If this has taught me anything, it's that I can use someone to watch my back.

I flash a smile back at Avery then look out into the hallway. It's about like I left it. Dark and scattered with shards of broken glass. Down at the far end, the door into the room above the army is open and light shines back into the hall. Shadows flicker back and forth in the dim light. I can hear the Horner's voice speaking in a harsh, angry whisper. We're not close enough for me to understand what he's saying.

I move through door and motion toward the observation room. "He's down there," I whisper back at Avery. I check my gun, wincing at it. Time to put this thing to use, whether I want to or not. I glance back to the door leading to the forest. "Forest is down that way. I don't know where the rest of these…" Before I can finish, a scream breaks through the hall. It's a mechanical sound that echoes in against the walls, setting off a vibration much like the one I had triggered earlier.

"Horseballs!" Avery yelps, backing into the stairwell. I cringe, looking down toward the observation room. It's Tick. Instinct kicks in, and I feel my feet moving under me before I can think better of it. I need to get in there and stop Horner. I take less than half a step before Avery's hand comes down on my shoulder, jerking me back. "Wait, stop," he hisses in my ear.

His voice brings me back to the hallway. I blink, staring down the length of the hall. Tick's echo does what my boot couldn't. Instead of shaking the walls so bad they could fall in around our ears, the doors along the sides slide open, revealing the rooms behind them. "Holy…"

Avery grunts, moving past me and toward the first open door. "Just go save the kid and I'll take care of the rest. Meet you top side."

He's right. It's all about business now and Avery knows how to take care of his part of it. I look down at the gun hanging loosely in my hand. I can't go rushing in like some idiot. I have to keep my head. "Right. Yeah." I look up at him and nod. "If I'm not back out by dawn, blow the place. Got it?"

Avery stops and glares at me for a moment. Instead of arguing, he nods. I don't plan to fail, but we both know well enough that plans never go the way they're intended. If something happens to me down here, that's the end of it and the only way to save Tick will be to get rid of everything. He might not like it, but that's the harsh reality of what we're doing. "See you at dawn," he says. Avery brightens his lantern and heads into the first of the open rooms.

"Good luck," I mutter to him, and myself. As I move past the room, I glance in. Avery's lamp illuminates a large, deep room with rows of file cabinets. He won't find many tools in there, but he might find a map of the compound or some kind of schematics. Might have been helpful to me last time I was down here.

No sense in worrying about it now. I fasten my lamp to my belt and start down the dark hallway. Glass crunches under my boots and I try to move slowly so Horner doesn't hear me. Ahead I can hear Tick whimpering, much like she did just after her hands were injured. I don't know what Horner's doing to her, but it can't be good. It takes all my will not to bust in there like a maniac.

The closer I get, the more I can make out of Horner's voice. He's barking commands at her – "Open it," "Turn on the lights," "Hurry up!" *Don't listen to him, Tick,* I think to myself. *Don't do it.* But something tells me she's compelled to help him. She's so eager to help, and not obeying may get her hurt. I can't bear to think about her helping that jackass.

Practically shuffling through the mess of glass, I finally reach the end of the hall and the open into the observation room. Horner didn't bother posting a guard as far as I can see. He was in such a hurry to get here, he didn't bother covering his back. Or maybe he doesn't have any more goons. If it's just me against him, I feel more confident about my chances. I lean up against the wall and look into the observation room.

Horner's there. His back is to me and his hand is firmly gripping the back of Tick's neck. He presses her up against the tall windows. Her hands are flat against the glass, and both are standing, as if waiting for a train. I can hear her whimpering. She's not helping him willfully. Horner hung lamps on each side of the room, and the fire reflects back from the glass, giving the place an eerie, haunted look. It reminds me of the sick feeling I had last time I was here.

And here I am again. I have to strike now while he isn't expecting anything. But the moment I move out from behind the wall, he's going to see me in the glass. I won't have much time to do anything. I lift up the gun and look at the cold metal. The last time I had used a weapon with lethal results was back in the war. Sneaking around is more my style, not killing people.

I don't want to shoot anyone. Taking a life isn't as easy as people want to believe. But this is Horner. This is Vann 'Asshat' Horner. And he has Tick. I shouldn't feel any hesitation. I should be able to turn into the doorway and put a bullet in the back of his balding blonde head. Yeah, it'll scare Tick. Maybe even scar her for life. She's survived worse, though. I can do this. I have to do this.

So why am I hyperventilating? Why does each short, shallow breath feel like the shards of glass, stabbing me in the heart? Why am I frozen in place? Inside the room, I hear a sliding sound. I manage to look back in time to see the windows slide open. Horner has stepped back a little, pulling Tick with him. On the other side of the opening glass is a platform with a pedestal sticking up in the center of it. The pedestal is a little bigger than Tick, with a concave surface, making it look like some kind of upright chair. It's too dark for me to see any details beyond that. This is what they were waiting for. And if I don't act now, it's going to be too late.

For Tick, I tell myself. I take a deep breath, cutting through the panic, and push myself out into the doorway. I hold the gun up and I can feel it shaking in my hands. Damn it. I need a clean shot. I need to get ahold of myself. My finger refuses to pull the trigger. Come on! When my hands disobey me, a new plan comes to mind. Maybe just the sight of me getting the drop on him will be enough. I call out, gun pointed straight at him. "Horner!"

He spins around, whipping Tick's small body along with him. His fingers are hooked into the cloth of her dress, nearly ripping the fragile fabric. By the look on his face, I know he's surprised. Pull the damned trigger already! But my fingers still won't budge. He glares at me, daring me to do it. I want to take that dare. I could hit Tick, but my bigger concern is knocking him backward through the opening and him taking

Tick along for the ride.

I look at Tick. The bright red glow of her eyes flashes as she recognizes me. "He wants them to walk!" she says, wiggling in Horner's grip.

"Shut up you little brat!" Horner hisses, shaking her.

Seeing that makes me snap. Forgetting the gun in my hands, I rush forward. If I can't shoot the bastard, I'll tackle him and beat his head into the floor. Again. He's ready for me. Horner takes a step back toward the opening and jerks Tick toward the edge. My eyes widen and I stop again. "You don't want to do that," I warn. "You need her. You won't let her drop."

A cruel smile crosses Horner's face. "How do you know I haven't already gotten what I…" He stops, the smile falling away. He narrows his eyes and tightens his grip on Tick's neck hard enough to make her squeak. "You're not supposed to be here."

Chapter 15

"You're not supposed to be here," Horner growls. Tick draws in a quick breath and stares, frozen by his grip.

"Yeah. I've heard that before," I reply, thinking it's a little late for him to be realizing it. Not only have we been talking, but he should have known I'd be coming. It doesn't take a genius to figure out I'm not going to roll over and give up. He must be as exhausted as I am. Maybe his brain is only now catching up to reality.

Then another voice comes from behind me. "He didn't mean you."

It's only then that I notice Horner isn't looking at me, but past me. I turn to see Samantha standing there. How the hell did she sneak up on me? How the hell did she even get here? Either she's better at breaking into places than I am, or I Horner is a distraction. Whatever the case, she's a different Samantha than the one I left tied up and screaming in the cave. The way she stands and the expression on her face shows her to be a stronger, more determined woman. She's wearing trousers and a long trench coat, and she's holding a gun, leveled at Horner.

"Release the girl safely, and I might let you live," Samantha says, focusing on Horner. She isn't timid and unsure like she was the other day. The change is startling. I have to wonder if I'm looking at a different woman with the same dark hair and rich brown eyes.

I suddenly feel like a spectator. My gun hangs loose in my hand, and I look between the two of them like I'm watching some kind of sporting event. I feel like I should contact my bookmaker and place a bet. On Samantha, of course. She may have betrayed us, but she's not Horner.

And she seems to be making up for it now. I hope.

Tick squeaks again, drawing my attention back to her and Horner. Horner is glaring at Samantha. Like a spectator, I'm largely forgotten in all of this. Horner pulls Tick a little closer to the edge of the drop. "Who the hell do you think you are, whore? I'm the one paying you. You don't give me fucking orders."

With Horner and Samantha engaged with one another, I decide to try to do what I can to help Tick. I slide back a little to get out of their tunnel vision. When they don't seem to notice, I start to inch toward the opening where the windows were. I need to get close enough to grab Tick while Horner is fighting with Samantha. Fortunately, Tick is also focused on her captor and doesn't give away my attempt.

"Ha!" Samantha snorts, stepping toward Horner and Tick. "Maybe you should have done a little more research before you made that move. You want to know who I am?"

I glance at her. I have to admit to being curious. I've lost track of who I thought she was, and she clearly isn't any of the things I had guessed. Samantha isn't an assistant or actress, and she's certainly not the whore Horner calls her. She is keeping him busy and his focus away from me, so I don't say anything as I keep inching toward Tick.

"Not really," Horner says. "You're just some streetwalker who's a little too full of herself." He snorts and looks toward me, freezing me in place. "He put you up to this, didn't he? What? Did he promise to save you? Give you a better life? How pathetic."

I'm about to defend myself when Samantha does it for me. In the worst possible way. "You think I need a man to save me?" She laughs and I feel my guts sink into my feet. That was exactly what I had intended to do right up until the betrayal in Portsmaw. The worst part is, the way she's acting now, I believe her. She doesn't need anyone. "Now, let the girl go."

And to prove she's serious, she fires the gun. The bullet whizzes past Horner's right ear, and off into the room beyond, making him flinch. Tick squeals and the echoing boom of the gun floats out over the open drop-off. I jump toward Tick, reaching out to grab her. She reaches back, her bandaged palms flailing in the air.

"NO!" Horner yells, jerking Tick back. He pulls her to him, using Tick as a shield. I miss by a long way, slamming down on the floor with a painful grunt. Glass covers this floor too, and I do my best to shield my face from it. The shards aren't enough to do much damage, but they cut and burn as they pass through my clothes. This could have gone better.

"Colton!" Samantha gasps. She wasn't expecting me to do that, and frankly, it hadn't been the plan exactly. Not that I'm running off plans any more. I have no idea what's going on or where to go from here, but they don't need to know that.

Horner isn't playing around. He pushes Tick back against the pedestal. She screams as the metallic click of gears fills the room. Her eyes flair, filling the room in red light. "You're too late, Reed!" Horner growls at me. "You can have the bitch! I don't need her anymore! You'll both be dead soon enough anyway."

The glass windows begin to slide close between them and us. My eyes go wide and I scramble to my feet, which slip on the glass-covered floor. Samantha is moving as well. "STOP HIM!" she yells. She can't get a clear shot without fear of hitting Tick. I'm a little closer, but I'm having troubles getting to my damned feet.

"I'm trying!" I shout back, making a desperate lunge for the closing gap. As I get there, the glass slams together with a rattle and I smack into it like some damned bird into a window. "HORSEBALLS!"

Horner is on the other side, grinning at us as Samantha reaches the windows. Tick is connected into the pedestal. Wires jut out of her skin and her face is expressionless under the red haze of her eyes. Her mouth hangs open as if she's still screaming, but if she is, I can't hear her through the windows. Horner mouths something, but I can't hear that either. Whatever these windows are made out of, it's too thick to hear anything through. Horner reaches up and waves as the platform starts to descend down toward the waiting automaton army.

"Damn it!" I shout, slamming my hand against the glass. "GOD DAMNED SON OF A…"

"Stop it," Samantha commands quietly. "That's not helping. We need to get down there. And fast." She pushes her gun into a holster on her hip, and turns to look around the room.

I pull myself away from the windows and turn. Samantha's right. I need to get myself calmed down before I make a mistake. She's already searching for what I know isn't there from my first time in this place. A way down. "So…who are you, really?" Not that I'm about to believe anything she says. We're way past that.

Samantha shrugs and grabs one of the lamps Horner had hung on a broken sconces. She didn't need the light. The lights out over the automaton army had long since been turned on, filling this room as well. But that light doesn't stretch out into the hall, and she starts toward the dark corridor. "Who I am doesn't matter, Mr. Reed. We're here for the same thing, and you'll either help me, or not. That's up to you."

I glance back at the windows. She's right again. Horner is quickly getting away with Tick. He's on the verge of accomplishing whatever he's up to. I sigh and pull my own lamp off my belt. I turn it up and follow her out into the hall. "Right. So no more bullshit. Who are you? If you expect my help, you're going to have to start telling me the truth." I want to know a lot more, but that's the best place to start.

Samantha turns into the first open doorway on her right. I pause, debating whether to go left or right. I decide on the left to make the search for a way down go faster. I hear her voice float from behind me. Her tone is cool and detached. "My name is Samantha Loral, but I'm not who you or Horner think I am."

The room I've wandered into is sterile. My lamp light reflects off a low table set in the center. I approach it and run a finger along the surface. The table is metal and cold to the touch, but there isn't a hint of dust. I have no idea how long the compound has actually been abandoned, but these rooms have been sealed since, keeping them clean. This room even smells like it's been recently disinfected, which reminds me how much I could use a drink.

Samantha's voice fades as we get further away from one another. This area is so quiet though, I could probably hear from the far end of the corridor. I assume she hears me just as well. "I know you're not some assistant to Dr. Wisen. And I'm guessing you're not the streetwalker Horner called you. I'd thought you were an actress at one point, but I'm guessing that's not right either. So, what is it?"

I shine my lamp around the room. Along the sides are cabinets and rows of medical instruments. The set up isn't so different from Dr. Kepling's practice. The tools look as if they're ready to be used, but whoever set them out never got around to doing anything with them. Finding nothing useful, I turn and head back out toward the hall only to hear Samantha call out. "Reed! Over here. Another door. It's locked."

I hurry over to find her waiting by the door – a normal one, like those downstairs – and holding out something toward me. As I get closer, I realize she has my lock picking tools in her hand. I frown, patting myself down. "How did you…?" Since I hadn't needed them, I hadn't noticed they were gone.

She smirked and stepped aside to give me access to the door. "Someone had to change your clothes after you crashed your airship. Mr. Nickols was more interested in Tick, so the job fell to me. You do keep some interesting things in your pockets, Mr. Reed."

I harrumph at her and grab the tools away. "I'll thank you to stay out of my pants in the future," I say, regretting it the moment the words came out of my mouth. I quickly turn away from her and crouch down next to the doorknob. Focus on the work. Don't think about her getting in my pants.

I set my lamp on the floor next to me and start on the lock. If this is anything like the locks I've already encountered, it should be easy. And that's good, because I'm not sure I could pick a harder lock at the moment. I try to steer the conversation back to more important things. "You still haven't answered my question though."

Samantha shifts behind me, holding her lamp to add to the light of my own. "Why should I? You wouldn't believe me anyway."

I pause in my picking and look up at her. All I can see is the glare of the light. "Maybe not. You've told me a load of cock and bull already. But let's just say I'm giving you another chance to come clean." I turn back to the lock, not sure what to expect of her this time.

Samantha sighs and shifts again, jostling the light. "If you must know, I work for the Invenio government. I've been investigating disappearances traced to this compound."

"Wait. What?" My lock-pick slips in key hole and snaps in half. "Horseballs." I pull the useless piece of metal free and look up at her again. I'll be damned if Avery's hunch about her is right. I still find it hard to believe though, especially with all the other lines she's given me. "You expect me to believe that?"

Samantha sighs and reaches into her pocket. She pulls out a small leather bound wallet and flips it open, holding it down so I can see. Inside is a picture of her and several official looking seals. Under the picture reads, 'Samantha K. Loral. Agent 3rd Class. R.D.I.' She gives me a little time to process it before flipping the wallet closed again and sticking it back in her pocket. "Now will you hurry up with the lock? We don't have time to screw around."

"Shit..." I mumble, hardly able to believe my eyes. She really is a member of the Republic Department of Investigation. A damned Reddie, just like Avery said. People in my line of work call them ghosts. The R.D.I. has a way of sneaking into our business and causing trouble. I've been lucky not to have any on my tail, until now.

"Relax. I'm not here for you," she says, motioning at the door to hurry me. I sigh and return to my tool set for a new pick. "All those things I told you? Some of it was bullshit. The rest borrowed from the investigation."

This woman is a piece of work. Part of me wants to put a gun to her head for all the crap she's dragged me through, and the other part of me finds her irresistibly attractive. If we weren't in this situation, I might lose control of myself. Then I'd have a gun to my head. Or somewhere else. "So, why all the crap then?" I ask, feeling the lock's tumblers fall to my work.

"At first, because I didn't know you or how you fit into this. After that, I needed you to keep after Horner." She sniffed behind me, the lamp in her hand moving and painting shadows around the walls. "You were supposed to bring me with you. I thought you might be more sympathetic if you thought I was in trouble. Turns out you're just another jackass."

"Hey! I'm..." the lock clicks, opening to me. I pull the pick free and look up at her. "I'm not a jackass, thankyouverymuch." I put the tools away and pick up my lamp as I stand. "You don't have any idea what I've been through for you and Tick. I've been trying to keep the two of you safe this whole time. And this is the thanks I get?" I open the door and look back at her. "You were going to shoot me!"

Samantha sighs and lowers her lamp. The space beyond the door is dark like everything else up here. Horner must have found a way to turn off the gas to this entire section of the compound. "That was for his benefit. Horner has no idea I'm not the person he thought he hired to convince you to do the hard work for him. He thought I was just a streetwalker, looking for a quick buck. If he hadn't reacted that way..." She shakes her head. "Look, sometimes my plans don't work out either. Can we get going already?"

"Fine," I say, seeing that she'd rather talk about anything but what happened in Portsmaw. I take a step through the door, distracted from my usual caution, only to realize there isn't a step to take. My lamp tells me the truth – the area behind the door is nothing but a shaft with a line of cables running down the middle – but I'm too distracted to see it. I gasp, my body falling forward with the lack of floor to catch my foot.

"COLTON!" Samantha yells. She grabs the collar of my shirt, yanking me back. The material rips a little and a couple buttons pop off, tumbling down the dark chute, but she pulls me back safely.

I catch my breath and steady myself as Samantha lets go of my collar. I can feel the crumpling of cloth where her hand had been. She's not a weak woman by any stretch. I look back at the shaft and adjust my shirt the best I can with one hand. At least I hadn't dropped my lamp. "Uh...thanks. Looks like we're not going down that way."

Samantha frowns. "Maybe. This looks like some kind of lift. There must be controls for it somewhere. If we can operate it, that will be faster than stairs."

As she speaks, a deep rumbling shakes the compound. We look at one another, the urgency rising around us. Whatever Horner is up to, he's in the middle of doing it. I nod in agreement and we both begin to search around the room for the controls. They're not hard to find in this mostly empty space. The only real option is a panel on wall next to the open door. The panel has a lever set in the middle. I grab it and look over at Samantha. "Here goes nothing."

I wince as I pull the lever, expecting an explosion. It would be my luck to get through all the crap I've seen over the past couple days, just to blow myself up. No explosion happens. I look around slowly, seeing nothing at all has changed about the room. A new sound echoes up through the shaft. Gears click and in the light of our lamps, we can see movement in the cables. Looks like I guessed right.

We wait silently for what feels like an eternity. The structure continues to shake every so often as something happens beyond our view. It's the most nerve wracking feeling I've experienced as I think about this place erupting around our ears. Did Avery screw up? Is it Horner? Something worse? The way Samantha shifts back and forth from one foot to the other, eyes darting here and there, tells me she's feeling the same. If this lift takes any longer to get here, I might explode. That's the real danger here.

Finally, the lift pulls up into the empty space behind the door. It's nothing more than a box, suspended by the cables that raise and lower the car. I've heard of lifts like this being used to transport miners into the coal and iron mines, but they aren't often used in buildings. Not even my building has a lift. I peek inside, looking for controls. It's nothing but an empty compartment. This thing was meant to be operated by more than just the people taking a ride. I glance at Samantha and shrug. "Get inside. I'll shift the lever and jump in."

Samantha raises a brow and steps into the waiting lift. "You sure about this? If you hurt yourself, I'm not carrying you." She turns around once she's in the car and watches me.

With her in there, I can see how much the whole place is shaking and that's more disconcerting than the thought of jumping into a moving car. I shake my head, doing my best to look confident. I'm pretty certain half of the shaking is coming from my own body. "I'll be all right. You ready for this?"

Samantha nods and pulls her gun free of its holster. "Ready as I'll ever be."

I used to live in a world that made sense. I got jobs, I did them. Someone got the item they were looking for, and I got paid. I'd buy some booze. I'd sleep for a while. I was happy. And then Samantha shows up in my life, and everything gets flipped on its head. Even she's upended everything I've come to believe about her. What's worse is that if I stopped to think about it, I'd realize that I like this version of her more than the one I was trying to save.

My eyes linger on her a little too long before I take a deep breath to refocus myself. The expression on her face is one of frustration. We need to get going. I kick myself into action and push the lever back up into its original position. As the gears begin to click again, I dart forward, surprised by my own ability to move so well. I fall into the moving lift, stumble past a bemused Samantha, and catch myself on the back wall.

Only the wall isn't actually the back of the car. Instead it's the wall of the shaft, and my forearm, which had caught me, scrapes along it as the car drops downward. "Ow! Crap!" I yelp, pushing myself away to stumble again to the center of the shaking lift. I cringe and cradle my arm to me. The motion is awkward at best with the lamp in my other hand.

Samantha leans against the side of the car, which is only really big enough for a handful of people, and grins at me. I glare at her and she gives me a look of mock sympathy. "Ah, I'm sorry. Did you want me to kiss it, make it better?"

"What I want is..." I snap at her. Then I stop and sulk back against the other side of the car. I'm not sure what I was going to say. Maybe that I wanted this to be over. Or to have never started in the first place. Something more than a kiss would also be nice, but this isn't the time or place. Instead I relax back and shake my head. "How about a few details? What the hell is going on here? And I want the truth this time. The full truth."

Samantha nods and lowers her lamp. She looks at me, her eyes showing a seriousness that I hadn't seen in them before. "Might as well," she says with a shrug. "If this is going all the way down to those war machines, we might be in here a few minutes." She pauses and I watch her, waiting to hear what I've been missing so far. She collects her thoughts and nods again. "This compound was established almost 20 years ago. Right after the end of the war. Records indicate that it was meant to research ways to repair the land. Reforest everything up there." She points upward to the land that's got to be far over our heads by now.

I nod. Nothing about what she says is surprising. Lots of places like this were built after the war. People like me came back with skills and ideals. Fixing some of the problems that led to the wars was only natural. It also explained Tick's forest, which obviously didn't spring up overnight. But that's not anything I didn't already know. I motion for Samantha to continue. I don't need the history of the compound. I need to know what got us to this point.

"Wisen was in charge," she goes on. "I don't know much about him personally. Apparently he was married to a botanist Dr. Darla Veital. While he ran the compound, she ran the research involving the forest."

I nod again. "Tick mentioned her. Said she worked with Dr. Veital in the forest. So what about the automatons? How does a place meant to fix the landscape, get into building an army? And who's really responsible?"

"It was all on Wisen," Samantha says darkly. She shifts as if saying his name makes her uncomfortable. "Harris Wisen, of course. I don't think his wife found out until it was too late."

"Too late for what?" I ask, not sure I want to know the answer.

"For her," she responds right away. "That army. It's made up of researchers." Her words hang between us for a few seconds and I see Tick's face flash before my eyes. She's nothing like the war machines, but I couldn't shake the thought that she might be involved somehow.

Samantha takes a slow breath and confirms it. "I don't know who Tick was before. But she's the result of the initial research. At some point, researchers started disappearing. And that's when R.D.I. got involved."

The whole thing is making me sick to my stomach. Or maybe it's the shaking of the lift car. Either way, I'm starting to see how deep I've gotten myself into things. "So, what happened with Wisen then? And how'd Horner get into this?"

"They're related," Samantha says with a dispassionate shrug. I recoil as if slapped by her revelation. "I don't mean by blood. Don't give me that look." She smirks slightly and turns her gaze to the shifting wall of the shaft. "Wisen had used up all his resources here. He'd accomplished what he wanted. For the most part. He just needed to find a buyer."

"And Horner was the buyer?" I ask. I had always assumed Horner came from money. But that had never explained how he got into smuggling. It didn't seem like the kind of life for a guy who has it all. I have heard stranger things.

Samantha shakes her head this time. "No. Horner was supposed to find him a buyer. We tracked Wisen to find out what he was doing. All we really had at that point was circumstantial. We needed more. Horner got Wisen to tell him everything. Then Horner got greedy. Decided he wanted the army for himself. We found Wisen's body a few weeks back."

"And that's where you came in?" I ask, watching her face and she nods. As far as I can tell, she's telling me the truth, but there's still a couple missing pieces. "So, why'd you come to me? Horner's got his own people. Hell, he knows this job as much as anyone. Why didn't he just do it himself?"

A broad grin stretches across Samantha's face. "You know Horner. Can't find his ass with both hands. He knew he couldn't get Tick, and that's what he really wanted. So, he went to the one person he knew would be able do the job. And if you died trying, all the better." Samantha laughs softly and smirks at me. "So, I figured I'd get you to grab any research you find too. As evidence against to show what Horner was after."

I frown, looking at the gun in her holster. She might have been trying to stay under cover when she threatened to shoot me, but that didn't explain why she went to such extremes to help Horner. I shake my head and look back up at her. "Something doesn't make sense. Why didn't you tell me all this before we left New Foundis? Or down in Portsmaw? You tried to stop me from going after Horner."

The lift came to a sudden and jolting stop. We both look in the direction where the door upstairs had been. Nothing but wall stares back at us. I frown and look to the other side of the car. The wall looks different on this side. I move over to it and hold up my lamp to investigate. The panel doesn't have a knob like the door upstairs, but there is a small opening that could be a lock.

"Think you can open it?" Samantha asks, shifting to stand behind me.

"We'd both better hope so," I reply. I set down my lamp and pull out my tools once more. "Why don't you finish your story while I'm working?" I'm not that happy to have her standing behind me with a gun in reach. If I keep her talking, maybe she won't remember it.

She steps back a little, giving me some breathing room. "You didn't bring anything but Tick back. We only have circumstantial evidence for Wisen's murder. I need more if I'm going to bust Horner. That's why I needed to come back here with you. You should be glad I didn't let him kill you first."

I glance back and wiggle my lock pick at her. "You should be glad I'm here," I snort back at her. "How'd you get away from Kepling anyway?" I had meant to ask her sooner, like when she magically appeared and shoved her gun in Horner's face, but the opportunity hadn't come up until now.

"It wasn't easy," Samantha said, her tone dark. "That old bitch didn't want to believe I was R.D.I. at first. Once I convinced her, and that bumbling lout of a sheriff, she let me go. I had to take the next train up the coast. I got a ride out here from a colleague…" she pauses and I glance back at her again. "You still have that device I gave you?"

I shake my head and focus back on picking the lock. "I gave it Avery. It's more useful to him than me."

"Perfect," Samantha says, no hint of sarcasm in her voice. "I meant for him to have it. I'm sure he'll know what to do with it."

"Which is what?" I say, hearing the click of the tumblers as the lock pops open. I smile and put my tools away again. I pick up the lamp again and turn to face her.

"You said you wanted to destroy this place," she says, smiling back at me. "I saw the way he fixed Tick. He's a smart guy. He'll know how to use the device."

I glance at her, raising a brow. "And the Reddies are okay with that? Destroying everything?"

Samantha sighs softly and shakes her head. "They aren't going to know. Of course the government would want the war machines. But you're right in wanting to get rid of them. This is something the world doesn't need. So, I'm giving you a hand."

"That device. It wasn't Horner's was it?" I ask, suspecting this woman is more devious than I give her credit for.

Samantha shakes her head, her smile returning. "No. But he has the other half. We'll have to get it from him." She pulls her gun out of the holster and motions to the door. "Now, we've wasted enough time. Let's go save the day."

I nod and pull out my own gun. Maybe this time I'll actually be able to use it. If it's not too late. "Ready when you are." I'm not ready. Not in the slightest. But we don't have any more time. I push open the door with my lamp hand and lead the charge, gun held out in front of me.

That sick feeling returns to me as I step out into the vast open space. I stop, my eyes sweeping over the field of automatons. Hundreds of mechanical soldiers loom overhead, each one a little more than 10 feet tall. My eyes follow them up. High above, the roof slowly rumbles open to reveal the night sky. We're already too late. Horseballs.

Chapter 16

"Colton! Over there!" Samantha's voice brings me out of my thoughts. I look to the right to see Horner standing next to the pedestal Tick is still hooked into. Samantha darts past me. She has her gun held up, pointing toward Horner.

Horner turns toward us as Samantha shouts. His eyes go wide, seeing us there. He turns back to Tick, grabbing her by her exposed neck. "Hurry up, you little piece of shit!" he yells in her face.

Tick's body twitches, but she doesn't answer him. I don't think she can speak. I glance back up at the ceiling, which is sliding open high above. It doesn't appear Tick has any control over how fast it opens, but we've wasted so much time getting down here, it's nearly exposed the entire length of the room.

Before I can react, Samantha takes a shot at Horner. She doesn't intend to miss this time, but running and aiming at the same time are nearly impossible. I had learned that much in the militia. If Samantha doesn't know it already, she's about to learn. At least she's already gotten rid of her lamp so she can use both hands on the weapon. Her bullet races toward Horner, grazing his right shoulder. He yelps in pain and spins around again to face us, gripping his wounded arm.

"Samantha! Stop!" I yell, running after her. "You'll hit Tick!" She doesn't answer me though, opting instead to take another shot. This one goes wide, ricocheting off the wall just above Horner's head. It bounces back and hits one of the automatons before disappearing. She's going to get us all killed at this rate!

Horner isn't going to wait for that to happen. "Stop them!" he shouts. Then he turns and runs into the army of waiting soldiers.

Damn it. This is not going well at all. Then again, what can I really expect? Horner to see the error of his ways, turn around, and give up? Of course not. "Samantha!" I yell to her as I catch up. "Get Tick out of that thing. I'm going after Horner." I turn and head into the waiting army before she can protest.

I toss my lamp to the side. I don't need it in here. Lights gleam down from the walls, making the room more than bright enough, even with the roof opening onto the night. Behind me, I hear a metallic clang and a scream. The floor under my feet rumbles and I glance back just long enough to catch sight of one of the automatons leaning toward Samantha. Its hand strikes the ground just in front of her, cutting her off from reaching Tick.

"Shit. Samantha!" I skid to a stop and peddle back around to run to her.

"No!" she yells back as another automaton reaches for her. "Keep going! I'll deal with this. You've got to stop…!" Samantha screams again as the second automaton swats her back against the wall.

I cringe and hesitate. Everything in me wants to help her. But Horner is still out there and at the moment, he's still in control. The automatons answer the question for me. The four nearest me swing around and loom over my head. The machines are human-looking, with armored heads, arms, and legs. I can't see any hint of flesh, but I know what's under that metal.

Except for their size, I'd think they were just people wearing armor. That's what makes them so creepy. I know Tick and I'm more than aware that she was human. Samantha had confirmed that these machinations had once been the researchers. Knowing all that brings home just what kind of mess we're dealing with. These are people. Just like in the war.

I swallow as the four machines look down at me. All around, others are coming to life. They have the same glowing red eyes as Tick, which flicker as their bodies begin to move. I give the four automatons a weak smile. "Sorry guys. Can't stick around to play." Then I duck between the legs of the one directly in front of me.

I hear the machines turn. Their bodies make a hell of a lot more noise than Tick. Whatever technology went into her to make her run relatively quiet apparently didn't make it into the big guys. As more of them start to move, the clanking and clacking of gears fills the area, obscuring one from another. I can only run now and hope I spot Horner somewhere through the mass of metal bodies.

I run between the moving monsters, weaving and dodging as they swing at me. Their large size makes them slow and clumsey. They bump into one another as they try to maneuver in the tightly packed room. I doubt Wisen intended them to be fighting anyone down here, so I use that to my advantage. I lure them toward one another with my zigging, making them crash together. I don't know if they can get up once they're knocked over. Even if they can, it will buy me some time. And it will be easier to see around them.

Just as I think I'm in the clear, I hear a booming sound behind me. I know that sound. I'd heard enough large cannons blasting airships out of the sky during the war. I don't bother to look back as the artillery hits the floor, blasting a large hole where I had just been. A pair of the automatons fall into the crater with a loud CRASH! I glance back to see their smoking remains sticking up out of the hole. I smirk. The soldiers are armed and they're firing with all the grace of blind monkeys. All I need to do is get these things to destroy each other and Horner's plans will be undone. That is, if I can stay alive long enough for it to matter.

I hear more explosions echo from somewhere else. My gut tells me the machines are firing on Samantha. She's shown herself to be a hard target, but I know her better as the soft, meek woman who needed someone to save her. Everything in me wants to go back and find her, even if only to make sure she's still alive. And what about Tick? If the automatons are firing near her, what if they hit her? That might stop them, but it will stop her too. She's the whole reason for us being here. I promised myself I wouldn't fail her, and I still don't intend to. I've got to find Horner and force him to end this madness.

I duck between a pair of swinging arms and find myself popping out on the other side of the room. The back flank of the army ends several feet from the wall, and most of the metal soldiers are pressing in toward the path I had just taken, leaving a larger clearing. In the open space, I spot Horner's white shirt diving into a nook. Got him. I rush forward, the automatons turning and following me.

Then the floor gives a rumbling lurch. I stumble and trip myself, falling forward. Several of the automatons are thrown off balance and they topple together, crashing just behind me. I jerk myself out of the way as one of them attempts to steamroll me. When I come around, I end up on my back, looking up at the ceiling. It's fully open. I can feel a heavy vibration under me as the floor starts to move upward. Things are going to get ugly if these bad boys get unleashed on the world. They may be practically useless in a tight space like this, but out in the open country, they'd destroy everything in their path.

One of the automatons steps on its fallen comrade and takes aim at me. I spot it in time to roll over backward and push myself to my feet. Pretty acrobatic for an old guy, but I'm going to feel it tomorrow. If I live through this. The floor where I had been laying is blown open. The rattling impact pushes me back and I only barely keep my feet. A couple of the closer automatons fall into the newly opened hole and slide down as the floor continues to rise upward.

"WHY WON'T YOU DIE!?" Horner screams from behind me.

I spin around to see him standing there, his face red with anger. "Horner!" I growl, glaring at him. "Stop this! Stop them! You're going to get us all killed!"

In confirmation, one of the automatons unleashes a blast, sending artillery into the wall over my head. I jump out of the way of falling shrapnel and toward Horner. He's stunned by the close blast. When he ordered Tick to send these machines after us, I doubt he thought he would get caught in the fight as well.

I barrel into him, knocking him back against the wall in the nook where he had been hiding. It turns out to be a rail for the rising floor. His back slams into the wall, pulling at his shirt as the floor moves upward. "STOP THEM!" I yell in his face as he screams in pain. I shove my arm up under his chin, forcing his head back against the moving wall. Let's just add a little more gleam to that bald spot!

The floor rattles past the wound in the wall with barely a protest and keeps slowly rising toward the world above. Horner doesn't cooperate. He grins and winces at the same time. "I can't," he practically laughs. "Only she can."

Tick. It all comes back around to Tick. I pull Horner away from the wall and swing him around, only to find myself face-to-face with a semi-circle of automatons. They have their weapons raised toward us. Their weapons are extensions of their arms, with variations from one to another. Some have small, gun-like attachments, while others have the monster cannons I've already experienced.

They look at us with their glowing red eyes and I hear their gears clicking in preparation for the next attack. This looks like the end of the road. But at least I can take Horner out with me. I look at Horner, swallowing back my fear. "Guess we're going out together then. I'd like to say it's been nice knowing you, but it really hasn't."

"Fuck you," Horner hisses. I brace for him to attack, but he only glares at me. If he doesn't want to fight our impending doom, who I am to argue? I would have made better use of my last words if I were him.

I look back up at the automatons, waiting for them to blast us into oblivion. I think about Samantha. Did she make it to Tick? Is she working right now on how to free the girl? Or did she get taken out with that strike I had witnessed? I think about Avery. Where is he now? Did he get the place rigged to explode? Was he outside already, waiting for me to show up with Tick? I think about Tick. She's an innocent victim in all of this, and once she's done commanding these machines to blast us, she's going to set them loose on the world. She might not have Horner's guidance, but she won't have anyone to stop her either.

All this thinking takes less than a second. It's like my life flashing before my eyes, only I'm just seeing the important parts. I've spent so much if it already dwelling on the past, I don't need to think about that any more. What did it matter anyway? I was nobody. I'm still nobody. I'm just a guy who has a talent for being in the wrong place at the wrong time. It's amazing I've lived this long. Guess I've had a pretty good run. Who would have thought it would end like this?

But it doesn't end here. Through the chaos of explosions and stomping metal feet, I hear a scream. It sounds like Tick. The floor shudders and rumbles as the gears grind to a stop. Ahead of me, the red eyes of the automatons flicker out. Their arms fall to the sides and they slump as if they're too tired to carry their own weight. My heart sinks as my brain goes to the only logical explanation. Tick is dead.

Horner begins to laugh, drawing me back to him. He's thinking the same thing. I can see it in his eyes. "Looks like neither of us are getting what we wanted," he sneers.

I want to punch that smarmy grin off his face, but first I want information. "And just what was it that you wanted? Why'd you do this?"

He continues to laugh, pulling free from my grip. He stumbles out of the nook and turns, falling against the unmoving leg of one of the mechanical giants. "I wanted what was mine," he says, reaching up to grab at the bullet wound on his arm. Blood had already soaked through the white of his shirt, making a streak like a militia insignia. A higher rank than he ever achieved. "I wanted what the world owed me!"

I raise a brow. Horner's taken a trip to La-la Land and forgot how to get back to the real world. "The world doesn't owe any of us shit," I grumble. If it did, Tick would be alive and free. Samantha would be in my bed. Avery would....keep being Avery. "Get over yourself. You've done enough damage already."

"THEY TOOK EVERYTHING!" Horner shouts, startling me. He charges at me, pounding his chest like the lead character in some overdone drama. He's in my face before I know it, covering me in spittle. "I WAS GOING TO GET IT BACK! I WAS GOING TO TAKE IT ALL!"

"BACK OFF!" I shout at him, pushing him away from me. He stumbles and falls once more against the automaton, making the large soldier reverberate with the strike. I want it to fall over on him, but it doesn't.

We stand there, staring at one another for the longest time, neither of us having anything else to say. I'm done with this. Tick is gone. Samantha is gone. Horner can't do anything else here. I've got to get out before morning when Avery blows this place. I start to walk past Horner in the direction where Tick had been. Maybe there's enough left of her for Avery and Kepling to put back together again.

I don't get far when Horner shifts to stand in my way. "You don't get to walk away," he says in a low, menacing voice.

I pause and look at him. "You really think you can stop me?" I shake my head, knowing I shouldn't take any bait from this guy. "Go home, Horner. Be glad you're still alive." Still free. If Samantha had gotten ahold of him, he'd spend the rest of his miserable life in prison.

I move to step around him and Horner takes a swing. His movement is slow and I easily duck around his fist. On the automaton's leg where he had been leaning, is a streak of red. I messed him up good when I had held him against the wall. I spin around to watch him stumble. His back and head are streaked with more blood. The shirt is in tatters. "You don't want to do this," I tell him. "Let it go. It's over."

Horner bends over, weakening with each passing second. He looks at me, glaring. He doesn't mean to give up so easily. I sigh as he moves to strike at me again. If this is the way he wants it, I'll put an end to his fight. When he gets close enough, I set myself and throw my fist into the middle of his face. His nose explodes in bright red, breaking in nearly the same place I had smashed it all those years ago.

Horner yelps and falls on his ass. He covers his face with his hand and moans. "No. No. It's not supposed to be like this. No."

I shake my head and turn. If Horner wants to stay here, so be it. He had until the morning. If he didn't move before then, it's his own damned fault. I can hear him moaning and muttering to himself as I weave my way through the motionless automaton ruins. Soon enough, his voice fades away, leaving me with eerie quiet.

I feel like the last guy left in the world. The automatons are like motionless ruins left behind by an ancient civilization. I felt like this during the war once. After I'd been downed by enemy fire and was left wandering a forest at night. The fighting never ended though, so I could still hear the sounds of airships and gunfire. I knew there were still people left in the world. But here? I'm not so sure. All I can hear is the creaking of metal bodies in their attempt not to fall over, and the wind blowing in from above. I feel alone. Lost.

I think back to what Samantha said about Wisen. How he had been responsible for making Tick and these machines. How he had been the enemy all along. Her lies stab the back of my head. She could have saved us so much trouble if she just told the truth in the first place. As it turned out, the truth probably wouldn't have caused any more harm, that's for sure. It might have even saved her life.

I shake my head. I can't think about these things now. I've got to pick up whatever pieces are left and find my way out of this hell. I move between the empty husks, watching the observation room windows above to make sure I'm going the right way. They're not as high up any more. Another 10 feet or so higher than the heads of the automatons. The floor had risen up a good way before it stopped. The cool night air has finally reached down into room, and I shiver slightly with the chill. It's been a damn long night. A long life. I don't know whether lasting this long is luck or misfortune. It definitely hasn't been a picnic for just about everyone else I've known along the way.

Toward the middle of the battlefield, the metal ground is empty. It seems about half of the machines came after me, while the other half, chased Samantha. The odds were against us from the start. But that's how it usually is. She took her chances the moment she decided to come here. A Reddie. Who would have guessed? Not me. I frown slightly. Someone is going to notice she's missing sooner or later, and then they'll be coming after me for answers. Horseballs. Maybe it really is time to retire.

 I pass over the empty area and into the field of automatons waiting on the other side. They crowd together like the ones that had been trying to kill me. And just like the other ones, they're motionless and silent. I start to notice a familiar smell. It takes a minute, but after a while, I realize exactly what it is. Burning flesh. Images of Tick's hands flash through my head. But this smell seems to be coming from the machines. Whatever is left of the humans inside the hard shells, isn't working well their sudden reanimation. Did Wisen know? Would these things have worked the way Horner had been hoping? It's a good thing the world will never find out.

 I get to the point where the machines are crowded the thickest. I stop to look at the strange patterns their bulky metal bodies make. Some are bending, while others seem to be aiming at some target beyond the mass. Some had stopped in mid-step and fallen against their compatriots, knocking each other over like dominoes. It makes finding a way through them, difficult at best.

 As I search through the tight maze of mechanical bodies, I hear familiar voices float from the other side. I pause and blink, leaning closer as if that will help me hear better. I can only catch a few words here and there. "Don't know…" and "Find…" But I don't need to know what's being said. I smile as I recognize the voice. Avery. I wait a little longer, and sure enough, a response comes back in Samantha's lighter timber. They're alive. I'm so happy, I don't even think about the fact that Avery was supposed to leave the compound after he set the place to blow. It's a good thing he didn't, because we're going to need him to get out of here.

"Avery! Samantha!" I call through the lifeless machines.

Their conversation stops and they grow silent for a few seconds. Then I hear Avery's voice respond. "Colt? That you? Where the hell are you?"

"The other side of these damned machines," I yell back. "Hold on. Let me find a way around."

They fall silent as I poke around the hulking machines, looking for an opening. I'd try climbing, but I'm exhausted and I don't know how stable the pile is. I also find something morbid about climbing over dead bodies, even if they're encased in metal. Touching the things is bad enough, but my best option is to squeeze between arms and legs and watch for any sign they're going to fall over. Some of them have stopped in awkward, unbalanced positions, but I don't even trust the ones that look sturdy. At one point I get stuck in the narrow opening between metal giants and I question why I'm even still in this game. A younger, more agile guy should be in here doing this crap. Someone closer to Samantha's age, who'd have a right to get hung up on her. As crazy as she is.

I tug myself free, and end up falling out into an open space. I stumble and catch myself before looking around to find that I've cleared the mechanical barrier. While the floor isn't a mangled mess of automaton bodies, there are more than a few that have fallen over. Their armor is smoking and blackened by explosions. Someone fought back and did a damn good job of it.

As I look to the left, I spot Avery standing there, watching me. He's got sooty smears covering him. I don't have to think hard to know he's the one who has been wreaking havoc on the machines. He also has a blackened piece of wood in his hand. I don't even want to know what he's doing with that.

Samantha is crouched down next to Tick, who lies on the floor. Samantha looks ruffled, but otherwise functional. Tick is back to being motionless. I can't even remember now what she's like when she's conscious, it feels like it's been so long since I've seen her moving. From this distance, I can't even see if her eyes are lit up.

I waste no time heading over to them. "Is she…?" I don't want to think the worst. We've been through so much to save Tick, I want the kid to have a happy ending. As I get closer, I can see the dim glow of her eyes, indicating that she's at least got some life left in her.

Samantha looks up, smiling weakly. "She's alive. If barely. I don't think getting her free of that thing did her any favors." As she speaks of the pedestal, I look toward it. Wires poke out in random angles, some of them flailing back and forth and sparking. I've never seen anything like it.

"What about Horner?" Avery asks.

I glance back in the direction I had come from and shake my head. "I let him live, but he's lost his mind. I don't think he's a threat to anyone anymore." I look back at Avery. "Were you able to work out a way to blow this place?"

Avery shrugs slightly. "I tapped into the main gas line and attached that transmitter device to it. But I need something to set it off. I thought maybe Tick could do it, but I don't know if she's in any condition right now." He looks up at the high windows above us. "I don't even know how the hell we're getting out of here."

I raise a brow as he mentions that. "How did you manage to get in?"

Avery smirks and pulls a roll of paper out of his overalls. He unrolls it and holds it up. "Found a map of the place. Made finding the gas lines easy. There're access panels all over that forest. And a doorway leading right in here. I managed to get through just before the floor started moving."

"And it's a good thing too," Samantha says, pulling my attention back to her. She nods to the piece of wood in Avery's hand. "Your friend realized he could do some damage to those things by using that stick to block up their exhaust ports. Gave me time to pull Tick out of that machine." She sighs, smoothing Tick's hair with her hand. "Anyway, did you manage to get Horner's transmitter?"

I frown and shake my head. "I didn't even think about it. He didn't give me a lot of options."

She nods and stands up. "I need to bring him in anyway. Let's go get him while Mr. Nickols thinks of a way out of here."

The last thing I want to do is fight my way back through the machines to haul an insane man to justice. He might not make it back out of here again, but I'm happy leaving him to his fate. Before I can voice my objection, a bang echoes through the massive room. Samantha ducks and Avery jumps back several more feet than I would have thought him capable.

I flinch, feeling the wind of a bullet zipping past me. The hell? I spin around to see Horner standing there. Blood drips from his nose and his eyes are a deep shade of purple. I can see the gun shaking in his weakened hands. The blood loss is the only thing that made him miss me. If he had been healthier, I'd have a bullet in my brain.

We stare at each other and I blink, wondering where the hell he got the gun. Reaching down, I pat my hip, realizing I must have dropped mine when we fought. Horseballs. A mad man with a weapon is just what we needed.

"Give me the girl," Horner mumbles, swiveling his aim between the three of us.

Behind me, I hear Samantha draw her own weapon, putting me in the middle of a gun sandwich. "Vann Horner. You're under arrest. Drop your weapon and come along quietly." Horner starts to laugh. I cringe and shake my head. She's not making any of this better.

"Horner, look," I say, trying to defuse things. I motion back at Tick, getting a quick reminder that Samantha is aiming right through me. "She's not of any more use. There's nothing you can do here." I look back at him, facing his gun again. "It's over."

Horner is still laughing. The insanity of it makes him shake more violently. I can only see the dark circles surrounding his eyes, but I doubt he's even looking at any of us. He's slipped into his own world and whatever he can see doesn't look a thing like reality. "Fuck you, Reed," he spits at me. Blood-colored spittle slides down his chin. "Fuck you, and that bitch, and your goddamned ass monkey!" He moved to look at each one of us, bobbing his head at me, then Samantha, and finally toward Avery.

But Avery isn't there. Horner frowns, wobbling slightly as he makes a confused, gurgling sound. I don't need to look over to see what has him stumped. I had seen Avery moving, much like I had when Samantha and Horner were having their stand-off up above. For a big guy, he's pretty damned sneaky. It's only too late that Horner realizes Avery's gotten behind him. Avery brings around the charred piece of wood, nailing Horner soundly in the head. Horner drops to the floor, the gun clattering out of his hand.

"Ass monkey," Avery says with a snort. He spits on Horner's bloodied back and tosses the wood to the side. "I never liked that guy."

"You had better not have killed him," Samantha says as she walks around me. She pushes her gun back into its holster and makes her way over to Horner and Avery. "He has a lot of questions to answer."

"Good luck getting anything out of him that makes sense," I say. If he manages to live, that is. We still have to get out of this place, and if Samantha has her way, we'll be carrying both Tick and Horner. Provided we can find an exit.

"Col-ton..." Tick's voice floats weakly to my ears. I turn to find her sitting up. She's shaking almost as badly as Horner had been, but her eyes are glowing a strong red as she looks at me.

I smile, a real, earnest smile. This kid's taken a beating and she's still going. I don't think I've ever been so happy in my life. I move over to her and crouch down, placing my hand on her back to hold her steady. "Hey kid. You all right?"

Tick looks down at her hands, properly bandaged by Dr. Kepling after Avery finished cleaning them. Something clicks in her throat and she shakes her head. "I have both right and left."

I laugh softly. I had forgotten how literal she is. "Yeah, okay." I look up and point at the revealed sky above us. "We need to get up there. Think you can do it?" I don't want to have to plug her into that pedestal again, but moving the floor up to the surface is the easiest way to get out.

Tick follows my eyes upward. Somewhere behind me, Avery and Samantha are arguing about what to do with Horner. Avery wants to leave him here and blow him up with the compound. Samantha is threatening Avery with a murder charge and interfering with her case if Horner's left here to die. Whether she's actually a Reddie or not, she's sure playing the part. She must have told Avery the same story because he doesn't protest her authority to arrest him.

Tick nods and looks back at me. "I can move the ground up," she says, her voice cracking and clicking with each word. Avery's going to have some work to do on her once we're safely out of here.

I point over to the pedestal, frowning slightly. "Do you need to be connected to that to do it?"

Tick looks at the pedestal and I can feel her shiver under my hand.

"No," she says, much to my relief. "Only to move the others." The automatons. I don't know how it all works and I don't want to know, but I'm glad we don't have to hook her up again. I'm not even sure if it would work, judging by the wild state of the pedestal.

"Good," I tell her, smiling again. "Then lift up the ground, and get us out of here." I pause, glancing toward the inner wall of the compound. The forest is still on the other side. As it is, if we manage to blow everything up, the forest will die. If the forest can be moved up like this platform, there's a chance its death can do some good for the area. I seem to remember hearing somewhere that forests thrive after they've burned. I don't know how it works, but it couldn't hurt to try. "Can you do the same thing for the forest?"

Tick nods again, smiling at the mention of the forest. "Yes. We can take the forest with us. Airika will love the forest."

"Uh…" What the hell do I say to that? Airika is still sitting up on top of the bluff near Portsmaw, in pieces. Even if she was here, I couldn't fit the forest into her cargo hold and take it with us. But the thought seems like such a happy one for Tick. I can't just dash her dreams like that. "Sure. I'm sure she will," I say finally. "Get us out of here." Tick nods and with a rumbling lurch, the floor starts to move again.

Chapter 17

Horner is still out cold by the time the floor reaches the top. Samantha and Avery come to an agreement. He isn't as opposed to hauling around Horner as long as he doesn't have to carry the asshat up all those stairs. As long as Horner keeps breathing, Samantha is happy. I'd be fine if Horner never wakes up, but he's Samantha's problem now. I end up helping Tick stand. She's weak, but at least she's awake and moving. Both good things in my book.

At the top, I finally figure out how this place is structured. I had guessed the borders extended beyond the barrier wall of the compound, and I'm right. The land had opened up on the north side, exposing the massive automaton room. The inner wall gives way to the barrier wall. I cringe, remembering the steam machines. We had parked them just by the northwest corner, but I don't know if they're far enough away from the opening to still be there. I hadn't noticed them falling into the automaton room, but then I was a little preoccupied.

"The forest?" I ask Tick as the floor comes to a rumbling stop.

She points to the east side of the compound. "There."

It's still dark, but as I look that direction, I can see a thin line of pink starting to come up over the horizon. Morning is coming, and none too soon. What I can't see is the yawning opening where the forest would eventually appear. I can hear the grinding of gears, proving that it's opening. It must have taken some brilliant people to make a place like this. Brilliant people who were destroyed by Wisen. They would never get true justice. I feel bad about that, but at least we can make sure no one else will abuse what remains of them.

I look over at Avery, who has already hefted Horner onto his broad shoulder. "Do you have everything you need?"

Avery nods. "Found the transmitter in his pocket. You sure we can't just leave him here?" He looks at Samantha as he asks, and she gives him the darkest glare I've ever seen.

I can't help but laugh. Samantha's glare turns to me and I choke it back. "Eh…yeah, well, we should go see if the steam machines are still up here. We'll want to get as far away from this place as we can."

Samantha's glare becomes a smirk. "I've got something better," she says. She picks up the lamp that Avery must have brought with him. Holding it up, she begins to adjust the wick back and forth, making the flame bigger and smaller in a short pattern.

"What are you…" I start to ask, then I hear the distant rumble of an airship echoing over the hills.

"Calling our ride," Samantha says, continuing the signal. "Did you really think we could get five people on two steam machines?"

I didn't, but it's not like we had that many options. Tick perks up in my arms at the sound of the airship. "Airika?" she says, her voice a little stronger with the thought that she's about to see her friend again. She pauses, slumping back once more and shaking her head. "No. She sounds different."

I sigh, hating to see Tick disappointed. "Sorry kid. Airika had a little accident. She's real sick right now, but we're going to make her good as new." I look at Avery, who nods in agreement. I spot a hint of excitement in his face. I suspect some of it's about getting Airika patched up, but the rest is about going back to Portsmaw and seeing Dr. Kepling again.

With Horner out of the way for now, I don't feel as insecure about the location. Going back even sounds nice. Wait? Did I just think that? All my memories of the city with its noise, and smog and light, suddenly feel stressful after the past few days. The truth is, I think I'm ready to give up the smuggling life. Especially now that I'm standing next to an R.D.I. agent. If she could get this close and not be after me, I'd hate to see what would happen if I crossed some invisible criminal line.

"Can I help?" Tick asks, bringing my mind back to Airika.

I nod slightly, though it'll be Avery who has final say on that. "I don't see why not. She'd like that." I can still see the old girl, sitting up there on that bluff in pieces, waiting for a little tender loving care from the mechanical child. I glance over at Samantha as the sound of the airship gets closer, and think about the night of the crash. "How exactly does our ride expect to land and take off out here? Landing'll be easy enough, but there's nothing elevated to use for take-off."

Samantha lowers her lamp as the bulk of the airship comes into view. It has lights set on the front, and it's a lot bigger than Airika. It doesn't even look like it's meant to fly, yet it has no problem. "How old is your airship, Mr. Reed? 15? 20 years? The technology's come a long way since then, and you can bet we have the best. Don't worry about it."

"She's not nice," Tick says, looking in the direction of the incoming airship. "She's angry. And cold."

I nod, looking at Samantha. "Yeah, what she said." Not so different from Samantha in my mind. And still, the cold hardness somehow makes her all the more attractive.

Samantha shakes her head and starts walking toward the west side of the compound, where the airship is destined to land. "And it's your ride out of here."

I sigh and start after her, helping Tick along the best I can. Avery falls in beside me, lugging Horner with him. With the sun approaching the edge of the horizon, the sky brightens and I can see the outline of the steam machines sitting right where we left them. "It's not the only option," I say, looking at them. I'm not that excited to take a long ride on those things again, to be honest, but they remain a choice. "Unless you're saying that it is."

Samantha looks back over her shoulder and raises a brow. "Hum? What do you mean?"

Something had been bothering me for a while, but with everything else I let it slide to the back of my mind. "You're a cop, right?"

"A government agent," she says with a shrug. "What's your point?"

Just beyond the edge of the wall, the airship swoops down. The sound of the engines fill the air and it rattles the fake flooring under our feet as it touches down. I have to move up closer to Samantha so she can hear me. "I don't exactly have a squeaky clean record. How do I know you're not going to take me in? Hand Tick over to the government?" And, I realize, I'm not going to see the other half of my pay either. A job I've put more time and effort, and even my life into than any other job before it.

Samantha stops and turns to look at Tick and me. Her voice and face soften as she shakes her head. "I think you've redeemed yourself, Mr. Reed. Keep your nose out of trouble, and I'll see to it you won't be bothered." She looks down at Tick and smiles an earnest smile, which has Tick responding in kind. "Tick…she's had enough. I'm sure my people would love to get their hands on her, but…" She shakes her head and smiles. That smile isn't the whole story though. I get the sense Samantha is going to catch hell for letting Tick and the automatons go. Maybe Avery and me too. She's making a sacrifice here, and my opinion of humanity rises just a little. "We'll take all of you back to New Foundis, and you can go on your way."

I nod, glancing back at the brightening horizon. "Make it Portsmaw, and you have a deal."

"Then Portsmaw it is," she laughs softly, holding out her hand. I give it a friendly shake, fighting off the urge to pull her in for something a little more. It's a good thing Tick is clinging to me, or I might have failed.

Avery keeps going on past us. Even with his load, he's moving quickly. He's forgotten about us and is focused on the airship instead, which looked to be nearly as big as a locomotive car. I'm not quite ready to hurry forward yet though. I drop Samantha's hand, knowing I had held it a little too long, and clear my throat. "So, uh…I really do appreciate you're help. You're doing a lot here, and I get that. But…well, I'm going to have to fix Airika, and set us up in Portsmaw." I glance down at Tick.

"And now I have her to take care of…"

Samantha's expression sours and she turns toward the airship. "I should have guessed. You did all this for the money, didn't you? If that's what you want, we'll pay to fix your ancient airship. You want a new one? We can do that too. We'll even take her off your hands. I'm sure there are plenty of people who wouldn't mind…"

"No," I say quickly, rushing after her. Tick stumbles slightly, but I manage to keep her upright. "That's not what I mean. And I'm happy you're willing to let Tick stay with me. It's just that you know about me. About my livelihood. I can't very well do that anymore, can I? You're giving me freedom and taking away my life."

Samantha drops her head forward and sighs. She looks up again as we pass the resting steam machines. "We could actually use someone like you. You can't be arrested for taking on government-sanctioned jobs, now can you?"

That's the last thing I expect. I stop, pulling Tick to me to keep her steady. "I…well…That sounds…"

"Think about it," Samantha says, getting further away. She shakes her head, her long waves of hair floating back and forth. "No. Don't think about it. Just be ready when I come looking for you."

Tick looks up at me and smiles. "I like her."

I take a slow breath, letting Samantha get far enough away she can't hear me. "Yeah. Me too." I shake my head, clearing out my longing thoughts and smile down at her. "Let's get out of here, all right? It's about time for some fireworks." Tick nods and we head around the corner of the compound wall toward the waiting airship.

Avery's already there, and the crew – the damn thing has a five-man crew! – is taking Horner from him to stow away somewhere aboard. Samantha is already half-way there and barking orders this way and that. If I had any doubts about her legitimacy, they fade away now. Reddie or otherwise, she's with some well-funded organization. Makes me wonder why she didn't have backup. And who she's going to have to answer to.

As I get closer, I hear Avery making amazed proclamations about the airship to one of the crewmembers. He turns as he notices me. "Colt! She's made of metal, Colt. All the way through. They call it al-lu-mini-yum. Say it's super light. Come look at this!"

Tick nods slightly, frowning. "Cold. She's cold. Airika is better. Airika is warm like the forest." She looks up at me. "Will we see Airika soon?"

I chuckle at both of them. What a pair I've ended up with. I nod. "Yeah, real soon." Then I look over at Avery. "What do you think, Av? Now that Horner's not a threat, we could retire in Portsmaw. I'll sell the building. You could get reacquainted with Dr. Kepling. I could teach Tick how to fly. Maybe do a little fishing." I decide it's best not to let him know that Samantha could come knocking any time.

He flashes a crooked smile and nods. "I think I'm ready for that."

"Everyone aboard then," Samantha says, coming over and shooing us toward the airship. "This one has windows. Once we're safe up in the air, you can set the charge and watch. I'll have the boys circle around a few times until we're sure it's worked."

We board the airship and find a long, low bench running along each side. It's not so much a seat as it is a railing, but there are straps that hang down from the interior wall to hold passengers in place. Along the hull are portal windows, much like on an ocean-going ship, but I can't see any way of opening them, and the glass is almost as thick as the hull. It doesn't provide for a very good view – even worse when strapped in – but it's better than Airika's dark cargo hold.

We settle in, not bothering with the straps for now. Soon the engines rumble back to life and the airship is rolling forward. I don't understand how it works, but I'm relieved when the airship pulls up away from the ground and into the air. Tick has pressed herself up against the window, watching the world fall away under us. Avery's doing damn near the same thing. I have to admit, the view from this angle, without goggles on, is something to see. The forest has fully emerged now. Many of the trees stand up taller than the compound wall.

The sun peeks over the horizon as we reach a safe height from the compound. Samantha appears through a little door near the front of the airship and makes her way over to us. "I'm told we should be a safe distance now. Are you ready, Mr. Nickols?"

Avery grins and pulls a small device out of his pocket. It looks like the one Samantha had given me at the cave, but this one has a small, red button attached to it. I nod to him, wondering whether Tick is going be upset about the forest. It's too late to worry about that now. He pushes the small button and gazes out the window.

Samantha leans into a window as well, and we all look out. At first nothing happens. The sun keeps rising, washing the world in an orange haze, but the compound remains silent. As we start to come around on the first arc, blue-white flames shoot up through the smoke stacks. Tick gasps, but she keeps her face pressed against the window. Smaller explosions burst out through the vents on the low structures.

Though we're high above the smoke stack flames, the airship wobbles slightly as we pass by. I understand thermals and this giant beast isn't immune to them. As we swoop around to the other side of the compound, the platform with the automatons is leaning heavily to one side. The metal soldiers fall against one another. The floor gives way, crashing back down into the hole and taking the automatons with it. The same blue-white glow of gas fire licks up from the bottom of the pit. I already feel better knowing those things won't be invading anywhere any time soon.

Finally, the underground violence reaches the forest. I wince as blue-white flames burst up through the dirt floor. The fire licks up around tree trunks, catching on the drying wood. Tick gasps besides me, and I look over to soothe her, but see that she's smiling. "Pretty," she breathes out, running a finger along the window. She has no idea what's happening to her forest.

I slump down to set on the railing, my back to the windows. "That should do it," I say, looking toward Samantha. "There's nothing else to see here."

Samantha pushes away from the window and turns to go back through the door. "All right. I'll let the boys know we can head for

Portsmaw." I smile and watch her retreating back as Avery and Tick continue to gaze out the window.

So much has happened over the last few days. A mysterious, troubled woman shows up at my door. She turns out to be so much more than what I expect. I find a strange kid full of tech I can't possibly begin to understand. And my best friend finds what he's been missing all these years. All in a little over a week. I lean my head back against the airship's side, feeling the vibration rattle around my skull. Damn I need a drink. And some sleep. I smile up at the ceiling of the moving airship. I'm going to enjoy my retirement for as long as Samantha lets me have it.

A Most Unfortunate Man

"Hey, John. Boss's taking us for Chinese. You in?" Keith bent over the top of John's short cubical, staring at him intently as he attempted to ignore the invitation and tried to look busy with his work.

John continued to stare at his computer screen, his fingers tapping lightly on the keys but not making any actual key strokes. "Er...no thanks. I have a lot to do." A spreadsheet sat open on his monitor with thousands of pieces of data already entered into it, but he had nothing to add. He had finished his work about an hour ago, and just kept the spreadsheet open to appear busy.

Keith sighed and folded his arms on top of the short wall. "Dude, how long do you want to stay some lowly data-entry guy? I mean, you've been doing this crap for how many years now? Everyone else has been promoted or left, and here you sit, surrounded by this boring bullshit."

"I like what I do," John responded, finally turning to look at Keith. He had practiced that response several times, having found that he needed to use it almost constantly. Every time a new promotion opportunity opened up, he had to justify why he appeared to the outlier in a group of go-getters.

"Yeah, right," Keith said, looking toward the full screen. "Just what do you like about it? The headache inducing lines of data? The potential for carpal tunnel syndrome? Oh, maybe it's the pathetic pay and constant fear that if you don't get enough done on time, you'll be fired?"

John frowned. Most people didn't push beyond that initial explanation. Now he had to think of something else. "Uh...no, of course not. It's…it's the independence. I can do what I like with no one breathing over my shoulder, and I don't have to breathe over anyone else's."

"Oh, of course. Right," Keith said, nodding sagely. "You know, that's probably a good thing. From what I hear, you're probably going to have lots of independence soon. So yeah, okay. Keep up the good work."

John narrowed his brow. "What do you mean? I don't understand."

Keith grinned and leaned over the cube wall once more. "See, you're out of the loop. You don't go to these lunches and no one talks to you, so you probably haven't heard. But Mr. Talbert uses the lunches to choose who he promotes, right?" John nodded slightly, still not sure where Keith was going on with this. "Well, he also uses them to choose who to fire. You don't go, you're putting yourself in danger of getting the ax, and from what I hear, Talbert is looking to cut a little fat."

John's heart began to thud in his chest as the realization swept over him. "But…but…I do good work. I'm always on time. I have a 90-percent accuracy rating."

"You're doing a job any monkey off the street could do," Keith said. "And you're getting paid more than most of the other data monkeys because you've been here so long. Why should Talbert waste his time and money on someone with no ambition?"

"I have ambition!" John pouted, folded his arms together. He began to wish he really did have more work to do, so he could use that as an excuse to get out of this conversation. He had been with the office for 7 years now, and he didn't really believe he could get fired for opting out of lunch. "Besides, what's it matter to you anyway? I mean, aren't you trying for a promotion too? Why make more competition for yourself?"

Keith shook his head and glanced up and down the isle of cubes. He lowered his voice as he leaned in conspiratorially. "Look, Talbert sent me over here, okay. He wants to give you a chance, but he just doesn't know you very well."

"Oh," John said, relaxing once more. He turned back to his computer screen, thinking he could probably bluff his way out of any further conversation. "Well, I'm pretty busy. These numbers don't input themselves, you know. If he wants to know me better, he can stop by himself." Though he had no idea what Talbert would learn that way. His space was Spartan – no decorations, no pictures of family, not so much as a calendar pinned to the cube wall. He also didn't have much of anything to make small talk about. All he really wanted was to be left alone to do his job.

"I just don't get it," Keith said. He stepped back, shoving his hands into his pockets. "You say you like this joke of a job and that you have some kind of ambition, though I sure as hell don't see it. What do you have to lose by at least trying to be a team player?"

John hung his head, looking down at his fingers resting on the keyboard. "It's not that I don't like the people here. Or anything like that. I just…I just don't like Chinese food. Why does he always insist on Chinese?"

"Wait…you don't…?" Keith was clearly flustered, making John look up again and nod. "That's it? It's just the food choice? Hell, you don't have to get anything. Plus, the place we go to has American food on the menu. Christ John, everyone thinks you're some kind of anti-social, homicidal maniac, who's just waiting for the right moment to whip out a shotgun and start blasting up the place. When in reality, you're just being picky for no damned good reason!"

"Anti-social, homicidal maniac?" John looked back up at Keith, concerned now that this went far beyond getting a promotion or keeping a job. "But I'd never…I wouldn't hurt anyone."

Keith took a breath and cleared his throat, calming down once more. "Look, I know that. That's why I'm here, talking to you. But you know how it goes? When something does happen, everyone always says, 'Oh, he was such a quiet guy. Never got into anyone's business. I wouldn't have expected this from him.' Now that's what people look for. The quiet, unassuming guy. You can't really help but wonder what kind of inner turmoil must be boiling in there."

John shook his head slowly. "There's none. I'm not mad or upset about anything. I'm just a guy doing my work."

"Then you need to prove it," Keith said. He glanced down at his watch, frowning slightly. "We'll be heading out in about 15 minutes." Then he turned, and walked back down the cube aisle toward his own desk, in an office with a door.

John watched Keith go and mulled his words. Was it really all that important to go to some lunch? He hadn't been to any of them all the years he worked here and no one had said a thing. He hadn't paid much attention when the office became deathly silent during random lunch hours and he had been left alone with only the sound of his keystrokes to keep him company. It had been bliss.

Now it appeared he had a choice and only a few minutes to make up his mind. He could remain at his desk, where he would be comfortable, or he could go to the lunch, surrounded by people who would be assessing his every move. Worse, it was a Chinese lunch that would inevitably end with the part he hated the most. Fortune Cookies.

The reality was he didn't mind Chinese food itself. He had no real desire for all the spicy and salty things, but there was always something palatable for the main course. It was the fortune cookies at the end he dreaded. Throughout his life, those rare times he had been forced into a typical American Chinese meal, he had to endure the humiliation inside the cookie at the end. It was something he would rather avoid.

But his preferred option of staying in the office didn't appeal much more. It could mean risking firing from a job to which he had grown accustomed. While he didn't hate his job, he didn't really like it either. It paid the bills and occupied his otherwise boring life. His home life was even more pathetic. In the times he couldn't be at work, he sat in an equally Spartan apartment, eating simple, microwavable meals, and watching a continuous feed of cable news. If he was fired from his job, there would be more of that. He would also have to make the effort to try to find a new job to buy microwave meals and pay for cable.

So the choice came down to facing the dreaded fortune cookie or finding a way to start over again. The cookie seemed far less daunting, and if he was lucky, maybe no one would notice if he ignored that part of the meal. John closed his eyes and nodded to himself. He would go and take his chances that things wouldn't be quiet as bad as he believed they could be.

John opened his eyes once more and looked down at his watch. There was only a few minutes left. Down the hall, he could already hear co-workers gathering and chatting noisily as they got ready to leave. He plucked up his courage and stood, stepping out of his cube.

And right into Mr. Talbert.

"Uhf...Hey, watch it there, tiger," Talbert said, laughing slightly. "What's the hurry, Smith? You planning on joining us today?"

John jumped back and looked down at the floor, nodding. "Er...yes, well, you see...I forgot my lunch today, so I..."

"No problem," Talbert said, slapping him on the shoulder. "You're always welcome, just like everyone else. Now come on. We need to grab a table before the place fills up. You know how it is on a Friday afternoon." He used his well-placed hand to start pushing John into the aisle and toward the hall.

"Uh, yes, thanks," John mumbled as he quickly moved in front of the boss. He didn't really know what it was like on a Friday. He actually didn't spend much time anyone beyond work, and usually didn't pay much attention to the habits of other people. But at least Talbert didn't seem to be as hesitant about his character as Keith made him out to be. Maybe this luncheon thing would be all right after all. Then he could go back to his regular routine.

"You're kind of a simple guy, aren't you, Smith?" Talbert asked, quick on John's heels. "Don't complain, don't rock the boat. Nothing wrong with that, of course. There's always a place in this world for people who just buckle down and get the work done."

John nodded slowly, doubting this adventure more as he got closer to the waiting crowd of co-workers. They were watching him and Mr. Talbert, some of them whispering quietly among themselves. Had Keith told them anything about his joining them? "Yes, Sir. That's kind of my thoughts. Can't complain too much about having a place, when there's plenty of people who don't even have that."

Talbert laughed again. "You must make your mother proud."

John tried to smile, but he didn't really understand what his boss found so funny about any of this. The whole idea of this lunch outing was to pretend he was "normal" and worthy of not only staying in his job, but possibly getting a promotion he didn't want. He was saved from any further answer as Talbert turned his attention to the others, laughing and joking with them.

Lunch wasn't quite as bad as John thought it would be. There were 15 people in the group all together, and they squeezed into a much too small table in the equally small restaurant. John sat on the far end of the table and listened as the others gossiped back and forth. There was apparently a good deal of dirt floating around the office, much of which John knew nothing about. He found he really didn't care about most of it as well.

Mr. Talbert was laughing the loudest, and acting in ways that were unbecoming of a division head. How he managed to get away with the bawdy jokes, John had no idea. He tried to smile and laugh quietly when the others laughed, following their leads in what they considered funny. As long as he acted like he was following what was going on, he hoped they wouldn't notice just how out of place he felt.

John ordered some plain chicken and rice and only answered questions thrown at him with simple yeses and noes and the occasional one or two word answer as necessary. The time flew by quickly, and he began to think he would get through this without too much trouble. Then the check came, carrying with it a pile of fortune cookies.

The check started on the far end of the table, the co-workers each grabbing a cookie as they mentally calculated whey owed. There was plenty of chatting and laughter surrounding this, but once each person made their payment, the contributor would open their fortune cookie and read the small message aloud. Everyone would chime in with "in bed" at the end, and break into a fit of juvenile laughter. Everyone except John, that is.

John watched the end of meal ritual silently, awaiting his turn to throw money into the pot. His mind turned trying to think of ways to avoid the cookie part, but he could see few ways out of it. Maybe they would be talking among themselves enough not to notice him skip the cookie? Once the bill reached him, he quickly tallied his contribution and reached for his wallet to grab the necessary cash. The group went silent and he could feel everyone's eyes fall on him.

John swallowed and pulled the money out of his wallet, placing it on top of the pile, then shifting to pass the bill along. Mr. Talbert cleared his throat before John could get far, however. "Don't forget the cookie, Smith. We're all waiting to hear your fortune."

"Oh," John sighed, looking down at the pile of cookies. "Er…I don't really like fortune cookies. I'd rather just pass, thanks."

"Eh, the cookie's not the important part," Keith laughed. Indeed, he had broken his own apart and set aside the crispy dough. "Even if you don't eat it, just pull out the fortune. They're good for a laugh." The others nodded and mumbled in agreement as they continued to watch John.

John cringed, seeing he wasn't getting out of this. Coming to the lunch had been the wrong move and now they were all going to know the truth. Part of him wondered if it was such a horrible thing anyway. Maybe they would all think what was about to happen would be a fluke, and overlook it. Though from the sounds of their jokes, they would certainly take the moment to make fun of him. Still, what else could he do but comply?

He set down the bill tray and put his wallet away before grabbing one of the cookies. They continued to watch him and he became quite aware of the other people in the restaurant. Most of them weren't paying any attention to the group, but he felt as if everyone in the world was staring and waiting to see the outcome of the irrelevant slip of paper. John took the wrapper off the cookie and closed his eyes as he broke the fried dough apart.

When he pulled the paper free, he already knew what he would find. Nothing. No text appeared on the greasy slip claiming he would find great wealth, have a happy family, or travel the world. No lucky lottery numbers, or words translated into Chinese graced the back. It was simply a blank piece of paper.

"Well?" Mr. Talbert asked, waving his hand to urge John to speak.

"Ha, it's blank," Tom from accounting said as he looked over John's shoulder. "Totally blank. He's got nothing."

"IN BED!" The group cheered together, breaking out in a rush of laughter that did have the other patrons of the restaurant glaring toward the table.

John wanted to wilt and fade away. Most of them would probably think it was just a mistake. A blank piece of paper thrown into the cookie by accident. But he knew the truth. He had never gotten a fortune from a fortune cookie. They always came out blank, as if they knew who was opening them. He could have picked any cookie from that pile and the result would have been the same.

"Oh, very unlucky." An older, Asian-accented voice floated over the crowd's laughter, something in it making them quiet almost immediately. Their eyes turned up to the older woman who stood next to John, looking down at the blank slip of paper in his hands. She clucked her tongue and shook her head slowly.

John swallowed, hating all the attention that had suddenly fallen on him. "Yeah, I guess so," he mumbled. "Printing error. Must happen all the time, right?"

"Oh no!" the woman exclaimed, reaching forward to grab one of his hands. Her grip was warm, and despite her age, her skin was smooth and soft. A nervous giggle floated through the crowd as they watched the older woman grab and begin to rub his hand for no discernable reason. "No, no. This no mistake."

"Su Lin," Mr. Talbert laughed. "You're scaring the poor guy. Look how pale he is."

And indeed, John had gone nearly ghost white as the woman manipulated his hand. He still gripped the paper between his other thumb and forefinger, letting it hang loosely as he gazed at the woman. He swallowed slightly, barely hearing Mr. Talbert's words over the din of his own thoughts. "I…er…it's always been like this," he confessed, startling himself that he actually said it aloud. All this time he had been worried the others would find out the truth, and here he was, admitting to it.

Su Lin nodded slowly, kindness and sorrow reflected in her dark eyes. "Yes. I so very sorry. They no understand. They can't understand."

"What's going on?" Keith asked as he stood and leaned over the table. His eyes locked in on the old woman's hands and a curious expression marred his face. The others were starting to whisper between themselves, asking the same question.

John shook his head, gazing back down at that same hand as the old woman's fingers rubbed back and forth over his pale skin. "I…don't know. I never knew…" He wasn't sure how to finish that sentence. He never knew why he only got blank fortunes, certainly, but he always felt it went deeper than bad luck. It was a matter of who he was the rest of the time – the Spartan, lonely existence, his desire to stay with the status quo. This was his very essence of being.

Su Lin looked him in the eyes and pressed her other hand against his forehead, frowning softly as she did. "You have no soul. Very sad. Very unfortunate. You come with me. We fix you." She dropped her hands and stepped back, looking toward Mr. Talbert. "You let him stay. He will be better man when he returns."

Most of the table looked at the old woman dubiously, John most of all. He wasn't sure he wanted to be fixed. What was so bad about living a simple life? Even if he felt he needed to hide this secret, it had worked for him all these years. But he was more surprised when Mr. Talbert voiced his thoughts. "Now hold on, Su Lin," the boss said, standing up as well. "You can't just go kidnapping my employees. He has work to do. And not having a soul hasn't made much of a difference in doing that."

Su Lin shook her head and grabbed John's arm, trying to pull him free from his seat. "No. This very serious. Man cannot exist without soul! He will steal other souls. All your employees in very much danger. He comes with me now."

Mr. Talbert smirked as another round of giggles filled the table. They had gone from concerned to amused at the old woman's antics. No one, including John, believed for a moment anything she was saying. He considered souls to be something of fantasy and he didn't really care whether or not he had one. John certainly had no intent on stealing anyone else's soul! "Hey," he protested as the woman pulled on his arm. She was deceptively strong for her age and stature. "I don't think this is necessary. Really, it was just a mistake. I'm sure."

Mr. Talbert changed his mind as a wide grin spread across his face. "Ah, go on and go with her, Smith. Take the afternoon off. You could use a break anyway." He laughed and the other started laughing with him as they went back to passing around the check.

"But Mr. Talbert," John protested feebly as Su Lin finally pulled him free of his seat. "I've got work to do. You said so yourself." Of course, that wasn't strictly true. He had finished his work earlier and didn't anticipate anything more for at least a little while. But he thought sitting at his desk and hiding from the laughing eyes of his co-workers was far better than whatever jeers he would encounter when he came back to work on Monday.

Su Lin seemed to be ignoring the conversation entirely as she kept pulling him further away from the table. "You come now. We find free soul. Fix you up real good."

"But I don't…" John tried to protest again, pulling back as the woman dragged him between tables and amused diners.

"Oh, go on, Smith," Mr. Talbert cheered behind him. The group finished their payment ritual and were getting ready to leave. None of them appearing the least bit concerned about John's situation, as if this kind of thing happened all the time. Mr. Talbert was already pulling his coat on and waved toward John through the sleeve. "See you bright and early on Monday morning," he laughed.

"You'll be all right," Keith called as he started for the door. "Su's an expert." Though an expert at what, he didn't say, and that worried John even more.

John walked half-sideways as Su Lin continued to drag him. His co-workers were quickly abandoning him, and the rest of the patrons watched the woman drag him toward the swinging kitchen doors. The entire situation felt surreal and he had no idea what to think of it. At least there was still a promise that he would have his job once this was all over.

Su Lin pulled John through the kitchen doors, chattering reassurances that he would soon be all right, though he found them less than reassuring. Inside the kitchen, the cook staff, who John noticed were mostly Hispanic, stopped their constant flow of talk and movement to see what was going on. John gave them a nervous smile as Su Lin waved a free hand at them. "Back to work! Back to work!"

She clearly had some power in the establishment as the kitchen workers quickly went back to what they were doing, albeit more quietly than they had been when John first entered. Su Lin hurriedly pulled him toward another doorway at the back of the kitchen. The sign on the door read "Authorized Employees Only," and she didn't hesitate in the slightest yanking him through.

John began to wonder if instead of being "fixed" he was going to end up as the dinner special. "Where are you taking me?" he questioned. "I don't think all this is really necessary. I'll be fine."

Before Su Lin could answer, however, the room erupted with a spat of screaming Chinese…or at least what John thought was Chinese. Another woman began to yell at Su Lin, causing Su Lin to yell back, her grip tightening painfully on John's arm. All he could do was cringe as Su Lin tugged and ranted. The other woman had been sitting behind a desk, working on the bookkeeping, but she immediately jumped to her feet when the old woman brought John through the door.

The senseless screaming carried on for what felt to John like an eternity. He hadn't wanted to be there before, and he most certainly didn't want to be here now. It felt like a private conversation he shouldn't have been listening too, even though he didn't understand any of it. Suddenly, the other woman stopped yelling in mid-scream. She looked at John with suspicion and he found himself gazing back, wishing he understood what was going on.

"You have no soul?" The bookkeeper asked. He thought she might be the old woman's daughter, or in-law. She was a little younger than Su Lin and restaurants like this were often run by families. At any rate, her accent wasn't as thick as Su Lin's when she spoke English. She had probably grown up in the United States.

John didn't have much of an answer for her though. He shrugged slightly, glancing at Su Lin, who was nodding emphatically. "Er...I guess. Maybe? That's what she's saying."

This was apparently the wrong answer, as it started the other woman screaming again and waving her hands in the air. She was very much upset, though he didn't know if was because of Su Lin's belief that he didn't have a soul, or the other woman also believed this and thought he might be about to steal someone else's.

Su Lin did her share of yelling in return, but this time she started dragging John along behind her again as she did. She pulled him through a bead curtain and into yet another room, decorated like some kind of shrine. The other woman followed them through, keeping up her end of the argument as Su Lin pushed John to sit down on a pile of cushions. He looked between them, deciding that if he wasn't going to end up as dinner, he was at least going to become some kind of ritual sacrifice to a god he had probably never heard of.

The argument died into a tense silence as Su Lin rushed around the little room, lighting candles and incense. The other woman stood just inside the beaded curtain, her arms folded together and a serious pout on her face. "You no worry," Su Lin said in a much more subdued tone. "My daughter thinks all this rubbish. She not care about the old ways."

"You're full of it," the other woman replied in her smoother English. "You're scaring this man with your voodoo. Let him go home, or back to wherever he came from. Leave him alone."

"She's right," John ventured, starting to stand up. "There's really no need to bother. I'll just get back to…"

Su Lin snorted and pushed him back down on the cushions. "You stay. You see. You both see. Soon you have soul. Life so much better."

The younger woman rolled her eyes and turned to head back through the curtain. "Whatever. Some of us have a business to run."

John watched the woman stalk out, feeling abandoned once more. He looked up at Su Lin, understanding now that whatever he said would make no difference. She was determined to move ahead with her plans. Maybe the other woman was also right that this was just some kind of voodoo, and nothing would actually change. If he just endured it long enough, he could eventually get out of here. At least Su Lin's daughter didn't seem terribly concerned he would be injured or killed by any of this.

Su Lin finished lighting everything and the room filled with a haze of scents that gave John a headache. She came back around to stand in front of him and reached down, cupping his face in her hands. "You relax now. Forget about world and work and everything. Just breathe slow, deep."

John found this easier said than done, of course. He had no idea what was happening and he was less than comfortable in the strange situation. "Wh...what exactly are you planning to do?" he asked, hoping that at least a little knowledge would help.

Su Lin smiled a genuine, grandmotherly smile, and released his face. "I send you to speak to great Ancients. Ancients will guide you to soul."

John reached up to scratch his head. The ache was still there, but a heavy feeling of drowsiness began to overtake it as the scented smoke circled around him. "You seem so sure," he slurred, not entirely certain what he meant. Sure that a soul was out there for him? That he needed one? That anyone needed one?

His parents had been deeply religious Catholics, and they had tried to instill that faith in him, but he could never bring himself to believe any of it. Now this woman was trying to send him to some kind of Ancients to find something that may not actually exist anyway, and she acted so sure this was the right thing to do.

"Shhhhh," she hushed him, kneeling down in front of John. Su Lin pressed her hands together and began to mutter in Chinese. John watched her as she closed her eyes, and he felt compelled to do the same. Perhaps it was smoke getting to him, or the rhythmic drone of her voice, but he slowly felt himself relaxing and falling into a peaceful trance.

The richly decorated room swirled away from him as his eyes closed. The heavy sounds of the kitchen dulled into the chirps of crickets and brooks. John wasn't sure, but he thought he felt a warm breeze trailing playfully along his face. He hadn't traveled much in his life, and rarely went outside if he could help it, but he felt as if he was sitting somewhere out in the wilderness, perhaps on a high mountain in some foreign country. It was certainly different than the world of the Chinese restaurant and his mundane life.

John forced his eyes open, hoping that what he was feeling was just a trick of his mind. He was sure he would see reality, the backroom of the restaurant, Su Lin sitting before him, the candles and incense burning all around. Everything would be over and he could tell Su Lin, 'Sure, he had a soul now. Have a nice day. Thanks for all your help. Got to be going. Bye!'

Despite John's wishes, this is not what he saw when he opened his eyes. He was met by the bright glare of daylight, which made him flinch. That was not supposed to be here. He blinked away the discomfort and looked up to take in more of the world around him.

John found himself sitting on a high mountain, overlooking a vast green valley, through which a wide river flowed. There was a stream running over a tumble of boulders, and cascading down the face of the mountain to join the river. Thin clouds and mist painted the valley and surrounding hills, giving the place a sense of faraway isolation. He had never seen such a grand sight, and found for the first time in recent memory, he was happy.

What brings you to my home? a deep, otherworldly voiced rumbled in his head.

John jumped at the sound, turning before he was fully on his feet, and nearly falling backward down the mountain. As he caught himself, a new sight met his eyes. Coiled up only a few feet away from him was a massive red dragon, covered in gems from nose to tail. It's long, serpentine body seemed to go on in infinite circles until it met the dragon's neck and large, lion-like head. Small tendrils of smoke rose from the beast's nose, but its eyes showed no sign of anger or violence.

I see, the dragon said. It rose from its position, stretching out the long body with a flick of its tail.

The strange words pulled John from his amazement. He shook his head, trying to get his brain to work once more. This was probably a dream, though he couldn't remember ever having a dream in the past. He doubted he would remember this one once he woke up. But for now, he was stuck here, so he decided to make the best of it. "You see what? Who are you?"

I am Fu Ts'ang Lung, the dragon replied. Its long whiskers floated on the breeze as it spoke, giving the creature a look of ethereal movement. *And that is your purpose.*

"Uh...what?" John focused on the multitude of gems that covered the dragons' body. There had to be millions of dollars' worth of bling covering the enormous beast, but that didn't help John understand what Fu

Ts'ang Lung was talking about. "How is your name my purpose?"

Fu Ts'ang Lung lowered its massive head, resting its chin on the ground. *Come. You seek a fortune only I can take you to.*

John hesitated, licking his lips slowly as he looked at the dragon. The monster could easily devour him in one gulp, yet it was inviting him onto its back. Yes, this definitely had to be a dream. "Uh…she…Su Lin? She said she was sending me to the Ancients and they would fix me. She said I don't have a soul." He spoke this aloud, reassuring himself that the strangeness of it all in combination with whatever chemicals were in the incense had just sent his mind into some kind of sporadic overdrive.

Fu Ts'ang Lung blew out a puff a smoke and glared at John. *Yes. Your fortune. Your soul. You will not find it here. It is far from this mountain, deep in the valley below, in the Cavern of Mists.*

"And you're going to take me right to it?" John asked, thinking it sounded as simple as going to the corner market to buy a gallon of milk.

The dragon raised its head for a moment, shaking it slowly. *No. I will take you to the cave. You must find your fortune yourself. You must figure out how to bring your fortune back with you. I cannot help once you enter the cave.* It lowered its head again, waiting for John to climb onto its neck. *We must go now. Your time in this world is short.*

"It is?" John asked, still reluctant to get any closer to the beast.

Fu Ts'ang Lung growled lowly, making a sound like an earthquake. *Were you not told? You have only until fires stops burning.*

The fires? John thought. Did the dragon mean the candles and incense Su Lin had lit? If that was the case, he was even more certain now this was just a dream; a hallucination brought on by the smell of the incense. At the very least when he woke up again, he would look into contacting the police and having Su Lin arrested for kidnapping and drugging him. He wondered if she had a regular habit of doing this to her customers. That would explain the ready shrine.

As John pondered this, Fu Ts'ang Lung growled again and moved, startling him. The dragon lunged forward and grabbed John before he could react, pulling him off the mountain-top and soaring into the air. Fu Ts'ang Lung's large five-toed talons held him in place, preventing him from so much as wiggling. He could scream however, and did so with more force than he thought he could muster. "STOP! WHAT ARE YOU DOING?! LET GO!"

You do not wish me to do that, Fu Ts'ang Lung's voice snorted in his mind. Tendrils of mist swirled past John's head and he turned it as much as he could, glancing toward the hillsides they were gliding by. Only then did it dawn on him that they were hundreds of feet above the ground and letting go would indeed be a very bad idea.

John pressed his eyes closed and muttered to himself. "It's all a dream. It's all a dream." But as much as he wanted to believe it, he could still hear the wind whistling past his ears and blowing his short-cropped hair in a thousand different directions. The only warmth he felt was from the dragon's talons, which were so warm he felt like he was sitting a little too close to a fire.

John continued to mutter to himself through the whole flight, which seemed to take forever. By the time the dragon started angling for the ground, his mouth had gone dry with his constant whispers. Fu Ts'ang Lung landed gently near the mouth of a cave from which the river was flowing, and set John down on the rocky shore. *We have arrived.*

John wobbled as the dragon released him, nearly falling into the river. He steadied himself and looked at the cavern entrance. Mist rose out from it almost as thick as the water that flowed below. "I'm…supposed to go in there?" he asked, not seeing a readily available path.

The dragon nodded slowly. *This is where you will find your fortune. This is what you have come here for.*

"Right," John said as he moved toward the mouth of the cave. The water didn't appear to be very deep here, though it was moving fast and there were several large boulders jutting out of the surface. He would have to navigate his way in through the watery path. "And what if I refuse? I mean, I didn't actually choose to come here. And it's a dream anyway. So, what if I don't want to go in there? What if my time runs out?"

You care so little for your existence? Fu Ts'ang Lung asked, lowering its head down to look John in the eye. John was surprised to find that while the creature radiated heat, it had no smell, or even a feeling of presence. Of course it wouldn't, since this was just a dream. *If you care nothing for your well-being, I will eat you and add you to my collection.* The dragon grinned and John glanced toward the mass of gems that glittered along its body. From this close, he could see the faces of people reflecting in the shiny surfaces.

A shiver ran over John's skin and he took a step back from the grinning maw. "I…er…that is…" He struggled to get his thoughts in order. This dream was making less and less sense all the time and all he really wanted to do was wake up. If only he could argue his way out going into the cavern and facing whatever was inside. "I just don't understand what's so important about having a soul anyway. I mean, it's never mattered before. People just leave me alone. I leave them alone. Isn't that enough?"

Fu Ts'ang Lung curled up on the ground, withdrawing slightly. *What is a soul? You cannot understand that which you have not experienced. What you seek is more than that which your kind has determined is something to be judged as good or evil. It is what allows your kind to create. To love. To hate. To seek. To yearn. To imagine. To fear. There is both good and bad with a soul, but that is what makes it worth having. Without a soul, you are but a shell. Without a soul, there is nothing. You have existed in your life for a very long time. But you have not lived. Is that enough for you?*

John looked down at his feet. "Maybe," he mumbled, not really sure there was any point in wanting more. "Why's it matter to anyone else?"

It does not, Fu Ts'ang Lung replied simply. *But what is the point of going back to nothing? Death is the logical option when there is nothing to live for. I can give you death, if that is your desire.*

John was silent for a moment, mulling it over in his mind. There really wasn't much of anything to return to. He had his job and a place to live. The basics, shelter and food, were covered, but there was nothing beyond that. And he had assumed he had been happy. Now he was beginning to realize that he didn't understand what happiness was. He didn't know what life was.

He looked up at the dragon, feeling the tug of survival deep inside him. He could let this creature kill him and end the banality of his existence. Or he could try to find what made life worth living and give it another shot. He didn't think he was ready to die just yet. At least not without trying. John nodded and turned toward the cave entrance. "All right. I'll go."

Fu Ts'ang Lung didn't answer, instead resting its large head on its coils and closing its eyes to nap. John didn't need an answer, however. He had made his decision and he moved forward, stepping down into the cool flow of water to start into the cave.

Almost immediately, the mists swirled in around him, pulling him forward while the water pushed against his legs. It was as if the cave was both welcoming him and shunning him at the same time. He knew he didn't belong here in this state, and yet the thing that would make him belong was waiting for him somewhere inside.

John stumbled as he took one slow step at a time. The mist and darkness of the cave made it impossible to see anything. He pressed his hands out in front of him and moved to the side, trying to find dry ground to walk on. The water wasn't as bad as he had expected it to be, though. The river was only about shin-deep and was warm and comforting, like swift moving bath water. But he thought he might have an easier time of walking if he could find some solid ground.

After several minutes of searching, he located a ledge and climbed up onto it. The mist curled around his body, compelling him to continue forward though he could still see nothing. John pressed his hands against the wall, feeling his way along and not moving nearly as fast as the mist seemed to want him to. How it could have such presence and feeling, he didn't know. It was as if the mist was alive.

He even thought he could hear it whispering to him. It spoke of memories from his childhood; things he hadn't thought about in many years. He had a lonely upbringing. His parents were not abusive, but they were distant, as if they didn't care he existed. He had no siblings and no friends he could remember. He wasn't bullied in school, but he was ignored. He had been a non-entity for as long as he could remember, and while he thought most people would be hurt by this, he felt nothing as the mist reminded him of what had been.

Ahead, the cave began to brighten. He thought it was just a trick of the mist at first until he realized that he hadn't been able to see anything but murky grey. Now he could misty tendrils pulling apart to reveal a larger space. John continued forward watching as the cavern wall began to take shape and the glimmer of tumbling water flickered past him. Eventually he was able to drop his hands from the cavern's surface and walk without trouble over the smoothed path.

The brightening glow was not the natural light of the sun, or the flicker of flame. Instead, it was a shimmering rainbow of different colors, some of which John had no name for. They played off the surface of the mist, painting with strange designs, often resembling faces that he thought he knew. At one point he would see Mr. Talbert, then parents, then Keith, then someone he knew from his youth.

Suddenly the mist parted, and he found himself standing in a great room filled with a multitude of gems. The gems rested on pedestals and shined without the aid of any external light source that he could see. They seemed to dance with their own internal light, generating all of the strange colors. In the center of the room, a fountain rose out of the floor, pouring forth the beginnings of the river that flowed down and out of the cave. This, apparently, was the heart of his journey, the place where he would find his fortune, if it was here at all.

"But how?" John whispered to himself. "Which one is the right one?"

He almost expected to hear Fu Ts'ang Lung's voice in his head again, but the only thing that came back to him was the bubbling laugh of the river. John frowned, feeling nothing that would tell him what to do. The gems simply stared back at him, gleaming away as if he wasn't even there.

Deciding the gems weren't the answer, he walked toward the fountain. It was a natural construction, a stalagmite that rose up to John's waist, with a conical formation in the top where the water pooled and was released into the river. The circumference was large, however, stretching about 20 feet. The mist came from the surface of the water coating the surface in a thick cloud before finding its way out into the cavern. He found it interesting that such a small amount of water could build into the river that had cut the expansive valley outside.

"So, this is the beginning," he said to himself as he leaned over the edge of the fountain. He wasn't really sure what he meant, other than this seemed to be where the river started, but he thought it was probably a more profound statement than he realized. Not only did the water begin here, but all the gems were situated in a way that they reflected on the surface of the pool, coloring it so brightly he couldn't see any further down than the surface.

The rising mist carried with it a heat that he could feel against his face as he leaned in. Despite the amount of steam, John ventured to touch the surface of the water to see just how hot it might be. As he poked it with his index finger, a series of concentric circles rippled across the surface, disturbing the colors and making the gems around him begin to sing. John blinked and looked up at the colorful stones. Each seemed to have its own tone that hummed with the ringlets.

"That's it," he whispered, suddenly understanding. He turned back to the water and leaned down until his face was inches from the surface. Though he couldn't remember ever singing in his life, he began to make a low, soft tone with his voice. It was a single note; one that sat somewhere in the middle of his range, though he knew nothing about music. The note simply felt comfortable.

His breath was enough to cut the tension of the water, creating yet more ripples. As they spread out across the pool, the colors of the gems began to flicker out, their singing dying with the color. He held the tone longer than he would have thought possible, watching as the color slowly went out of the room and finally there was only one gem remaining. This gem sang back to him in the same tone, flickering with bright excitement.

John stopped singing and reached down into the water, closing his hand around the spot of glimmering color. As he covered it, the cavern when dark again and he could feel the gem in the palm of his hand. He pulled it free from the water's surface and opened his fingers to look at it. Once more, the other gems in the cavern returned to life, no longer singing, but glimmering as brightly as they had before. The gem in his palm also flashed with its internal light, reflecting all the colors of the rainbow across his face.

You have found your voice. Your soul. Fu Ts'ang Lung's voice echoed in his mind. *What you do with it now will be up to you.*

John nodded slowly, wondering how he was supposed to get it inside himself. Perhaps if he ate it as Fu Ts'ang Lung had threated to do to him? Or would it be enough to just put it in his pocket? Perhaps if this was just a dream, as he still thought it might be, it wouldn't really matter anyway. He would wake up and life would be just the same as it had always been.

But then, he wasn't sure that was true. Even if this world was just a drug-induced hallucination, he had learned something here. With or without a soul, he now understood that life was what you made of it, and living the way he did meant nothing. He had no impact on the world and in return, the world did nothing for him. At the very least, he would go back with the desire to find a purpose and pursue it. John would chose to live.

He slipped the gem into his jacket's breast pocket and held his hand over it as he looked up the swirling mist above. "I'm ready to go back," he said softly, watching the mist dance and churn. As soon as he spoke, the gems surrounding him began to dim once more and the mist started to descend. The moving cloud circled around his body, wrapping him in warmth and he closed his eyes.

Darkness enveloped John and the acrid smell of incense replaced the earthy scent of the cavern. The clanking of pots and sizzle of cooking food covered the bubble of the river. John gasped as his eyes popped open, revealing the shrine in the back of the restaurant.

Su Lin sat before him, smiling gently. "You find new soul." It was not so much a question of his success, but an assurance that he had indeed found what she had sent him to find.

John looked down, finding his hand was still resting over his jacket pocket. Under it, he could feel a small lump. He reached into the pocket and drew out the gem, wondering how that was even possible. Had he really been to another world? Met a dragon? Found his soul? The gem no longer gleamed with its internal light, but instead had become a deep, brilliant green emerald. He smiled, feeling the light within him, leaving only the precious stone as evidence that he had really experienced the journey.

He nodded slightly, looking up to Su Lin. "Yeah. Yeah, I think I did. Thank you." He held the gem toward the woman, intending to pay her with it. It had to be worth something after all; much more than anything else he had.

Su Lin laughed and reached up to curl his fingers closed over the stone. "You okay now. Go home. Live your life. You have much to catch up on." She let go of his hand and stood up, moving over to the bead curtain to open it for him.

John smiled and put the emerald back into his pocket. He stood and followed her to the curtain. "Thank you again," he said quietly, giving her a slight bow. "If there's ever anything you need, let me know. I want to repay you somehow."

Su Lin shook her head. "You use soul wisely. Do not let it go to waste. This will make me happy." She patted John on the arm and nodded toward the office and kitchen beyond. "Go now."

John nodded once more and smiled in earnest. He couldn't remember having ever been inclined to really smile about anything before, but this was the dawn of a new day. He started out toward the kitchen and found Su Lin's daughter at her books once more, glaring at him as he went by. All he could do was smile in return, knowing what he had just experienced was both fantastical and real. She didn't have to believe any of it if that was her choice.

With a skip in his step and a new outlook on life, John left the restaurant to start again. He was going to do it right this this time. He knew there was both joy and heartache ahead, Fu Ts'ang Lung had said as much, but he was looking forward to it in a way he never thought possible. His life was now in his hands and he was already thinking of a thousand different ways to spend it. John stepped out of the restaurant door and took a deep breath of fresh evening air. It was time to start living.